UNKNOWN
SOLDIERS

Also by John Rolfe Gardiner
Great Dream from Heaven

UNKNOWN SOLDIERS

John Rolfe Gardiner

E.P. Dutton | New York

Library of Congress Cataloging in Publication Data

Gardiner, John Rolfe.
Unknown soldiers.

I. Title.
PZ4.G2227Un [PS3557.A7113] 813'.5'4 76-30635

ISBN: 0-525-22675-3

Published simultaneously in Canada by
Clarke, Irwin & Company
Limited, Toronto and Vancouver

10 9 8 7 6 5 4 3 2 1

First Edition

To my father and mother

UNKNOWN
SOLDIERS

1

Clayton, Virginia, will not reveal itself in the little secrets of wallpaper under wallpaper. It hasn't that sort of pretty antiquity. Rather imagine it sprang full formed as village not aspiring to town, and before that, a place people passed through, not one they stopped at: the crossroads of Wye Bridge Pike and Station Drive.

It was the roads that mattered. For the truth about Clayton you would tear up the roads, not the wallpaper; the story would be in the layers of fill dirt, under layers of gravel, under alternating bands of white and gray stone, these eventually bound with tar, now all of them under a perfectly smooth, black macadam, machine painted with white lines.

A cross section of Wye Bridge Pike would tell you, year by year, which contractor had run strongest with the court house gang at Stilson, the county seat, and, thus, which held sway at the state house in Richmond. A band of gray meant Earl Jackson had the road job—the gray stone came from his cousin's quarry. White stone from Winchester meant Jewel Lamartine had been favored. A reddish stripe toward the middle of the strata meant something had gone wrong for both of them just after the war.

From Clayton the Pike ran a curvy course west to Stilson, and east over hills before bending down into Carlton County, across the Potomac at Wye Bridge and into Washington. The transverse Station Drive would reveal almost identical leaves of evidence. But its oldest secret lay visible at the surface, a series of gently graded straightaways, these broken by no more than a dozen easy bends—the path of least resistance between Washington and the Indian Falls of the Potomac. It had been the line of a country trolley, covered in 1931 with the first loose layers of fill dirt.

A shallow excavation could tell you not just who'd prospered off the roads or by what conveyance people traveled them, but how fast they might have careened down the Drive and through the intersection on their way to somewhere else; there was no stop sign then. After pavement one could approach and depart Clayton almost without noticing the change there; before, when there'd been little to see anyway, daytrippers from Washington could reach and escape the corner unaware of what they were being obliged to leave so slowly. Though as early as 1936, when the Drive was still loose gravel, the Lewis brothers from Small Hill corner to the north had achieved seventy miles per hour on one of its downhill straights before spinning into a ditch.

By 1942 the village had hardly discovered itself; its ruralness locked into the tightly held farms surrounding it and the scattered homes set back from its several streets. A mule and wagon in the middle of Station Drive were a nuisance, not illegal; the community still hiding its rustic secrets from the warring nation's capital only six miles to the East.

In late May of 1942 Junior Panimer came hell bent down Station Drive, then tar-bound white gravel, in one of Lamartine's dump trucks, accelerator floored, his bad arm braced between window frame and steering wheel. He was coming for his son who was being held after school again. Junior swore at the grammar school principal who was still two miles away in Clayton.

"God damn you turn him out now or I'll get him myself."

2

Imagining defiance, he smacked the smart aleck teacher man upside the head, which was just the dashboard, then grabbed the wheel to correct the swerving truck. He cursed the road though the hauling of its white surface had been his recent livelihood, then swore again at the principal who'd been keeping his son late, and at the boy himself, his namesake, Panimer.

Almost a month before this, the boy had sat in assembly with the rest of the Duncan Kimball School while Payton, the principal, called attention to his navy, cardboard ships sailing across the auditorium above them, each on its own taut wire, each driven forward by a sponsoring class's war bond effort. "I notice," Payton said, "the fifth grade's destroyer is somewhat ahead of the eight-X battleship *Victory*. I should have thought . . ." Payton's voice became lost in cheering from the fifth grade section, that and a single shrill note from eight-X, from Panimer, head down, who had the first and fourth fingers of his right hand in the corners of his mouth, whistling as he and only two others in his class knew how. Never mind that his own class had just been shamed by the announcement; any occasion would do to show the talent—this time for Johnny Roe Pride on his left, who didn't know how, but mostly for Nancy McConkey, two rows in front, whose head swung around for just a moment, a little amused, a little scandalized. Mrs. Cuttrell reached from behind and cuffed his ear.

"Class paper drive leaders meet after this assembly in Miss Nicely's room. The scrap rubber teams meet tomorrow after lunch. By the way, Miss Nicely tells me her room already has four tons of paper." Cheering again from the fifth grade. Panimer's fingers went to his mouth reflexively. He was still whistling when Mrs. Cuttrell grabbed him by the shoulder and shook him. Payton's announcements were lost on the boy. Subdued, he stared overhead at the school navy, the ships that sailed forward with every ten-cent savings stamp purchased at the pain of two unbought, unlicked popsicles; the stamp to be licked and fixed in a war bond booklet. Bonds were To Have And To Hold the posters said. He looked up and imagined his class boat floating far behind all the others. He had nothing to

3

spend on the battleship, but he hated to see it lose a race. He could outrun anyone in the school.

Several days later in their home room period Mrs. Cuttrell told them, "I'm ashamed. Aren't you ashamed? I'm ashamed for all of us." Their ship was falling further back in the school convoy. She asked for suggestions. Hands stabbed the air as for an easy spelling word. Mary Kopese proposed a bake sale. Stephen Callisher, whose family had given up deserts for the duration, proposed giving up deserts.

"We could just eat less," he said, "and then the money we saved . . . we could get it from our parents. And then we could all buy at least one stamp every day."

"What else?" The ideas came faster, until Johnny Roe Pride offered himself.

"I could just fight any boy in the class who don't want to help in the war," he said. "I mean after school. Outside."

"That's enough," Mrs. Cuttrell said. Through all this Panimer sat mute. The ten cents in his pocket was going for candy at the Jew store.

"Panimer," Mrs. Cuttrell said. "I want to see you after school today." She made him miss his bus waiting for him to explain what was the matter, which he could not do. "Well, you can just sit there until you can tell me something," she said. A half hour later he'd still said nothing. She called him to her desk. "I want you to take these home and plant them," she said, holding out several packets of vegetable seeds.

"We already got a victory garden," Panimer said.

"You take these home," she insisted. Panimer accepted them as his ticket out of the room. On his shuffling way up Station Drive he sowed the longest row of vegetables in Clayton—without benefit of furrow. First turnips, which he hated, then radishes, and finally carrots, which his father said didn't grow so good around there anyway. While he scattered the seeds behind him he muttered plans for the school navy, which had caused him to have to walk three miles home.

The next afternoon at lunch time Panimer snuck out of the

4

cafeteria, back to the auditorium. He took the janitor's stepladder from the broom closet and carried it to the eight-X battleship. Standing on the top step he could reach the boat. He shoved it hard; it slid along the wire all the way to the victory wall. He carried the ladder back to the closet, then hid in the latrine, shutting himself in a toilet stall. He could hear them coming back from lunch through the auditorium. Someone noticed right away. Mr. Payton was informed. Before the first afternoon period began the boat was moved back to its lagging position.

The next week holes were discovered in the hull of the PT boat. Then the sixth grade's cruiser Roosevelt was found sailing in the wrong direction. Repairs were made. There was a teachers meeting in Payton's office. Panimer heard Payton tell a teacher it was sabotage. He wished Nancy McConkey knew what he was doing for their class.

The battleship moved, but other ships moved faster. One morning the fifth grade marched past the open eight-X door for an early recess and one of them yelled into the room, "Eighth grade is losers." Every day Mrs. Cuttrell made sure her class walked together through the auditorium on their way to lunch, and the saboteur walked behind her, hot with his secret, at war with his courage. If he were going to do it he'd have to wait one afternoon till everyone had gone home; he'd have to miss his bus again.

Panimer was standing with the wire cutters in one hand and scissors in the other. The savaged navy lay in pieces all around him. It was a thorough Pearl Harbor he had managed; not a wire uncut, not a ship unsunk. He was the enemy frogman, traitor, and did not even know it.

"Look what you done, boy." It was Lester, the janitor. He'd been watching from behind the broom closet door. "You're Panimer, ain't you?"

For a moment the boy could not answer. Then he said, "I'll give you a quarter. It's all I got. I'll bring it tomorrow." Lester shook his head. There was no way to bribe him. He just wanted to be left alone by Panimer, by Mr. Payton, by the fifth grade's Miss Nicely. He was content to be ignored by the whole Duncan Kimball school, which would know how to deal with traitors.

Panimer sat forward in his school chair, staring down at the obscenities and loves departed eighth graders had carved into its single arm—"Phyllis + D.B." and some third party's opinion of what Phyllis would do for anyone. This amid a maze of initials, arrows (some feathered), ampersands, plus signs, some pairs wrapped in hearts punctured by more arrows, all overflowing the flat surface. He looked up at the one unfrosted pane in the eight-X door where any moment he expected the face of Mr. Payton, thin and flushed. It was too close to the end of school to rebuild his navy—but he would find the saboteur and make him pay.

What were they waiting for? A confession? On this, the first afternoon after the school's Pearl Harbor, a half-hour detention for every class, while outside, bus drivers waited, raced their engines and cursed.

"Hey," a whispering behind him, "Payton's got the janitor in his office and . . ."

"Johnny Roe, don't let me call you down again. Panimer, sit up in your chair. If anyone knows who did it, you'd better tell right now," Mrs. Cuttrell said. Silence. "I can't believe anyone in this room could have done it." Panimer could tell she was not certain. "But one of you may know who did it. No one knows who did it? This is just a terrible thing," she said, "it's like . . . like a crime against the country," the class squirming in recognition of something so awful their teacher could not explain it. "We'll just wait then," Mrs. Cuttrell said. This producing nothing, she tried, "It's a shame we all have to suffer for . . . sit up, class." Then, "If anyone knows, they can tell me after school." They sat silently for the rest of the half hour, as much in awe of the crime as the threat of punishment, frightened for themselves. "All right, get your wraps," Mrs. Cuttrell dismissed them.

On his way down the hall Panimer could see Lester still standing in front of Mr. Payton's desk. He wanted to run but two teachers stood in the front door watching him. What chance did he have against a whole school of good citizens, eight whole classes of coerced informers. The teachers in the doorway were talking about him as if he couldn't hear them: "Hasn't that boy shown a change? When I had him I couldn't trust him to clean erasers."

He edged past them, wishing it was still that time long ago in her third grade. Lucky for her it wasn't; back then when there was such hell to pay and he was glad enough to pay it—when he was boss bull Panimer of the third grade, scourge of the Jew store, little thief and no-hands Schwinn knight errant, entered secretly in the lists for Nancy McConkey. Champion cyclist of grades one through six, he could steer all the way from his house to the Duncan Kimball door never touching handlebars—a one-mile no-hands rider (a half mile but for the detour past the McConkeys) guiding his Schwinn through Clayton's several streets, in and out of parked cars, over boards he'd placed along the route to lift him onto the village's frost-skewed sidewalks, cursing drivers who pulled in front of him, like Mr. Stockstill, manager of Chain Food, always in his official trance, never watching where he was going, almost spoiling the no-hands ride. But Panimer would balance, almost at a standstill, then speed as the way cleared, arms flying out behind him, and finally the double S twist where lesser riders grabbed to steer, around one culvert, over another, dropping his shoulder for counter balance, up into the schoolyard where mates, too proud to applaud, awaited instruction in the day's mischief. That was back when he used to sneak off the school grounds during recess, over to the Jew store for a pair of wax jaws to chew till the sugar juice ran sweet in his mouth. And he would forget in class, chew loud and hard, trying to make the crumbling wax stick together.

7

"Panimer. Swallow that gum. Now."

"I ain't chewing gum."

"You swallow it."

"No ma'am," he'd say because even in the third grade he'd known that whether you called somebody Miss or Mrs., or Miz to avoid the choice, it might cause a teacher to go red, or angry, and the reason had to do with whether or not they went to bed every night with a man; some of them embarrassed if you thought they did, others if you thought they didn't.

"You defy me?"

"Ma'am?" I'll throw it at you before I swallow it, nanny goat.

"You call me Miz Vines," unable to bear the distinction herself.

Johnny Roe Pride, sitting behind him, said, "It ain't gum. It's nigger wax. Panimer's chewing nigger candy. Ha. Blue gums. Nigger jaws," then the room in giggles until her three-ply yardstick snapped down.

"Quiet. It's not your business, Johnny Roe. Panimer, whatever it is you're chewing, swallow it."

"No ma'am." Like hell he would, not in front of Nancy McConkey, unamused. Not for Johnny Roe either. He coughed the broken wad into his cupped hand, turned and hurled it toward the window, which was not open. Wax and sweet saliva ran slowly down the panes.

The next day, another detention for the whole school. Again Lester was questioned in the principal's office. Mr. Payton called another teacher's meeting. "You've got to find him," he said, assuming now there had been only one and that it had been a boy.

"We're going to find out who did it." Mrs. Cuttrell passed the message to her class. "We're going to find him." They were being forced to see that whoever had done this awful thing lived, sat, studied, ate among them, that such a sickness must surely reveal itself among the healthy, its trembly fever alone must betray it. Again all the classes were dismissed, and as they spilled into the halls, hurrying for their buses, Panimer saw how

8

angry they were. He heard Johnny Roe say, "I know who done it," and Rodney Paley, the biggest boy in school, who drew lines in the dirt at recess and dared anyone to step over them, promised, "If I find out I'll beat him up till he can't walk." The whole school seemed to be trying to get through the front door at once, the oaths and yammerings of their injured innocence echoing in the hall, wild in their belated freedom, culprit among them, all shoving to be outside at once. Panimer was almost pushed into Lester, but the janitor did not see him, only following in his push broom's swath, ignoring the flow of children who passed to either side.

Two days more, Panimer's hopes rising; in time he might relax completely. But while he gained confidence the whole school began to take on the shame it was accused of. Regular troublemakers shook their heads against false accusation; all of them were beginning to accept their complicity because the thing had happened among them.

"We cannot let him get away with it," Mr. Payton told them in assembly. "We have all been careless. Now we've all got to pay for it. Until we catch him. This is war time." Panimer felt the shame enveloping the school, but took new comfort in the shared guilt.

The story spread into the town, a conversation piece for the ladies who sat in the notions store window, a relief from their regular concern with the men who passed along the same sidewalk at the same hour every day on their way to their discussion of the war on the counter stools of Peterson's Drug Store. The incident had even spread to the next town. When it was week-old news on the village tongue the Clayton Journal dared this:

School Navy Sunk
Principal Seeks Saboteurs

Now a matter of public record, it would be difficult for the village to let it pass unresolved. If Lester had thought it would be forgotten he'd been mistaken; it was not just the village's sense of undeserved shame that refused to let it die. It was

Payton. The principal would not relax his promise of universal discipline. Until the guilty came forward or were found out, they would all pay for the act against his school, his country. And while he stood fast in his anger the parents of the unjustly punished grew ugly in their untoward shame. After the first week of detentions and brow beatings they no longer wanted culprits, they wanted Payton's job.

The second week he did not come from his office on his usual rounds of halls and classrooms but sat prisoner to his telephone, over and over explaining the thing to the querulous and the outraged; with each call his implacability growing and the community temper stretching tighter. "We cannot make even a small allowance," he said again and again until the children themselves had heard more than they could stand and as they moved through the last forced motions before their summer freedom—classroom to recess to classroom to lunch to classroom to recess—Lester saw the venom that begged his secret surround them all and grow; girls covered their mouths in obligatory horror at the unspeakable reprisals their heroes promised on the body of the traitor should his name be found. And the janitor who for years had dusted and swept around their carelessness and the carelessness of unnumbered classes before them—long since inured to their mindless acceptance of his travail—heard the meanest among them boast they would beat whoever it was to death. Again he was called into Payton's office. He was scared now.

Panimer sat in his home room making no pretense of attention to Mrs. Cuttrell's remonstration. Three days away from summer, perhaps safe now, a little exhilarated, a little incredulous at his direct hit on the school. He'd only been aiming at cardboard ships. In his alert seclusion he scanned the room. No distraction. Just the letters and designs in the arm of his chair, which only served his anxiety, the carved and scratched messages of a past that seemed so full of forbidden intimacies. A girl named Phyllis had led a whole class of questing, fumbling, speechless boys, pimpled and erect, on a vain chase. They'd even chiseled her into walls and windowsills where new layers of paint had begun to heal the record of their affliction—and cut her into the line of tall sycamores along the schoolyard fence, into the bark's round patterns of gray and tan that always reminded the boy of army camouflage; the same open secret of their devotion, now disappearing as the trees' scar fiber healed around the names and hearts that had bled sap for Phyllis.

Panimer pulled a stub of pencil from his pocket and set to work on the chair's arm. There was space enough to wedge the name between a fat heart and a crude female torso. She would have to suffer that proximate indignity for him, for herself, to be recorded in one small corner of the school's furniture. Nancy McConkey. He stopped, cocked his head, considered his progress. **NAN.** Unsatisfactory. Not deep enough. He'd have to begin again. But carefully, an eye on Mrs. Cuttrell. Now the pencil dug deeper, through layers of varnish, into the wood. He shielded his work behind the cupped fingers of his left hand as the lecture on honesty continued. Thirty other bodies in the room no more attentive than he; eyes shifted, heads turned, notes passed, lips moved. They were progressing from a silent squirming to a low hum and finally a defiant buzz of voices.

"People." Mrs. Cuttrell interrupted herself without rancor or frustration. It was a reflex, no more than a running pause in her lecture; and the class's immediate silence, a perfunctory response. They would be quiet for a moment before the cycle of their defiance began again.

Decisions. Should the first c in McConkey be capital or small? He worked without fear now, his delinquency covered by the general mutiny of his classmates. McConkey, he repeated. If he said it a lot of times quickly it became just a funny noise. Should he let the end of her name run into the adjacent heart or squeeze it out of scale to avoid contact with the common Phyllis? He could see his late effort on Nancy's behalf was meager compared to the declarations of love and lust surrounding it. My God, he thought, every day must have been Valentines Day back then.

"Panimer!" The name split the aisle, knocking apart heads

11

that had been leaning to whisper to each other, and knocking the pencil from Panimer's hand, snapping him to attention. "Panimer! Are you writing on that desk?"

"I'm not doing nothing," his hands already moist, moved slowly over the pencil.

"I'm not doing anything."

"Anything," he agreed quickly, covering both the pencil and the newly carved name now because Mrs. Cuttrell was coming down the aisle toward him. Then she was looking down at him and demanding,

"What are you hiding?" He did not answer. "Move your hands." He did not move. She was about to pull at his arm when she relented, or remembered, "Panimer, you're wanted in Mr. Payton's office. Right now," and the announcement seemed to shock her as much as the class. The room grew quiet again, then a gasp from behind him, then absolute silence as fear seized them all. For two weeks they'd been made to walk through their routine, abused, while they waited for the name, for someone other than the janitor to be called into the principal's office. Now the name had been spoken—Panimer. And eight-X had heard it first. They sat in the awe and shame of association with the boy who knew he was in double danger, not just from principal and teachers but from the children around him. If he suffered their silent shame for him now, it would not be long before he suffered their abuse. No time at all in fact because as they watched him stiffen in his chair, Johnny Roe Pride said,

"He done it. Panimer cut the boats down. You done it, Panimer." And Panimer did not turn to deny it, but sat trying to control the tremble in his hands, which were sweating freely, making a brown paste of the varnish dust carved from the name which they still concealed. No defense but the voice of Mrs. Cuttrell, saying, "No one asked your opinion, Johnny Roe." He could see the pity in her as she stared down at him, no longer concerned with what he'd done to the chair, but waiting for him to move. They were all waiting for him to move. He was waiting to move, knew he had to rise and leave, was rising and leaving,

12

but could not feel himself doing it, spastic on the hot guilt and heart racing absolutely out of control.

2

Junior Panimer was the father and Panimer, the son. The man had been given only one name—Panimer—which served him double duty, or triple, as first, last, and middle if occasion arose. School records had the boy's name as Panimer Panimer. The father's driver's license showed the identical first and last names. He had tried to call his son Junior Panimer but when the boy was old enough to understand what had happened to him he sulked against ''Junior'' until his father said, ''All right, you call me Junior,'' partly as a joke, partly to prove ''a name can't hurt you.'' But the joke became habit and the habit, fixed.

If the father had known more about his given name it would have hurt him more. His mother had made a marginal living in the northeast corner of Tennessee, not exactly as a whore but with occasional gifts of food and money from a half dozen consorts, among them several miners, a religious cowboy, and a union organizer. Since none admitted paternity—and she was not sure herself who the father was—all could share the guilt and secret reparations.

Then came the name, Panimer. It had started as Panama,

14

when someone suggested that was where the father must have run to; then it passed through mutations, stretching to Panamerican when a candidate for Congress introduced a rally of drunken miners to hemispheric foreign policy. It shrank to Panamer, then back to Panama, and finally settled on Panimer, easier to say and sounding more like a name.

But it wasn't a name, which annoyed his mother only briefly, until she realized that being no name it was all names, that her options in child support were as wide as her liaisons. A name ought to have at least a trace of paternity in it, but this one told the men less than they could have hoped about a father and the women more than they cared to know about the mother.

For a while they had suspected the man known as the organizer and they had called the infant "the little communist baby," but Tosie had objected so strenuously that they eventually honored her denial. Then, unsolicited, the town had undertaken a kind of collective adoption, humored the little boy as a nephew though never as a son. As he grew they saw he was oddly favored in looks (still no trace of a father in his face), handsome in a black-haired, off-centered way that would attract women. His cheekbones were high but slightly out of line with each other. His mouth took on a slight, conscious sneer, offsetting the larger imbalance of the face. What had seemed close to deformity in his infancy ("Ain't his face pushed kind of sideways?" someone asked Tosie) grew less pronounced as he matured, became the focus of schoolmates' fascination with his looks.

At ten years old he left school, went into the Fraterville mine as a mule boy. But he grew too fast to hold the job long. At twelve he was sorting coal at the tipple, a year later he was working the face. Already close to six feet tall, he was well muscled. His own quick glances at his shoulders pleased him.

Then the mine exploded. Junior Panimer had been walking out of the mine when it happened and was spit from the drift while one hundred and eighty-six others were burned or blown beyond recognition or trapped by gas. Only he escaped, and he came to take pride in that escape the way a man might be proud

15

of winning a lottery. It was not just that he was the lone survivor; the mine had spit him out for good.

They found him in a clearing outside the driftmouth vomiting blood, one of his eyes a bloody place, several ribs broken, and his left arm twisted crazily in its socket. Dr. Elkins predicted death. The boy's resilience fooled them; these were simply new deformities to be outgrown, or assimilated. He recovered, blind in his left eye, his left arm partially unhinged; he never again raised it above his shoulder. It swung a trifle out of phase when he walked.

These things that at first seemed grotesque gradually became natural, grew familiar as his name Panimer, through use, until nothing else would have seemed right. The slightly twisted things about him simply drew the more attention. He was clever in a way they did not see. If he did not do well in school—well, they had not expected him to be a mind too. Because after his recovery he had gone back to school, where they had not demanded much more than his daily presence. They could not hold him long. He was three years behind and larger than any others his age.

Already self-conscious to distraction, knowing he was a bastard and knowing that everyone else knew, he saw that girls could not keep their eyes off him. How many times did they entice him to lead them—into barns, woodsheds, fields, woods, empty shacks, abandoned coal drifts? He lived a kind of furtive idyll, secretly romanced and secretly pitied.

At seventeen they still thought him a strangely beautiful if retarded school boy, supposing he couldn't read because he only mumbled his responses, refusing to compete, or to be seen competing. Their pity showed through their deference and he made love to that pity with a vengeance, fornicating all over the countryside with at least a dozen girls and women, most older than he. The village and those to either side in the valley had lost one hundred and eighty-six in the explosion but Panimer was not just filling that male vacuum; he would have been promiscuous anyway.

Still, he couldn't stand the men who came to his mother's

cabin—they came less frequently now—and could no longer abide knowing their intermittent generosity had been his support. Exhausted, disgusted by the women who sought him, Panimer left home. Maimed and handsome, cursing that corner of Tennessee, he began a slow migration—east and then north—that would take him through three states, a succession of jobs, three woman, maybe children, until in Perryville, Maryland, he found a woman he could not or would not leave.

By the time he arrived in Perryville, age thirty-four, he knew just how to take a new community by shy ingratiation. His humility when he asked for work was balanced by his size and strength. He had stopped growing at six feet three inches, and weighed close to two hundred pounds. He called himself "just a broke-down miner, a ordinary laborer," but by then he was an adequate carpenter, auto mechanic, stonemason, plasterer, and all-around handyman. When they found he had talents far beyond his self-assessment they sought him out, paid him what he asked. It was always too late when they discovered he was a drifter. He would already have stolen their confidence, or their affections, or the affections of their women.

At Perryville he worked in a Veterans Bureau warehouse, loading and unloading trucks, and attracted the manager's daughter who hung around the office. She was educated, had been to a boarding school in Virginia, where they let her ride horses and speak French. He gathered this much from the conversations of her father, Mr. Rossom, and the men who came to do business with him. While Panimer loaded and unloaded hospital sheets—far too many hospital sheets—she sat in the office, looked through magazines, and stared at him.

There were irregularities in the warehouse, Panimer noticed. He supposed they were the usual mistakes of government people—sheets coming in one day, leaving the next, loaded on the same truck that brought them, sent back to where they'd come from. The inefficiency amused him at first. Once the same load arrived and left and arrived again, all within a week, which might have been funny except that by then Panimer was foreman and his crew complained about the extra work. He decided to tell Rossom about it—it was a way to get inside the office, where the girl would see him. He walked in and said his piece. "Yes sir," he said, "crate number's same as yesterday." But Rossom did not seem interested, looked instead at his daughter and told her, "Paula, you go on home."

She was watching Panimer over the top of her magazine. He left the office, wondering aloud what the United States Government was coming to.

Panimer's naivete was not without curiosity though he never suspected the truth of the place because all he saw were the truckers' invoices, the lot numbers and sizes, never the prices for which the goods entered and left the warehouse. But daily he grew wiser to the inefficiency until he had lost his usefulness to Mr. Rossom. One day he was gone, and he had taken Paula with him. Mr. Rossom didn't try to stop them.

It was more than Perryville's tedium that Paula fled—the endless magazine reading, the seeking after something, anything, which her mother had called "waiting for someone nice to come along," and her father, "staying decent until she finds a man with prospects." It was the prospect of a man with prospects she fled, a man like her father, always boasting of the money he made, of how much more he could be making if he wanted to, of his real estate. She was not really aware that she disliked her father. In fact, the night she drove away from Perryville, sitting beside the rough man she had chosen so suddenly—she did not even know he was blind in one eye—contemplating her flight, a hand under her chin, her eye on distance, in her first long thought of home, she said, "Panimer, where are you going?"

"Does it matter?" he said.

"I mean, honestly, do you have any prospects?" After which he attacked her so viciously with silence she cried until he threatened to take her home.

It had been a brief, furtive courtship, right under Mr. Rossom's nose. The girl's apparent unconcern with her beauty had confused Panimer; her baggy sweaters and lumpy skirts, her auburn corkscrew curls that fell always tangled to her shoulders, her short body wriggling in her chair, waiting for a more comfortable position to come along. Her round, unrouged face, against all this, was still winning. But this was not a temptress who had been sitting in the office every day, peering at him over her magazines; she was a distracted woman looking for safe passage from boredom.

The day he saw her alone in the office and spoke to her for the first time he was immediately aware of his mistake. He had not teased her vanity by ignoring her till now; he had simply postponed the day he would find she could not be bought for his mere existence. He took her a lime soda, which she accepted without affectation. "Thank you, Panimer," she said, with no hesitation in acknowledging his name and no signal she cared to talk.

"Guess you like those glamour magazines," he said.

"They aren't glamour magazines," she answered. "They're about politics and social problems. And books." She went back to her reading.

"Books," he said. "Guess I know what's in every book was ever written." She looked up, pained by the arrogance of this second interruption. "Words," he said. If this amused Paula she did not show it. She shifted uncomfortably in her chair and Panimer retreated. His first pass had been an embarrassment to both of them.

Paula had supposed someday she would write for magazines—witty, thoughtful articles that would catch the eye of a famous Baltimore journalist. And when he and the public cried, "Author," she would stay hidden behind a pen name. It would be an anagram of Paula Rossom, so well hidden no one should guess. She jumbled the letters dozens of ways before deciding on Alors Maupos. Then she waited for the ideas to write about. The ideas did not come. Or if they did she did not write them down because she did not know how.

After several years these notions had worn so thin any outsider might have punctured them, though Panimer, tramping over her reveries in muddy shoes, hardly seemed the one. Had he been aware of the tender place he trod, he might have backed away completely but the next time he found her alone he asked, "You remember any of that stuff you read? Or you just moving your mouth?" He had caught her spelling aloud—Maupos—as she wrote it in a magazine. She flipped the page quickly and demanded, "Don't you have manners?"

He apologized but persisted, "What you reading now?"

Resigned to a polite, if brief, explanation, she said, "It's about vitamins. People in the cities aren't getting proper vitamins. America is a very badly nourished country."

"That's right," he agreed. "But more surprising is the farmer. Now you'd think he'd be about fed as good as any, but he's one of the worst. He's about starved for your whole line of B vitamins," and before Panimer had finished he had given her a complete explication of this article and two others in the same magazine. In the middle of his performance she tried to argue a point but forgot the fact on which her case turned and trailed off. Panimer rescued her and went on.

Paula, as dislocated as the letters in her pen name, was angry, humiliated, amazed. The attendant in her father's warehouse had invaded her intellectual preserve. She didn't have to ask more about him; he was already telling her the story of his early deliverance from the coal mine. He could see she did not believe him.

"Watch," he said, raising his left arm until it stretched straight in front of him. "There. I can't lift it any higher." She pressed her lips together to keep from grinning. "Go ahead," he said, "you try to push it higher." She moved toward him, hesitated. "Go on," he said, "It's crippled but it don't hurt." She put both hands on his wrist and, using his whole arm as a lever, heaved upward but only succeeded in bending him back at the waist. "Easy," he said, "no cause to knock me over."

They talked a good deal that month but his interest in her magazines died as suddenly as it had appeared. And Paula never learned how he had mastered that one issue, how he had gone to the Perryville library at his lunch hour every day for two weeks and read and reread those articles, seeking the librarian's assistance when he stumbled over words, engaging her in long discussions.

At the end of that month Paula knew the maneuvering around her presumed intellectuality was over. And by then each seemed to understand that circumstance rather than proposition or assignation was going to be their signal. One Friday afternoon Mr. Rossom left early. They lingered until they were alone. Then, without asking or needing to, he led her up to the loft of the warehouse and there, behind an eighty-year supply of floor wax, whose eventual discovery would contribute to the ruin of her father and help send the Veterans Bureau administrator to Leavenworth Penitentiary, the two of them slowly undressed each other, and, with honest moaning, sank into a pile of excelsior and consummated their new love.

3

Guilt-hot, Panimer headed toward Mr. Payton's office, his mind racing over the building, bouncing off blocked exits. The hall narrowed to a tunnel in front of him, keeping his feet honest. The fire escape was no good; he could only reach it through the fifth grade room upstairs where Miss Nicely would still be talking to her class. He had glanced back at the front door, but Lester was standing there, trembling on his broom. He could go down the back way to the basement latrine, maybe hide in the boiler room, but there was no exit from the basement. And he did not want to hide. So his feet took him where he did not want to go, and he was not thinking whether to admit or deny it all; he assumed Lester had told. There would be no denying it.

A few steps from the principal's door he heard his father's voice: "You better damn well make allowance," then Mr. Payton saying, "We cannot make even a single . . . ah, hey, eh . . ."

Panimer could not see what was happening in the office, but he knew that Mr. Payton had stopped in frightened mid-sentence, and the boy could imagine the way his father was holding his right hand in Payton's face and getting ready to

22

swing his left flipper of an arm at the principal's head. He turned the corner into the office, saw his father's arm drawn back and Payton's glasses on the end of his nose where, a moment later, they might have been broken but for the boy's sudden presence in the room.

The two men relaxed, passing backward from the edge of combat, to embarrassment, to the original postures of their argument. The father spoke first, turned to the boy and said, "I'm taking you home."

Payton began again, "Mr. . . ."

"Junior. You can call me Junior."

"Yes, if you take Panimer now, you'll have to keep him home for the rest of the year." There were only two days of school left before the summer vacation, but Payton was at a loss for some further sanction. "The case will have to be taken up with the superintendent."

Through all this Panimer sorted his position, moving backward from guilty to accused, to suspect, and finally to just another student—just another child of another angry parent. He had decided it would be better to stick out the last two days than to be assumed guilty because of his absence. But it was too late: his father was pushing him out of the office.

Several years earlier Junior Panimer had moved his family out Station Drive, three miles north to Small Hill corner, "out amongst a bunch of coons," Jewel Lamartine said, and Junior had not seemed to care, even though Lamartine was right. The colored were clustered around the corner itself and Junior's was one of four white families surrounding them, each set back from the center, each in its own quadrant of the corner cut by Small Hill Road and the Drive.

Now they were coming up the Drive, Junior punishing the truck—no hitch hikers today. The June air came warm through the windows out of the forest of tulip poplars, pin oaks, locusts, and walnut trees, which made the road a tunnel of green shade. Wind blown, half blinded—Junior's one good eye strained for a piece of the road.

"Daddy, I done it," Panimer yelled.

Junior swerved around a wagon, whose hunched driver had heard the commotion approaching behind him, but had not had time to guide his team to the side of the road. "Get that goddam mule flesh out the way, Kreutz." Junior yelled looking back over his shoulder as mules and wagon skittered along the ditch, "Damn buzzard food." As an afterthought he leaned again on the horn, and turned to the boy.

"What did you say?"

"I done it," the boy said again. "I cut them ships down."

Panimer had not misjudged his father completely—he was an ally—but he had misjudged the limits of his alliance. He stood unflinching under the man's strapping, given behind the truck as soon as they were home, even before Paula had come to the door—ten strokes that stung his buttocks and legs, counted without venom and received without fear, because Panimer knew his father was angrier at being told than at his having cut down Payton's ships, angrier at having to know it. In the middle of the beating the man said, "Anybody see you do that?" And when Panimer lied, "No," he could feel the blows softening. The strapping with his own belt was a way of telling him that if he was going to get into trouble with Payton, he'd better do it on his own, had better not come crawling home with confessions or apologies, had better not shame his family.

Paula stood waiting for them in the doorway. She had on a modest flowered dress, its short sleeves bunched at the shoulders, maybe two years behind the catalogue in her fashions. Her hair hung in neat corkscrews already made up for the carnival that night in Stilson. Junior did not notice.He brushed past her into the small living room, turned and waited for the boy. He was not deciding whether to tell her; there was no question of that. Here Panimer had misjudged too. He had hoped his father might keep it a secret, but he might have known they'd sooner argue than keep secrets from each other. Junior hesitated because he was preparing arguments to meet her arguments.

Panimer came in, went to his room, and was already lying on

24

his bed when his father called, "Get back in here." He got up, walked back and stood straight and shameless between them, his face hardened by the punishment already received. His father was saying, "Your son here, he's the one they been looking for at the school." She grabbed her shoulders, her arms crossing her chest against calamity, and looked pitifully at the boy, as if begging to be told, but gently. But Panimer just stared at her; he could see she was going to cry, and his father, unrelenting, said, "He's the one cut them ships down, what they been talking about, sabotage and that." She said nothing. "Ask him."

She looked away from the boy, afraid he would confirm it, but asked, "How'd you find out?"

"He told me."

She began to cry in little spasms of grief, sobs that came at such odd intervals that the boy was not moved to pity but afraid he might giggle. He was relieved when she began to speak.

"What will they do to him? Will they expel him?"

"They don't know about it."

"He's got to tell them."

"Got to tell 'em nothing." His defense had begun.

"I never taught him that," Paula said. " I don't know where he ever learned that."

"Nobody taught it to him," Junior said. "He taught himself."

Not satisfied, Paula said, "He doesn't get that from my side."

Junior could see she was not going to let go of it, and his silence now was a sort of kindness because he was thinking, "Your daddy was a pretty good thief."

Panimer was watching his thumbnail and fingernail as he snapped them back and forth across each other, making a little display of boredom, pushing his mother past anger to sobbing again. She turned to her husband. "You're going to let him stand there and defy me?"

"I whipped him once."

"Can't you see it didn't do any good? You don't even care."

This was more wailed than spoken. Their helplessness moved the boy to contempt. But this shrank to pity and then just guilt; it was all right if they were weak with him but he could not stand to see them weak with each other. They continued arguing in front of him, trying to decide what to do (nothing, because she would not tell the principal herself against her husband's command). Still she had to know why her son had done it, what had got into him—absolutely unanswerable questions that they put to Panimer over and over.

"I don't know," the boy said, and "I just felt like it," and "I don't know why I felt like it," only frustrating them until they were reduced to arguing with each other again, once more making the boy uneasy. Then his mother began to yell at him, which stiffened his silence. It was not just anger; she was afraid. "Don't you give me that look," she said. "Don't you ever try something like that again." She suspected his act had been in spite of patriotism. And in a village of patriots. Her fear was for him.

"Don't you let me hear any more of that about you down at Greene's store either." This was just a blind cast for trouble against the chance of recent or future delinquency. Panimer hadn't run a scam at the Jew store since they moved out of the village. But her remonstration sent Panimer riding back into that two-wheel, no-hands world at the corner of Wye Bridge Pike and Station Drive where the Jew store sat—an easy mark—across the Pike from Lamartine's Mobil, the garage where he had spent whole days with Johnny Roe Pride and the Stevens brothers, busy around the air pump, their bicycles stripped into mingled piles of parts; pestering the mechanic for screwdrivers and valve wrenches, mending an inner tube—more patch than tube—while they planned the next attack on old man Greene.

It was not just penny-candy theft. Panimer was in charge of the collection of soda pop bottles—one case was all they needed, the case itself to be swiped from behind the garage and the bottles collected along the road. He was the only one with nerve enough to talk right to Mr. Greene's face while robbing

26

him. Johnny Roe said: "It's not robbery. It's just the Jew store." But when the time came he stood outside with the others, supposedly standing guard, but just waiting to run if anything went wrong. He and the Stevens brothers and Willie Jackson stood at the side door and watched as Panimer went in the front with the bottles. He walked right up to Greene and, leaning back against the weight of the case, said, "Bottles for deposit."

Mr. Greene, who was fussing around his vegetable counter, muttering along behind the muttering of a picky customer, said, "No deposit on Hires bottles."

"No sir. This is the only case got any Hires in it. Got more outside that's nothing but Coke and Royal Crown."

Greene ignored him. The case was getting heavy now and Panimer pushed it gently against the storekeeper's leg.

"Well take it on back to her," Greene said. Panimer carried the case back to Mrs. Greene at the cash register and she separated the no-returns and Panimer volunteered to carry the accepted bottles back to the storeroom.

"Got a lot more outside," he said.

She didn't even seem suspicious, but let him carry them himself to the back room, where he rested for a moment before picking a case of empty Cokes. A minute later he came out the back door with the new case, then along the side of the store where his mates stood fixed to the handlebars of their bicycles in a tension of guilt and glee that might erupt any moment into laughter, or sudden flight, or both. And then he was in the front again presenting the stolen case to Mrs. Greene for her second accounting, then back to the storeroom for the next case—a different brand this time—out the back and along the side of the store where his friends were fairly choking on their silence now, and in the front again. Mrs. Greene sighed at the inconvenience, but automatically checked the bottles by twos, so that he supposed there were at least two more trips left in the game, and he said, "Just two more to go."

"Your mother buy all them here?"

"No'm. Been collecting along the road."

27

"Don't have time for all these bottles." But she finished her count and Panimer, hearing irritated resignation but still no suspicion, was already on his way back for the next case, hurrying this time. The boys were giggling at the side door, which should have been warning enough, but he meant to amaze them and Nancy McConkey too, who, when told, would marvel behind her total boredom. He wanted the money too, which wouldn't even come to two dollars (to be split five ways) if he didn't get the fourth case past old lady Greene. And this time she just waved him past, disdaining to count. He whistled with the ease of it and was still whistling when he came around the corner with the last case and saw his watchmen scattering on their bicycles. Johnny Roe yelled back, "Get on in your store, you old bitch," at Mrs. Greene, who was standing, arms akimbo, in the thief's path.

4

An unlikely couple on the surface, Paula and Junior were tightly wed behind their facades. It might appear she had married beneath her; she had always known it was not so. She was not a fallen woman but a runaway—from a self that had never been, a writer who had never composed a memorable sentence, daughter of a man who had aspired to a bureaucrat's life and never attained petty bureaucracy. At first her husband's crudity had excited her. Eventually she had come to understand it as the mask he wore over his intelligence—to avoid responsibility. It was this refusal to be what he could that frustrated her. She suspected he was infecting her son with a careless ambition. Now her crying gave way to a feisty silence, interrupted at intruder's peril. She would not allow the subject to be changed and she would not allow it to be talked about.

"I never been sorry I found you," Junior told her on the way to the carnival.

"Never mind that," she said.

"You look so pretty," he told her.

"Don't talk to me, please."

He gave up.

"It's you let him get away with it. That's why," she said. When he began another gentle defense she did not want to hear it. So he brooded too—injured and defiant.

Whenever Paula brought up Panimer at Green's store Junior suspected she was tempting an argument she did not really want—that she was just daring him to mention her father. Four years earlier, on the night Mrs. Greene called and told them how she had been cursed and nearly robbed by their son, Junior had been angry only briefly, at first frightened at the nerve of Panimer's deceit, but concluding the thing was a youthful prank. The boy had been only ten. Junior admired the scheme, proud that Panimer was foreman of village mischief, even boss of Earl Jackson's boy. Paula saw through that admiration and was outraged.

As Panimer explained the technique—the bottles going out the back and in the front—Junior's memory was joggged back to the Perryville warehouse where the same shipments had gone in the front and out the back and in the front again. But then he had been unwitting errand boy of an extraordinary fraud, directing the loading and unloading for Mr. Rossom, knowing something was wrong and only discovering when the scandal made the newspapers—long after he had fled with Paula—that all those goods had entered the warehouse at one price and left at another, that hospital sheets sold at surplus for twenty-five cents were being bought back the same week for over a dollar.

"He doesn't get it from my side," Paula said again. Junior turned on her.

"What side did you have in mind?" She did not answer. "What side, I said," but he could not provoke her to say, yours. "What about your old man?"

"He was innocent," Paula squeezed through tightening lips.

"Guilty as hell," Junior said. "Why do you think he never sent the law after us? Why do you think he let his precious run off with me?"

"Don't talk like that in front of him." She nodded toward the back seat where Panimer sat, a little amazed at what he had uncovered.

"Why don't we ever see my grandfather?" Panimer said.

"You be quiet," Paula said. Then turning back to her husband she said, "You see? You see what you do to him?"

Junior suspected his wife's feverish patriotism, her extra hours of bandage rolling—all her war chores—were little payments against that family crime she had never allowed herself to admit. "Why don't you stop trying to win the war single-handed?" he said. He swiveled to tell his son: "She won't give up till she's got half the world fed and the other half on a committee."

"Watch where you're going, Junior. I give the Kreutzs vegetables because they've got nothing else to eat."

"And that's not enough but she's got to be rolling gauze every week with the ladies. And if it's not something else, she's on the telephone." Paula's citizenship had begun to annoy Junior, her careful cultivation of their victory garden, bandage making Wednesday nights at the fire hall, obedience to rationing, committee organizing, hitch-hiking to the village for groceries to save gas. He did not begrudge her her patriotism, but he did not want her judging his. With all her work he could see she was still dissatisfied with him, with Panimer, even with herself.

"She wants me to join up." He winked into the back seat at his son. "How could I surrender?" he said. "I can't even get this hand over my head. And only one eye works." Paula turned and saw her husband and son smiling at each other.

"Watch the road, Junior." How could he talk like that she wondered. Never mind that he was fifty-one years old, with crippled arm and blind eye. "Look out."

"Damn them, " Junior said, steering the car back to his side of the road to avoid the Lewis brothers' approaching roadster, which had not even slowed.

"Where do they get their gas coupons?" Paula said. "I don't want you hanging around with them," she told Panimer. "I don't care who their father is." She turned back to Junior. "We're breaking the law right now. You know that? We're pleasure driving."

The carnival was alive, spinning when they got there, grounds crowded, parking lot full. Curved strings of lights lined the field; everywhere electric bulbs moved in large circles and small, turning their discrete signals into solid rings and back again as wheels sped and slowed, and stopped and sped again—thrill wheels and wheels of chance, burning through the warm night's tobacco haze.

But Panimer refused to get out of the car. Instead of just leaving him, Junior and Paula sat, thinking they would outlast his stubbornness. Junior turned the radio on. Panimer was not fooled; they would, at last, plead with him. "I got nothing to spend," he said. His father gave him a dollar and said, "Don't spend it on them vomit cars," and his mother, "That's too much. He doesn't deserve it." He would go with them, lose them as soon as he could, then come back and wait in the car. The radio was saying: "and carelessness with fire in war time must be considered an act of sabotage. A careless cigarette or match can do as much damage to life and property as a carefully set blaze of an expert saboteur. There is . . ."

"Turn that off," Paula said. Junior had already reached for the switch. They were both staring into the back seat, trying to read the boy's face. Panimer was looking out the window, trying to recognize faces in the crowd, afraid he would. His father ordered him out of the car. He got out, followed behind them, using them as a shield. But right away he saw two boys from school and one of them had seen him and looked the other way and moved off in the crowd with his friend.

"Take a chance on a radio . . . give what you can, but make it hurt a little. Put your license number in that drum right there. Take a chance on a radio . . ." A line of men stood across the entrance encouraging donations. Junior got up some change but didn't want to bother with the raffle. Paula made him. When they looked around again, Panimer had disappeared.

Junior wanted to throw leather balls at lead bottles, win Paula something soft and furry so she would calm down. Then he could go and play the gambling machines. But she was pulling him up to the Civilian Defense booth where they were recruiting trainees. Junior could not credit what he saw—Harold Johnson, who'd made a profession, since the age of sixty, of one continuous headache, forever described and forever treated in Peterson's Drug Store, was sitting there with Doc Peterson and two other drug store regulars, all of them in a row wearing white shirts and blue arm bands with yellow circles that contained lightning bolts.

"Messengers," Paula said. They've been trained as messengers. It's for after an attack. They went to Richmond for training." Junior felt a little embarrassed—for them, for himself. He tried to lead Paula away, but she was pulling against him, saying they ought to find out more about it, that he ought to sign up for something.

"But how could I surrender?"

She spun away from him, leaving him shamed, but free to go and play the gambling machines. Friends were calling to him as he got into a long line behind one of the machines.

"Don't get in that one. That one just paid off."

"Hey, Junior, when'd you get here? Hey, Billy, there's Junior. He's a one-armed bandit. Go pull his lever. Hey, Junior."

They'd all been drinking but him; beer he guessed.

"Get in this line. That one don't pay at all."

He walked over to join Billy Paul, another of Lamartine's men.

"D'you drive?" he asked. Junior nodded. "Shoulda drove the company truck." Then seeing Junior was not going to ask why, he said, "State man's in the parking lot with Osmond. Taking license numbers." But Junior's attention was fixed on the machine in front of them, which had become stuck in one cycle, paying two nickels for every one inserted; the player feeding it as fast as he could, but pulling the lever without emotion, as if he had found something that belonged to him, though it might take a little while to claim. The line had broken, was pressing around him, shouting, "You been there long enough," and "Give someone else a chance," and "Quit shoving, buddy"; behind them all, the owner of the machines watching—also without emotion, because if the man pulled two for one all night he wouldn't have more than twenty-five dollars, and his quarter machine was making that much every fifteen minutes.

Junior, bored with another's steady trickle of success, turned back to Billy Paul. "Osmond?" he said. "Osmond's the fire chief's brother. It's his carnival, ain't it?"

"That's right," Billy said, "but they just put Osmond on the county price board. Says he's got to do right by it."

Panimer ducked around in the shadows of carnival machinery, then sat for a long time behind the electric calliope. A generator started behind him and spoiled the music. He got up, drifted through the crowd, using strangers for shields now, sliding away from faces he recognized. He caught sight of his mother entering a tent, under a sign that said **CLAYTON WEL-COMES TRIUMPH. SIGN UP FOR VICTORY.** She was talking to Miss Nicely, the fifth grade teacher. Across the way, Valerie Jackson, who dozed by day in the window seat of the notions store, was registering women for something. She was Mrs. Cuttrell's sister and had been married to Earl Jackson's brother. Or was it the other way around? Panimer couldn't remember. He backed up though, and moved over to the next row of concessions, almost walking into his father's boss, Jewel Lamartine, who was talking with Redmond Clarke, the fire chief. Again he stopped, and watched as Lamartine spit discreetly, and discreetly covered the obscenity with a little dust nudged with the edge of a shiny white wing tip.

All these intersections of conversation, kin, and enterprise knit the carnival ground, thwarting his participation, blocking his escape. He tried the center fairway, well lit but crowded. As he came out into the full light he saw three older boys lounging in front of the recruiting tent. One of them saw him and pointed. He did not recognize them, but turned and walked in the other direction. He looked back. They were following. Moving faster, still walking, he circled half way round the merry-go-round, looked back through moving horses and saw them separating, coming around in both directions. He began to trot, looked over his shoulder and saw they were running too. He broke into a run, and was almost at the end of the fairway when he turned sharply into a tent. Someone grabbed his arm and said, "You can't go in there," but he pulled away, inside, and pushing through a silent crowd, reached a platform which he crawled under. Where he would have stayed, but for a new commotion behind him, someone shouting, "Get that boy out of there. He's too young for this." He wriggled under the back of the tent, looked around and took off running again, toward the parking lot. At the fence he fell to the ground, catching his breath. He had lost them.

Moving between the rows of autos, trying to remember where they had parked, he was surprised to see his father and Billy Paul. They were bent over, one at the front of the car, one at the back, trying to remove the license plates, laughing and cursing the rusty bolts. There was a bottle on top of the car. Panimer moved back through the lot and sat down against the fence.

An hour later the sirens sounded. The sheriff's car and panel truck the county used for collecting stray men and dogs came racing along the dirt road beside the fairgrounds raising clouds of dust against the carnival lights; car and wagon, red lights blinking and spinning, turned into the fairway, their sirens screaming at each other—the people had already cleared a path—turned again and stopped in front of the gambling machines. A man ran in front of the sheriff's headlights, and jumped the fence behind the machines; nobody followed. Then, as if someone had tipped the fairground, the crowd rolled to the end of the field where the deputies were loading the one-armed bandits into the panel truck. Then a siren from the other side, and the people came tumbling back again, all the way to the front gate where smoke was pouring from the raffle drum. The raffle numbers had burned. Someone had already emptied a fire extinguisher into the drum and the biggest engine from the fire department across the road was sitting there looking silly and Redmond Clarke was yelling at the driver to cut the pump motor and get the truck out of there because it hadn't been enough to piss on. His brother Osmond was arguing with the state price man about what had happened; how, or why, the drum full of license numbers, which the state man had meant to commandeer, had been turned into a charred mush, even before a winning number had been picked. By the time the people began to flow back again the last of the gambling machines were loaded and already being driven off the fairground, sheriff's car leading, flashing lights still protesting urgency.

Panimer was waiting by the parking lot fence, out of sight, when they came back. His father's arm around his mother, he heard him saying:

"Wheels. Look at em . . . issa ferris wheel . . . turn . . . and look where it takes you. Right back, thass where. Anna merry-go-round . . . issa same."

"Be quiet, Junior."

"You be quiet . . . anna vomit cars . . . jess another get off where you got on . . . without yer supper."

"You should be ashamed."

"Shame on *you* . . . issa same. Anna gambling wheel . . . give em some anna wheel go . . . an get some . . . annit go again an you give it back . . . an' back where you was.

"So?" But Panimer could see her smiling through her disgust and he knew she was glad the arm was around her.

"So *you* should be ashamed."

"Shut up, Junior." Then whispering, "Be quiet. There's Mrs. Jackson."

The boy caught up with them; they turned and saw him and immediately his father seemed sober again. On the way home they all sat in the front seat. Their independent ways at the carnival had spun them farther apart than they cared to be. Even the boy was content that his mother's arm should be draped across the seat behind him, that her hand should rest on his shoulder, and he could see his father's hand leave the gear shift to caress her leg. Which pleased him too.

They all had confessions—to make and to hear. Only Panimer unable to explain. His father began:

"Damn right I took the tags off," in response to no one's accusation, even question. "Got 'em right under the seat here. None of the state man's business."

Waiting to be scolded, he gently rubbed his wife's knee, but she said, "Guess I could go to work. Seems the least I could do," and before that could settle she was saying, "Redmond said would we mind if they put the Small Hill siren on our house and I told him that's the least we could do was let them put it there. Because he said we're on top of the hill and that's where a siren ought to be, up high."

"Siren?"

"Wait a minute. And he wouldn't mind if one of the colored took it, but all of them are down at the corner, and besides, he wasn't sure any of them had a telephone and it's as easy as that. When there's an air raid they call you and you sound the siren three times for the black out and when it's all clear they call you again and you give it one long signal."

"I don't mind," Junior said.

"Have to buy shades black on the outside for every window in the house."

Panimer said, "Couldn't we just turn the lights out?"

"I'll be working evenings at first," Paula said. "Then the day shift when they get to full production. It's sixty-eight cents an hour, and they're going to run a bus all the way out Station Drive three times a day. And it's not even dangerous." Paula would not let them interrupt her. It all had to be explained at once, and better while she had Junior at a disadvantage. There wasn't going to be any arguing about it. She had signed up and that was that. "And the Stilson bank's insuring everyone who works there so how could it be dangerous? There's going to be thirty-five buildings and none of them can have more than a pound of powder in it at one time. It's just for small parts, just fuses and what did he say—detonators."

Junior said that was fine, sure they could have the siren on their house, not bothering to respond to these other notions, which he supposed were just more war dreams, because Clayton didn't have enough people left to work in a factory and this thing in the village about an explosives plant was just talk, but he said, "Besides, you can't have an explosives plant in a village."

"You weren't listening, Junior. It's only for small . . ." but Junior wasn't listening, only thinking, not even enough colored to work the farms, so who's gonna work in a factory; the boys already enlisted and the new people worked on the war, in Washington, the government people, the price people, who'd come in because the job had got too big for the ones already there, like their neighbor Mr. Lewis, who'd been in government for as long as anyone could remember.

Junior said, "Put Osmond on the Price Board and look at. His pants is already too small. Ain't this a shame?"

Panimer said, "They didn't need your license number. They could just take the number off your ration sticker." Junior glanced at the A sticker on the windshield.

"That got a number on it?" he said.

Paula, hoping it would, turned on the overhead light.

"It's on the outside," the boy said.

"Don't matter," Junior said. "Nobody's business. D'you see that Florida man jump the fence?"

"You aren't drunk at all," she accused. He laughed. She laughed. Then Panimer. Then all three, at the sequence of their laughter.

"Don't matter if he got away," Junior said. "They took his machines and busted 'em all to hell."

"Who said?" Panimer asked.

"That's what they told him they'd do. Billy Paul said the high sheriff warned the man yesterday. If he didn't have 'em outa there by tonight, they'd take sledge hammers to 'em."

"I bet they squirt money every which way," the boy said.

"And the money goes into savings bonds. For the town. Sheriff said it was the least they could do."

"How did the fire start?" Paula said. This met silence, embarrassing them all. Junior took the corner at Small Hill too fast and his front tire caught the edge of the culvert. Right away the car was thumping along at a tilt. They pulled over beside the baseball diamond. Junior got out and looked at the tire. "Ain't this a goddam shame?" he said, but quietly, so Paula and Panimer decided it was safe to get out and look too. "Ain't this a goddam shame?" he said again, louder; thinking he had a spare but that he couldn't get another tire, or maybe he could because he worked for Lamartine, but didn't want to ask, and was just wondering what he *would* do when Paula said, "You can fix it, can't you?"

"It ain't just punctured," he said. "It's tore."

"Can't you change it?"

"I told you don't tempt me with talk. Not when I'm driving."

"You were going too fast."

Quiet for the moment, they heard a harmony, high and close, colored women singing,

> . . . and get into position
> Praise the Lord, and pass the ammunition
> And we'll all stay free . . .

carrying through the night, across the baseball diamond. The boy wondered where the colored Pin and Dog and Phoog and R.B. and Amos and the others from Small Hill were, having heard that coons were generally put in a motor pool because that's what they knew best (this overheard from Earl Jackson) and that they always went to the European Theatre (this from the Lewis brothers), but suspecting both sources of what his mother called "just prejudice." The Army wouldn't let them spend all their time just swimming and going to movies. He wasn't about to ask, to be caught ignorant about the war, something everyone else knew by heart.

"Isn't that beautiful?" his mother said. "They sing so beauti-fully."

Junior was looking for his tire iron, rummaging through the trunk, remembering the bumper jack was no good. It would go up but not down and he'd had to drive off it last time and had bent the whole thing. But he found it and set it up and began to crank. He stopped. The singing had stopped. He began again. The click of the jack was carrying across the field to where the colored girls sat at the edge of the woods. There was a tittering, "Shut up, girl," a smothered laugh, then general mirth, maybe derision—of the jack, or of him and the jack, more likely the predicament of his whole family.

He grabbed the tools, threw them in the trunk, and slammed it shut. "Get in," he said.

"Aren't you going to change it?" Paula asked.

"Get in."

He raced the engine, spun into the road, the tire thumping wildly, jerking the steering wheel, and him, as if he'd grabbed hold of a paint-shaking machine. Before they reached the driveway they were riding on the rim, throwing sparks from the pavement, the iron screeching down through the hollow.

5

Paula had been right. They were going to build an explosives plant in Clayton. In fact, Junior worked on it himself, put the tarpaper roofs on every one of the thirty-five little wood frame buildings and supervised the installation of the fiberboard walls in half of them, because Jewel Lamartine got the construction job. Earl Jackson's company did the grading and put in the gravel road and built the chain link fence, which turned out to be the bigger contract since so much earth had to be moved.

It was built on one of Lamartine's tracts, a marshy flat behind the town, which made Lamartine one of the partners in the new company, along with Charlie Stockstill, manager of Chain Food, and Hiram Johnson, who ran the Ford agency (looking for investment opportunities for the duration), William Roehmer, manager of the Stilson Bank, and Arthur Settle, Clayton Mayor and Civilian Defense chief, who was made president. It was the mixed fortune of all but Settle to have at least one son in service and they named the corporation Sons of Clayton Explosives Inc. The opportunity for patriotic enterprise had fallen to them from the Action Defense Corporation, a Maryland fireworks manufacturer that had turned its plant to munitions and now had more work than it could handle. They agreed to send their surplus to Sons of Clayton on subcontracts.

All through July, Jackson's trucks carried fill down Station Drive to the site and by August the construction had begun. Lamartine moved fast. By the time one end of the tract was graded the buildings were going up. The plant had to be ready by the end of September. It was. And Paula worked on the swing shift as she had promised. Junior didn't fuss about it. Some of his friends' wives did the same thing, and Paula's salary and his own overtime wages would make them rich.

Paula had been right about the siren too. Redmond Clarke sent his men to install it the week after the carnival. It looked like a little squat silo and the firemen built a small platform for it on the peak of the roof. They put the switch outside the kitchen door and when it was connected, gave it a trial blast, which brought Panimer and the Lewis boys running up the hill from the corner store to see what had happened.

Paula had never quite relaxed in the Clayton community. She had forced Junior to move out of the village. People thought she had run away from their society, supposed she thought herself too good for them. There had been gossip of Junior and another woman. Then the woman moved away and the gossip passed and Paula regretted their move. She had isolated herself. Now she wanted the village's approval and friendship. But the harder she struggled for it, the more they withdrew, reading her advances for a hypocritical snobbery.

"Junior and I would love to get to know you better," she told Mrs. Pride in the check-out line in Chain Food. Mrs. Pride turned away and Paula heard her repeat what she had said to Mrs. Johnson.

The new times suited Paula. She was patriotic to a fault and the war would give her a chance to win back the village. For a start she meant to win the county victory garden prize.

When they closed the carnival three days early, Junior was annoyed. "I catch hell from you," he said to Paula. "But what about all those others using their gas rations to drive to the carnival. Ain't this a shame? A whole bunch of people that was

42

nobody is somebody all of a sudden, and looking into all us nobodies' business. And the worst is Osmond Clarke, but he won't stay the worst. And a lot of 'em are just looking for a bigger ration of gas, one lie jumping on top of another so they can claim some kind of B sticker, as if they couldn't possibly do their war duty with the three gallons a week they get with the A."

"And what about you?" Paula said.

"So?" Junior said. "I work for Lamartine, don't I? I can get filled up at the Mobil any time I want. So long as I don't flout it."

"Flaunt it."

"Yeah. So long as I don't flaunt it."

To Junior the first year of the war seemed to be one long false alarm. People were touchy. The Germans were winning in the desert on one side, and on the other the Japanese were taking islands. When people looked at the sky every little cloud looked like a parachute. One night Osmond Clarke woke up to see explosions across the river and his wife had to beat him with a hard pillow before he'd believe it was just heat lightning.

Panimer was not going to be as big as his father. He was smaller boned though well proportioned. His long, black, usually dirty hair hung over a face that seemed a compromise between the round outline of his mother's and the crude features of Junior. When Paula studied the boy she saw Junior, when Junior looked he saw Paula; just as each discounted their contribution to Panimer's mischief in favor of the other. The father thinking, if the boy was mixed up, even devious sometimes, it was no wonder with a mother so confused she could cry or get angry about the same thing, and Paula supposing that a father who could whip his child for a deed he tacitly admired was certain to confound him, that any delinquency was taught by, or inherited from, Junior. Like most parents they failed to see the child did not think of himself as a product of either's influence; he was Panimer, who secretly loved Nancy McConkey, and who had sunk the Duncan Kimball navy—for reasons of his own.

The boy's charm lay in a disguise of talent, something he *had*

43

learned from his father. He was fast and bright, athletic, but he talked with the slow speech of Small Hill corner and moved in a slouch and shuffle. Though still unlicensed, he was already expert in the Small Hill salute, a single finger raised from its grip at the top of a steering wheel as he sped up Station Drive in the Lewis brothers' jalopy. And he could hit a baseball sharper and cleaner, with more consistency than anyone he knew, colored or white, if not as far. And when he broke out of his slouch into a run, when he really meant it, he amazed them.

But this was shuffling season; hot breezes out of the hollow carried the sick-sweet sassafrass from the fresh-dug garbage pit in the woods and voices from beyond the corner riding the noise of a small engine every day, somewhere across the skin diamond, behind the long hill full of junked cars, Lloyd Marcum's junkyard, where Panimer would roam nights with James and Roland Lewis, smashing old, milky windshields, busting headlight glass, searching parts for their jalopy, and rolling derelict autos down the hill to collision with still other rusting skeletons until the light came on in Marcum's window above his garage, and they ran.

It was so humid that a game of pitch and catch could be finished with one overthrown or misjudged ball, the pain of chasing it a dozen yards greater than the urge to continue, enough even to make him wonder why the game had begun at all—too hot even to argue who owed change from yesterday for sodas at the corner store where they heard a customer inside trying to negotiate the price of a roll of toilet paper and demanding of Mrs. James, "This ain't the kind feels like sandpaper running up and down your behind?" Almost too wasting hot to giggle at that.

But the three of them, Panimer and James and Roland finished their sodas and walked across to Marcum's where they meant to present themselves as legitimate, daylight customers for some part or piece of junk, just to hang around the garage, to see what was new, in case there was something they really needed. But Marcum wouldn't have a conversation. And he wouldn't let them inside the garage. And he didn't want them hanging around his field. Which is where they wandered anyway, moving slowly, slapping the bodies of dead cars, goading Marcum's patience until they were up the hill where he couldn't see them. Then they saw for the first time where the engine noise had been coming from, and the voices. Down the far side of the hill in the hollow two men were building a cinderblock wall, one of them running a power mixer, the other laying the block. The boys couldn't agree what it was going to be. Panimer thought a house, but Roland said nobody was building houses, that anybody coming to live around there was coming to work in the new plant and none of them had any money but would live in a trailer park in Clayton, and his father, Mr. Lewis, didn't like it a bit, because the town didn't have a proper sewer for them and their business would all be running into the creek.

"More likely another garage," James said. "Marcum couldn't fix a scooter."

They sat down against the running board of a car too decomposed to identify and argued what kind it had been. Tired of that, Roland said "cinderblock's the strongest there is."

"It's got holes in it," James reminded him.

"That's what makes it strong," Roland said.

"Wouldn't take nothing to knock it down," Panimer suggested.

"It ain't built yet," Roland said, and they looked at him, guessing his meaning. They hadn't thought of that before, that this row of junks at the crest of the hill could be rolled down the other side, away from Marcum's garage, into the hollow—to test the strength of cinderblock.

They came back several times that week to check the wall's progress. It didn't seem to be getting any higher, only longer; three blocks tall and already fifty blocks long. Still no corner; their speculation began all over again.

"Maybe Marcum's going into chickens."

"Who ever heard of a cinderblock chicken house?"

"I did."

"It's not Marcum's property anyway. Belongs to a man in Washington."

"Then it's a factory," Panimer said.

"It's a secret," James said, "a war secret, and that's why you don't know what it is."

Sometimes they could make out the voices of the mason and his helper, drifting up to them on the noise of the mixer engine, and it finally occurred to them the men themselves did not know what they were building, only the dimensions of the thing. Which were still growing. The flush-string had been stretched all the way to the woods but still no corner had been laid.

Most of the time they just worked without talking. And the wall grew higher—six blocks tall when they began to build the scaffolding. A bulldozer came and started pushing more trees down. That seemed to be the signal for help. When the dozer had cleared another hundred feet into the woods, a crew of two dozen arrived and whatever it was turned corners, began to grow in earnest in three dimensions—a great gray shape in the hollow, covering square acres, four stories high, so that from Panimer's house on the hill at the other side of the corner it was going to be visible through the woods in winter. And from the Lewis place, further back in the same quadrant of Small Hill Corner as the new structure, it would be seen all year long. By the time Mr. Lewis's curiosity turned to anger it was much too late; the sudden size of the thing alone was enough to discourage any hope that it might be stopped or undone.

But he meant to find out who was behind it, went to the Stilson Court House and discovered the property had been bought by a Delaware company. He called the principal listed on the record of transfer, but only reached a lawyer who told him the real principal was in England on war business, he thought, and even if Mr. Lewis succeeded in reaching him, he would only be talking to a representative for a number of others, the lawyer implying the project was a secret and would have to remain so. Enough to discourage further investigation but it left Lewis still annoyed, thinking they better damn well win the war if these desecrations were ever going to be undone. This and the trailer park behind Clayton, visible from Station Drive. It had

46

already begun to fill in anticipation of jobs in the explosives plant.

The community knew Mr. Lewis was a government man. It didn't know much more about him. Until the war started and he began to talk about paper. The radio told everybody scrap paper was important. The President told them it was important. But Mr. Lewis had been heard to say that the paper business had dishonest men in it who were undercutting the people's efforts.

Panimer overheard Mr. Lewis tell Jewel Lamartine, "It's a scandal. They're getting away with it. We can't stop them." He saw Lamartine shake his head in sympathy with Lewis's concern. "They're making hundreds of thousands of dollars," Lewis said. "They're cheating the ceiling price."

"It gives the children something to do," Lamartine said. "I mean collecting the stuff. It gives them a part in all this."

"They're the ones getting cheated," Lewis said.

The crew working on the huge cinderblock building suddenly doubled, strange men arriving each day in two buses that did not even have license plates, and the boys sat on the hill and watched as the men crawled over scaffolding and began to rivet the steel superstructure that was going to support a great pitched roof of corrugated gray metal. No windows, just a solid gray mass that would have dwarfed the competing shape of any building they had ever seen before except that it was tucked into the hollow of Small Hill corner where nothing was going to compete with it.

The Lewis boys brought the word down to Panimer from their father that the thing was just a monstrosity and beyond that he couldn't tell them what it was.

"He knows," James said, "he just can't tell us." So they supposed it was going to be used in the war, which would make Small Hill a very important target. "That's why they put an air raid siren on our house," Panimer said.

They watched as enormous rolling steel doors were hung from each end of the building, with huge hasps that would be fastened with sliding steel bars. They almost forgot they meant to test the strength of cinderblock.

Roland was the oldest of the three—seventeen and facing his last year at Stilson High, after which his father intended to send him to a preparatory school for the military academy. He wanted the boy to be an officer, or maybe a slowed academic career would create the longest possible distance between then and the possibility of combat. One could not be certain of the father's motive inside his love for a son, even a love so aggravated as that one. Roland cared little for school, was addicted to Small Hill indolence and to the freedom given by his jalopy, which he shared with his brother James because James was his mechanic. The car had no single name—an oversized Chevrolet engine was somehow made to propel the rebuilt chassis of a Ford Phaeton, and only James could explain the little miracle of power transferred from transmission to incompatible drive shaft. Too much power; they had broken one axle.

Sometimes they drove all the way to Washington, to pawn shops on M Street where they exchanged things taken from their own home for cash. James, at fifteen, thrilled to ride shotgun to this homemade thievery only because there was no shotgun, complementing his brother's joy in a running car, since his own delight was in making the car run.

It was the end of the jalopy that altered their summer; the last wheeze and explosion of the engine, its pistons perforated, that left the Phaeton powerless on Station Drive, and Roland trying desperately to start it, unaware of the internal damage already done. It did start once more, ran just for a moment, until a final explosion tore through the head gasket. It never turned again—not even James could change that. They got Marcum to come and haul it to his garage, and when they had the engine stripped down James knew it was finished.

When he convinced Roland, it only remained to bargain with Marcum for a price; the brothers supposing they had something to bargain with. They didn't. But it took them half an afternoon to realize Marcum was not teasing them, but actually refusing to pay even a dollar for a car whose engine was now scattered all over his garage, a vehicle that would never move under its own power again, only waiting to be towed to the top of the junk hill.

Marcum had them, and they knew it. He could see they knew it, and so became disgusted with their persistence, threatening to call their father and charge him for the towing, and by the time they left the garage the man had them thinking they might actually owe *him* something. As they walked up to the corner James said, "We don't owe him nothing."

"We don't owe that son of a bitch a thing," Roland said.

Without the Phaeton they were stranded in Small Hill for the rest of the summer, left to traipse through August, from home to corner store, to garage, to skin diamond, to the junk hill where they watched the gray building grow; left to loiter with Panimer, who was only fourteen, only starting high school that year, and whose father was a laborer.

Roland was a thin, blond boy, not athletic but bold. He was graduating that summer from sodas to beer in bumper bottles that Farmer Kreutz would buy for him at the corner store in return for small change. He wondered how soon he would be a soldier? His father seemed to know everything about the war. It was a dangerous irritation, though not something to panic over; he would not wear patriotism on his sleeve. That was for children, for the schoolboys who sewed division patches on their coats. Clayton's patriotism pleased Mr. Lewis; its rhetoric amused him. His sons' delinquencies were annoying but trivial, busy as he was with national priorities.

James, trying against instinct to imitate his brother's indifference, found it harder to accept compromise or abstraction where action and vengeance belonged. Sketches he spent whole class hours on, pictures showing each intricacy of emblem and mechanical detail of a P-38 spitting bullets at a Zero, would never be shown to Roland. He resented his father's preference for his older brother—Roland, who would say, yes, then disobey, or ignore, sometimes even keep his word, whatever his whim, while he, James, would argue at the outset, shirk a chore and make no secret of his shirking. He did not wish their victory garden to go to weeds, neither did he care to weed it.

49

The brothers had tolerated the younger Panimer at first; then, grown a little dependent on his summer company, were charmed by his own diffidence and by the speed and coordination they knew hid beneath his shuffle. They were unaware their friendship harbored the Duncan Kimball saboteur, just as Clayton, continuing its preparations against enemy attack—its delegations of emergency responsibility, its bond and scrap drives, its construction of Sons of Clayton Explosives—was ignorant of this cell of cynicism and sabotage in its satellite corner Small Hill.

6

As he turned the corner in Clayton each morning, on his way to Washington, Mr. Lewis's gaze always caught the window of the notions store. There in fading gold letters was his favorite village sign: **CLAYTON'S NOTIONS,** and under that, **OCEANS OF NOTIONS**, and under that, Wilma Settle, Prop.; and now in fresh red paint in a bottom corner: If They Land Here We'll Take Care of Them Ourselves. Lewis smirked as he read the new line for the first time. The store had always amused him anyway, as one of those places whose existence must be less than marginal, though its cash register, graying stock, and the constant attendance of a proprietor protest solvency. Absurd to think Clayton could support a notions store even then, much less ten years earlier when Wilma Settle opened it. Nor could it be losing much since her nephew, Arthur Settle, now town manager, owned the store and let her have it for nothing. Lewis's amusement was rekindled each time he passed because he knew the real commerce of notions in Clayton was in fact transacted there, the daily tattling and clucking of the oldest village tongues. He always said the place might have been better named The Notions of Wilma Settle and Friends.

One of the friends in that nonsewing circle was her maiden sister, Jane Settle, who had taught at the Duncan Kimball School and once, years earlier, had called Mrs. Lewis at home to tell her that her son Roland, then in second grade, had grabbed and kissed a girl whose mother would also have to be told. Such outrages told and retold, year by year, were the stuff of Clayton's mythology, and all from the source—Clayton's Notions.

The village did have notions of self-defense against the enemy. Arthur Settle, chief of civilian defense, ordered a survey of the community by the town clerk. He was to record every rifle, pistol, horse, cart, auto, and truck that might be called into local service. The clerk took his task earnestly, first in the village itself, then in the outlying homes. At Small Hill he sensed resistence. First Marcum didn't want to tell him anything, least of all his most intimate trade secret—which of his jalopies would run. The only honest answer was none, but he said, "Couldn't tell you, from one day to the next."

"Mr. Marcum, maybe you could estimate."

"No. I couldn't even do that."

He asked permission to walk up through the junk field to look for himself.

"Couldn't tell much by just looking," Marcum said.

The man started past him, up the hill. He had only gone a few steps when Marcum caught up with him from behind and said into his ear, with some menace so that he jumped sideways, "I said you couldn't tell much by just looking." The young clerk had not seen a car yet with a tire on it; most of them were up on blocks and missing some mechanical vital. He gave up, walked back to the corner to take inventory at the shacks around the store. Settle had told him, "Every house, colored or white, I don't care," but he might have known after failing with the first woman that his survey of the other shacks at the corner would yield nothing. But he persisted shack by shack and might have left Small Hill with nothing added to his defense inventory had he not remembered one of Lamartine's men lived there, and asked his way to Junior's house, where he found Paula, effusively cooperative, volunteering everything she could think of—their car, Junior's shotgun, the dump truck, even a farm wagon rotting behind the house. "The truck belongs to Lamartine," she said, "but you know in an emergency . . ."

"Of course," said the clerk, so delighted with this small trove and Paula's enthusiasm that he never found the Lewis place.

It was time to test the strength of cinderblock. The construction crews that had worked double shifts on the great gray building in the hollow had been packed off in their buses, moved on to another project. Tractor trailers arrived daily. The steel doors rolled open for them and closed behind them: no use to try to see what went on inside. Huge curtains had been hung across the entrance. Eventually the trucks would come out the rear doors, wheel around the building, empty of great weight. Panimer knew that much by the sound of their engines, the ease with which they rolled up Station Drive. They came from all directions and left in all directions, trucks carrying the license plates of ten or fifteen states; some of them double semis that could hardly negotiate Small Hill corner.

"Cinderblock's the strongest thing you can build with," Panimer said. "It isn't," James said.

"You don't even know as much as Panimer," said Roland.

Their crippled roadster was at the top of the junk hill, waiting to be picked over, sold piecemeal by the man who had taken it from them for nothing. Already a headlight had been removed, giving the Phaeton a blind, lopsided aspect, more than James could bear. But neither brother realized Panimer meant to make this assault on the wall an incendiary attack, much less that he would be willing to steer the car most of the way down the hill himself, before jumping clear, to insure head-on contact with the target, even risk kamikaze collision, to prove his zeal, or nerve; they would not be sure why he did it.

That afternoon the three of them lurked around the garage. They saw a man drive up to the garage door in a black sedan. He had a coat and tie on and called from his window to Marcum, who came out straightening his overall straps and wiping grease from his hands. They talked, Marcum leaning on the man's door. But before long the stranger was out of his car. And the boys could hear what he said because he was almost shouting, "Why won't you sell?" and "It's nothing but junk anyway," and "I'm giving you top price." Then a silence, and they could see the man was just waiting, maybe supposing his appeal had taken hold because Marcum was working his cheeks in and out with his mouth closed, and the boys moved closer to hear the answer, all three thinking it must be the Phaeton in jeopardy of sale since it was the only think on the hill with tires on it. But there was no answer. Only Marcum standing there, sucking his cheeks in and out, until the man said, "I'm offering more than the ceiling price. For all of it," gesturing widely at the junk field.

"Don't want more than the ceiling price," Marcum said.

"Marcum," the stranger said, a little incredulous, "you got the only junk lot in northern Virginia that hasn't been sold for scrap. Now I ask you as a patriot, what do you want for it?"

"Nothing."

"You'd let it just sit there? Just rust into the ground?"

"Just rot where it sits," Marcum agreed, turning and walking slowly into the garage, not even looking back when the man spun his wheels in the gravel.

The boys met on the skin ball diamond. They took the back way to the junk lot, through the woods. Panimer carried a gasoline can, which surprised Roland and frightened James.

"No percentage in doing it half way," Panimer told them. Loath to speak their misgivings, the brothers followed behind the younger boy to the top of the junk hill where the Phaeton sat, a single shiny moonlit form in a row of decay. It was already facing the target, only needing the removal of wheel blocks, the release of its brake and a slight coaxing to send it on its hundred-yard course to the wall, which stretched below them, a long dark shadow in the hollow. Panimer put the gas can on the front seat and climbed behind the wheel.

Roland and James, their back against the back of the Phaeton, heels dug into the ground and their hands turned under the bumper, lifted and pushed, until the car slowly began to roll. They turned and watched as it gathered speed, caught the steeper grade and again accelerated; waiting for the pilot to bail out, never doubting he would, even after the car was moving much too fast for safe exit. Even after it had crunched into the wall they supposed they had missed his jump in the darkness. And they were running down the hill, calling to him, when they saw the woods light up at the back of the building. Stopping in the middle of the hill they watched as two men came around the corner and along the wall to what was left of the Phaeton.

"There's someone in here. It's gas running all over."

"Look out, it's gas."

"Is he dead?"

"Can't tell."

They heard no more; the two men had lowered their voices, but the brothers stood there waiting several moments, watching the ground beneath them, just keeping their balance in the dark. Two shadows lengthened in front of them, their own. They turned into the beam of a flashlight coming down the hill, and ran to the edge of the woods. It was Marcum. They watched the light swing in wide arcs in front of them as he stopped, moved, and stopped again. Until the beam caught the demolished Phaeton and he hurried forward. The two men had vanished and the light at the end of the building had gone out.

"Your name's Panimer, ain't it?"

Panimer was hurt. He came to, his head cradled in Marcum's lap, the junk man mechanic sitting on what was left of the Phaeton's running board. Blood still ran from the boy's head, and Marcum was asking, "Who done you this way?"

"I don't know," but the interrogation had already begun to create its own response.

"Well, what happened?"

"I can't remember nothing." This continued to be his answer to all questions about that evening. How had he come to the junkyard? He could not remember. How had the gas can got there? He could not say. Who had put him in the car? He could remember nothing about it. The brain had been slightly concussed; who could argue that the memory of one evening had not been permanently dislodged? Junior and Paula knew well enough his amnesia had been extraordinarily selective, saving all that went before that night, even the bush beans he had not picked for the supper he had not eaten the evening of his accident, but nobody believed it was an accident. Who could believe he would have put himself in the car with a full ten-gallon gas can and rolled himself to what might have been his death? They had to assume it had been done to him, either by adolescents who had not quite reckoned with the consequences of their act, or by adults who had.

The Lewis brothers had seen Marcum take off his shirt and wrap it around Panimer's head, then lead him slowly up the hill. Marcum had taken the boy back to his garage and telephoned Junior, who came and drove him home. The doctor arrived, examined Panimer quickly and sewed him up—eleven stitches at his temple, fifteen in his jaw. He left, accepting his patient's word that he could not remember how it had happened.

7

Panimer started at Stilson High School that fall with stitches in forehead and jaw, two dark, cross-hatched lines that made his face a bit frightening, as if it had been stuffed and zipped up, an unfortunate aspect for a new scholar. But scholarship was not much on his mind; the war all around him was getting closer. He was not sure where he stood. The Stilson police questioned him about his accident but no one asked him about the sinking of the Duncan Kimball navy.

To get to his new school he had to change buses at Duncan Kimball. He imagined Mr. Payton standing on the grammar school steps, waiting to intercept him, to send him home before he could change to number 47 for Stilson. Or maybe it would just be Lester, stooped over his broom, still spying on him. He saw neither of them, but followed the Lewis brothers onto the second bus, slid way down on the seat behind them, and turned the stitched side of his face away from the aisle. Johnny Roe Pride swinging onto the bus, using the door lever for a trapeze, saw him. "Hey, Panimer," he called. Panimer did not turn, pretended not to hear. Johnny Roe sat down beside him. "Hey, Panimer. D'you hear Payton got fired?"

"Didn't get fired. Got transferred," a girl behind them said.

Panimer turned. She looked away, and Johnny Roe tried not to notice the scars and black threads but could not help himself.

"You got in a accident, hunh? We heard you got in a accident. How many stitches?" Panimer turned his scars to the window again. "Everyone thought you done it."

"Done what?"

"When they sent you home last year."

"I went home cause I felt like it."

"They sent you," Johnny Roe said. "You carved on your desk. Miz Cuttrell showed everyone. She said it was just the same as vandalism and you'd have to fix it before they let you come back. You carved Nancy McConkey. She's in back."

"I didn't." Panimer said, uncomfortable with his lie, afraid she might be listening behind them.

Nancy McConkey watched as he examined his reflection in the window, as he felt tenderly along the stitches, even winced for him before she looked away to wonder which of her old classmates would be her friends this year. Nancy was changing. She would not be a tall, thin woman as her lithe pre-adolescence forecast. Now, in puberty, there was already a fullness about her, a heavy-legged, closeness to earth that announced sex, and the announcement embarrassed her, coming too early, before she was ready for it. Her blond hair had become rather darker; she had let it grow longer. It gave her eyes something to hide behind. Her face was softer, had shed its prim, grammar-school satisfaction and taken on a rather more endearing aspect of timid confusion. At the moment she was annoyed by a blemish on her chin and by an older boy who had fallen into the seat beside her, his back and elbows shoving carelessly against her as he demonstrated a bayonet maneuver to a friend across the aisle.

Panimer was more than satisfied with the changes in Nancy. But there seemed no chance to speak to her. Or if there were, he made up reasons why it was impossible. They avoided contact for the very reason they might have spoken—they were attracted to each other. It was not an old acquaintance they would

58

presume upon, but an old awareness: acute awareness. They had never carried on a conversation, not even in their first years of school; only that child-code of masked affection, betraying itself through threat and indifference, accusation and denial. He had always performed in her presence even when performance had passed comprehension, as in the playground rhyme:

> Take off your hats, you Republican rats,
> And make way for the Democrats.

but mostly acts of nerve, skill; Panimer on his Schwinn, saving his no-hands double twist into the schoolyard for her.

Now they had come to a second stillness—the silence of adolescence. How could he tell her that only last year he had carved her name on a Duncan Kimball desk; or she, that she didn't mind the stitches, that she would like to touch the scars.

Once he knew his way around halls and lunchroom, Panimer found Stilson High School much like Duncan Kimball. Boys boasted of brothers and fathers, all of whom seemed to be winning the war singlehandedly, though the principal and teachers still begged nickels and dimes for war bonds and saw that everyone had a scrap drive assignment. "Paper's just as important as anything else," his homeroom teacher told him.

"I can't be class paper warden," Panimer told Mrs. Fernanda. "I work after school. In the garden." A lie. Or mostly lie.

"I'm going to speak to your mother. I don't see why you can't contribute like the rest."

"She works in the explosives plant. She can't come after school." Was Nancy listening?

"Yeah," Johnny Roe said, "she works in a building with the colored."

"Is there something wrong with that?" Mrs. Fernanda asked.

"No'me," Johnny Roe said.

"And this doesn't concern you. I was talking to Panimer." If she was just talking to him why couldn't she keep her voice down? "Panimer, I'm going to write a note to your mother."

59

Let her write a note. He wouldn't deliver it. Why should he be messenger of their secrets about him? He didn't have a lightning bolt on his sleeve, or a town spotters emblem either. That's what he'd wanted. Town spotters got extra gas coupons. They went away and learned the sounds of enemy planes and when they came back they had an armband, the extra gas ration, and a tire certificate. Johnny Roe's older brother Ronald, who worked the door lever on bus 47 every morning and bossed younger riders, was a spotter. He drove around wasting gas and his old man's tires and wearing the armband. But he only worked at the spotters post one hour a week because it bored him.

The year before, Panimer was told he couldn't be a spotter until he was fifteen. Now he didn't care any more about the job's privileges. The Phaeton was gone and the Lewis brothers wouldn't let him drive their parents' car. They got it too seldom though they seemed to have all the gas they needed. He couldn't bribe his way behind the wheel with gas stamps; they didn't really trust him any more, weren't quite sure what he'd do.

It came down from the principal that all students, in turn, would make short speeches in their home rooms describing their contributions to the war effort. Panimer squirmed as his time neared. Each day the stories grew longer. Mary Beth Alton, who began the cycle with a shy blurt about knitting, had been left far behind by the end of the first week when Susan James read from a long list beginning with knitting and ending with "bandage making, letter writing, making signs that say 'war worker sleeping' and half my allowance is for savings stamps."

After that all the girls read from lists, which won Mrs. Fernanda's approval. Most of the boys got up and told how many pounds of paper and tin cans they'd collected, then sat down quickly. Nancy McConkey was absent the day of her turn and Mrs. Fernanda said she could wait till last.

"Panimer." Would Nancy understand if he said nothing?

"I couldn't do nothing for a while because I got hurt."

"Stand up," Mrs. Fernanda said. "Is that all?"

"Yuh."

"Well," she said, "when you're better . . . you can tell us what you're doing when you're better. Johnny Roe Pride."

Everybody knew Johnny Roe's father was a Seabee. They'd heard it often enough. And always another story to go along with it. "My father runs this bulldozer in the Seabees and he was making this airplane runway and a Jap shot a machine gun right at him and he just put the dozer blade up in front of him and all the bullets ricocheted and one of 'em killed a Jap sniper up in a tree and my father just went on and finished what he was doing without even shooting a Jap. Once two men in my father's company got killed by ricochet and bullet one didn't touch my father."

"What are you doing to help your father?" Mrs. Fernanda asked.

"My brother and I, we're ready if the Germans parachute here. He's got a four-ten and I got a twenty-two and we wouldn't even have to see 'em if they was hiding behind Chain Food. We could just shoot at the wall and ricochet would get 'em."

"That's enough, Johnny Roe." The recitations continued. But they were interrupted that day by bursts of laughter from the senior room above them. Panimer and forty classmates, subdued, wondered what fun they were missing. Later they heard Roland Lewis had been sent home for what he told his class about war contributions—even after the teacher told him to stop telling it.

That evening he got off the bus at Small Hill and went with James to the Lewis house. Roland was rocking on the porch with some whiskey stolen from his father's liquor cabinet. He let them beg a while before he explained what happened; how he'd told his class about the Honolulu women and the man from the price office where their father worked. How these Honolulu women were the kind you could buy so they'd touch you and whatever. And the price man was over there to see prices didn't get too high. "That's when she told me to stop," Roland said, "but I told her it was true and if she didn't believe it she could ask Pop." He had continued against her protests, knowing well the trouble he was talking himself into, telling how an admiral had come and got this price man his father knew and taken him to a room where all these beautiful women were sitting who ran these places where you could buy the girls. Their prices had gone way up and it wasn't fair to soldiers and sailors.

This brought the classroom to uncontrolled laughter and a second warning from the teacher. Roland had argued gently that he didn't mean any disrespect, that he thought she would see the serious point of his story when he was finished. She let him continue to tell how the price man asked the women how long it took their girls to do what it was they got paid for, and suggested if they took less time they could handle more customers at the old prices. And everyone would be happy. All the while Roland trying to imitate the feigned innocence of his father who told these stories at the dinner table over his mother's objection. Even after the teacher dismissed him, Roland, still pretending confusion, said, "My father says it's just economics."

8

In Clayton's Notions there was more news to tell, less time to
tell it; Wilma Settle's friends were busy much of the time with
war chores. By the fourth week in September the town's fall
rhythm was changed by the new plant's schedule—two shifts,
day and evening, with many working overtime. When the first
six hundred workers became accustomed to the new routine the
number was expected to double as the factory went to three
eight-hour shifts. Almost all the new employees were women.
Most of the younger ones came from neighboring counties on
buses each day. Others moved their families into the new trailer
park behind the village.

The influx was making Clayton rich—even business in the
notions store was crisp. Mr. Greene kept his grocery open from
eight in the morning till eleven at night, still couldn't accommodate all his trade. Charlie Stockstill, manager of Chain Food,
closing his doors at six each evening, watched enviously as
customers entered the Jew store, wishing he ran his own business. He was grateful he'd been asked by Lamartine and the
others into the explosive plant consortium. Explosives made
him nervous, but the thing made sense as a business venture.

The contracts were assured and if the war was successful the government would take care of its patriotic businessmen.

Charlie Stockstill supposed everything would be all right on the home front if Congress would just stand up and renounce all the socialism the country didn't need any more. If there was less meddling, the people would do their jobs. As it was the inspector had warned him twice that month that his butcher wasn't keeping the rules. Stockstill read through the meat cutting regulations—all twenty-eight pages. "They can't be followed without a ruler in one hand and cleaver in the other," he said. "So what's he supposed to hold to the meat with? Why don't they check Greene's meat?" But when he calmed down and took stock of his enterprises he knew he was getting rich.

The three women in the notions store watched Paula through the window as she walked by with Claudelle the colored woman. "Look at her," Wilma said. The others usually let Wilma speak first; it was her store.

Her sister Jane said, "Arthur says there's two things you have to allow into a war plant—pants and the colored."

"There go both of them now," Wilma said.

"It's a shame about her boy," Valerie Jackson said. "The way he's turned."

"He's mental," Wilma said.

"Mental," Valerie repeated. "What in the world does that mean?"

"Since his accident," Wilma said. "He can't remember a thing."

"He remembers how to stay in trouble," Valerie said. "Sister had him in her eighth grade. She couldn't make him sit still."

"Don't argue, Valerie," Wilma said. "He's not right. You can see that. He'll look right at you and defy you."

"I think he's dangerous," Jane said.

"He is dangerous," Wilma agreed. "Mental and dangerous. Stares at girls and won't do a thing for the war effort."

"Pants and the colored," Jane said again, watching Paula and Claudelle disappear through the Chain Food door.

64

"She just rides the bus with those colored from Small Hill," Valerie explained.

"If he's not mental," Wilma said, "you tell me what."

"He's just mischief turned bad is all," Valerie said.

Mr. Lewis always said there ought to be a recording device in the notions store because Wilma Settle and her friends were daily compiling a history that escaped into air—births, deaths and near deaths, details of real estate transfer and construction contracts, character assessments. It would have been too simple to dismiss them as gray-haired gossips. Their minds were agile, their censure feared, their predictions generally accurate and moving beyond their circle to the leadership of the village, with which they were well connected. Wilma and Jane were aunts of the mayor Arthur Settle. Jane lived in Stilson and was a senior member of the fire department's ladies auxiliary. Valerie had been married to Earl Jackson and was Mrs. Cuttrell's sister, and thus well informed of school matters.

They were not mean spirited; they might be as generous as they were opinionated—to all who walked within the pale of their opinions. They upheld Clayton's mores because they *were* its mores. But the wartime village stretched their tolerance.

"Sister was just so sure the boy cut those boats down," Valerie said. "But she couldn't prove it. And she felt just so bad about Mr. Payton leaving the school on account of one troublemaker."

"It's worse than making trouble," Jane said. "It's just like sabotage." She let that sink in before starting in another direction. "Arthur says Clayton itself makes a right smart army. Without help from anybody."

"There's over two hundred cars and trucks pledged for emergency. For the evacuation convoy, saints forbid, but never mind that, he said, because there won't be any evacuation. Not here."

"There was only a few wouldn't pledge," Valerie said.

"The junk dealer," Jane remembered. "Marcum wouldn't pledge. Wouldn't cooperate at all. A field full of cars, and if there's a one that runs, he's not telling. And if there isn't, why doesn't he sell the lot of them for scrap. Arthur says the man's harmless, but I've an idea he . . ."

"It's one of his cars the boy was in," Valerie said.

"No, that car belonged to the Lewis boys," Wilma said, "and I said after it happened, now those boys had something to do with it, and I always wondered what kind of family it was they came from could let them carry on the way they do. No, the car belonged to them. It was sitting in the junk man's lot, but he never had title to it." Her precision impressed Jane and Valerie; they sat still for a moment in homage to the new detail. But the reference to the Lewises had reminded Valerie of something she could hardly wait to tell while Wilma finished, "Arthur says if the man's got to be dog in the manger with his junk, well let him. The war can be won without his like . . ."

"I didn't tell you what . . ."

"Don't interrupt, Valerie. Marcum found the boy in the car but he told the police there were two others there before him. Two men."

"Two men. Now what could that be about." Jane said.

"The Lewis boy" Valerie interrupted "the older one you know, Jane, the one you had to send home."

"Yes?"

"He told just the filthiest story. Right to his teacher's face. Right to her whole class. And do you know he said his father told it to him."

"I don't know what kind of people they come from," Wilma said. "That Mr. Lewis telling Johnny Roe Pride he might as well be pulling weeds in his garden for all the good he was doing as class paper warden. Imagine telling a child that."

"What kind of people are they up there?" Jane asked, and with that doubt cast, not even Wilma's observation on Paula's dogged conscientiousness could loosen their new hold on Small Hill. And Valerie, who had been saving this, said, "It was about whores at Pearl Harbor." They drew short breath.

Small Hill was the more mysterious to them, with its new cinderblock structure larger than an airplane hangar. It seemed

66

impossible it could be that huge without their knowing what happened inside, what was stored or made there. But like the rest of Clayton they referred to it only as the war building, its size and secrecy attesting legitimacy, overwhelming the rumors that rushed into this void. Wilma Settle and friends, familiar with all the stories, believed none of them. The secrecy at once piqued and appealed to them; they made sport of the wild guessing. Harold Johnson said the building contained "one each of every single part of every single kind of United States military equipment. Just in case." The notion of a Noah's Ark of armaments caught Wilma's Christian sensibilities and if she laughed at Harold's idea she laughed gently.

Someone else said there was a giant plane being built inside that would fly faster than noise, so high the Germans wouldn't see it, which idea hardly survived the moment. How would they get a plane up Station Drive? A submarine theory failed the same test. Some thought people lived inside the building. But when did they come out? At night? If it was some kind of factory, why wouldn't they see the shifts going and coming? For a while the notion caught hold that special teams from Washington, scientists and such, worked on secret projects inside. The size and number of trucks passing through the building at all hours were just part of a disguise. A corollary held that technicians arrived and departed inside the trucks—hard to prove or gainsay since the truck drivers never spoke except to yell people away from their secret cargoes.

At various times the building was said to contain: the eastern United States' total reserve of copper tubing, the whole United States supply of silk for parachutes (which were being made right there by seamstresses who came in the trucks), magnesium and other sensitive metals whose location must be secret to foil saboteurs, all C rations for shipment East (which theory gained when a soldier returning to Clayton via California said the building had a twin on the West Coast), a training center and obstacle course for attack dogs (barking was sometimes heard from the building and a German shepherd had been seen trotting its perimeter), studios and sound stages for training and

67

propaganda films, the manufacture of incendiary bombs (sometimes connected with the magnesium theory), parts for new high-speed tanks, and a depot for innumerable kinds of weapons.

Real inquiries were few, and direct questions at the premises impossible; a German shepherd *had* patrolled the area ever since Panimer's accident. The dog was not really needed; Clayton supposed maintenance of the place's secrecy a piece of its own duty. Villagers might enter community conjecture, but an outsider's questions would be ignored.

Wilma Settle and her friends played with all these ideas until the game became serious. Jane suggested that whoever put the boy in the car and rolled it down the hill was trying to knock the wall down, to get a look at the secret behind it. "Else, why the gas?" she asked. "Unless someone was trying to blow the place up," which stopped them for a moment. But the concept of a foreign agent in their midst was too fanciful; they returned to familiar names.

"None of them wanted it there," Wilma said. "They all fought it. Lewis told the board of supervisors they were letting the county ride war fever right to hell in a hat box, allowing such a thing." Again Jane and Valerie were impressed, not so much astonished by Wilma's repetition of the man's language as by her recollection of a detail they had forgotten.

"And Marcum wouldn't sell a part of his junkyard for it. They were all against it."

9

"His mother takes rides from the colored," Panimer heard, climbing on bus 47, "hitch-hikes with the colored."

"What's it to you?" he said as he went down the aisle. Someone shoved him as he passed and taunted until laughter closed around him. He pushed his way through the laughter to the back seat where no one could watch him from behind, where *he* could watch everything. Everything was Nancy.

From oldest at Duncan Kimball to youngest at Stilson was a dangerous transfer. Roland and James gave some protection. They were not especially tough; formidable as a team, but more out of tenacity than strength. He couldn't depend on them all the time—they had torments of their own. Panimer would have kept to himself had he not been pushed beyond patience, even beyond anger. What he said when the same boy came back through the bus to taunt him again came from a mindless depth. "Your father's going to die," Panimer said. All the way from Stilson to Clayton he wished he could suck the words back into him. He did not know the boy, or his father. How could he have said a thing at once so familiar and cruel?

"Oh yeah?" the boy said. "How do you know?" The children around them had grown quiet with the exchange; waiting for a fight.

Through that fall Nancy had watched Panimer in retreat, more in sorrow for lost opportunity than in anger or suspicion of his ways. He had been reprimanded more than once for his indifference to patriotism; his only response, a mumbling denial of interest. It was that pained mumbling she hated, supposing it hid some secret that might vindicate him, even wishing he would stand and yell at Mrs. Fernanda, no matter what it was he had to yell. How could she spend her attentions on him if he could not speak his mind? Each tension that passed between them, anything that might have led to conversation, a seat beside each other on the bus, an almost innocent touching of fully clothed bodies, was poisoned by whatever unspoken thoughts constrained and left him vulernable to the patriots around him. They attacked, he retreated, Nancy maneuvered, moving from her usual seat in the middle of 47, where she knew Panimer watched her every day, to the front where the older boys welcomed her. And one of them began sitting next to her in a more than casual way. Flattered by his age, not especially taken with his face or manner, she decided, on balance, to accept his daily company on the bus, offered him a clipped conversation full of "not much," and "not really," for his advances, which she thought a little crude.

Paula got a note from Mrs. Fernanda, sealed and taped to Panimer's report card. He wouldn't hold his hand over his heart while he pledged allegiance, it said, and he would only mumble the pledge if he spoke it at all. And he had been familiar with a girl.

Paula, a little sad and searching, showing the note to Junior, asked: "Honey, wasn't he all right once? I mean wasn't he innocent? Where did he change?"

She had caught her husband in a particularly blunt, beer-soaked moment. Maybe remembering something of his own spray of seed in that northern corner of Tennessee, and a childhood of no innocence he could remember, he said: "Gonads."

"What, honey?"

"Wasn't ever a boy lost any innocence. You just wait for your gonads to drop so's you can use 'em."

"Junior!"

When it happened it could not have been a reconciliation, since no argument, or any real conversation, had ever taken place between them; Panimer moved from day to day in furtive expectation. His wheeling world had been brought low, everywhere the evidence of lost rubber, from the naked spokes of his discarded Schwinn to the junked cars in Marcum's field, all brought low, sitting on bare axels or rusting rims, while Nancy drifted from him.

The school had been pushed out of shape by the war, the freshman class swelling with the younger children of new war workers, while some students who should have been seniors had taken summer jobs and never returned from them. The younger were moved into upper-class rooms; war was promotions. For those who fell into phase with this shifting world it had suddenly become fun, making grownups of children (now they went to work) and children of adults (now they played with guns). Panimer saw the pleasure, even envied it, and found distraction in the dislocations. His class had shifted rooms twice and seating assignments three times. Which is how he came to touch Nancy for the first time, their desks wedged together in the crowded classroom where the teacher had finally insisted that students alternate seats. "Boy, girl, boy, girl," she said. She grabbed the hesitant Panimer by the shoulder, who would never have dared the approach on his own, and pushed him into the seat beside Nancy. He was stirred to crimson by the suddenness of it. Mrs. Fernanda had only been trying to make her students stop talking.

There was no talking. So close, the two of them were tensed against the chance of touch, their arms and legs drawn in tight to

71

avoid that embarrassment—a tension too uncomfortable to last. Contact began as a click of shoes, Nancy's foot moving ever so slightly, whether to relieve cramp or unconsciously seeking its neighbor she could not have judged, and Panimer's moving ever so tentatively to meet it. Until that slight knowledge of flesh, even wrapped behind two thicknesses of leather, brought a mutual recoil, surprising both of them. Nancy's foot disappeared under skirt, like tortoise into shell, and Panimer flinched, and regained his tight-wrapped posture. It had been done, unmentioned but recognized, because they returned to that classroom the next day in anticipation of the same excitement, and were not disappointed.

On that day their ankles touched for an unconscionable moment, then separated, then regained contact and remained warm against one another in the full knowledge of both of them until the continued sin of it became insupportable. Still unmentioned and unmentionable. But their daily expectation of shared sensation became their sensational secret, unbelievably private and forbidden. And they went through all that semester, never even admitting their secret to each other. As if when she rubbed her calf so delicately against his shin it could have been the unconscious act of a mind fixed on the blackboard problem as she stared, mindless, straight at Mrs. Fernanda. And as if Panimer could have been answering such an unconscious signal with an uninformed tremor of his own, though he quivered in the knowledge of it. They allowed each other every ready guise of innocence, unable to admit affection, much less its physical affirmation. If acknowledged it might all have to stop.

The intimacy continued, advanced to knee and thigh until, unknown to them, it became visible to classmates around them. The only one they'd been hiding from, other than themselves, had been their teacher. And then it became an unspoken declaration of affection between them, not without embarrassments, the daily teasing of a tumescence he could not always hide. Once Nancy stared at what was happening to him, causing him to edge away for the rest of the period and to reject her attempts to reestablish contact; with probing foot she tried to explain what she could not say, that she had not been offended, that it was all right, even that she was fascinated.

It took most of the next week to reassure him, or for him to convince himself, but, once convinced, Panimer allowed their affair a new abandon, returned each pressure of her leg with a firmer pressure of his own. Again he thought he caught her watching his swollen pant, and was sure he heard a little cry as she looked away. This time he did not withdraw and their assumed secret took on new license. Mrs. Fernanda was the last to see, though the careless pursuit of their new mysteries was bound to lead her to the discovery made by their classmates weeks before. But when she noticed it she was no more able to punish than cite the offense, only said: "All right. Everyone sit up straight." Panimer and Nancy were unaware they had been caught. But later in the same period when Mrs. Fernanda said, "I said sit up straight," there was no doubt because she was looking right at them and continued to watch as, straining for innocence, they edged apart.

Mrs. Fernanda's note home brought no response from Paula. The news left Stilson for Clayton's Notions, though not before new seating assignments left Panimer and Nancy at opposite corners of the room. Without agency of a third force they were unable to reestablish contact. Teasing classmates only widened the separation. And though the two could now speak to each other of homework and other irritations, their season of tactile pleasure was lost.

10

Paula did not get the straight-day assignment when the explosives plant went to the twenty-four-hour schedule in November. She could have, but when she heard volunteers were needed to watch drying ovens on the midnight shift she sacrificed again. "Only till they find some others to take it," she promised Junior. But others did not come forward and her all-night shifts continued into the early spring.

Stilson High School children had made War Worker Sleeping signs for the plant workers and the foreman passed them out to the night shift women. "Who's gonna disturb your sleep, honey?" Claudelle asked her on the bus back to Small Hill in the morning. Paula had been amused with the sign too but was taking it home anyway. They laughed at the idea of having your doorbell rung or your sleep disturbed in Small Hill. Claudelle lived at the corner and was mother of Phoog and R.B., who were driving trucks in the Army. Working in the same building, she had befriended Paula, who had anxiously answered the colored woman's friendship, awkwardly at first, asking, "Your name's French. Did you know that?" then trying to recover with "I was going to have a French name once. Just for writing."

Claudelle had broken through the white woman's formal attempts at informality and now they could relax together on the shuttle bus. Some afternoons they would hitch-hike together, to the village and back, for groceries, but they would only get rides from a few colored drivers. Sometimes they had to walk the whole three miles to Clayton. Paula would try to get her new friend to shop with her at Chain Food, but Claudelle would use only the Jew store.

They were not really comfortable in the village in daylight together—Paula, nerved up, parading her camaraderie with the colored woman past the notions store; Claudelle, a little afraid, sensing the white woman was putting her on parade, but both relying on the notion that war and war work gave them license. Claudelle would do her shopping, then sit on the Jew store steps waiting for a friend to offer a ride back to Small Hill. "Come on, honey," she would call to Paula, "there's room for you too."

Tired, happy, Paula loved that year, working all night in the factory, never mind that all she had to do was move casings on and off the drying trays, set a timer and wait. She came home each morning exhausted, proud. Junior would already be gone to work, but she would get Panimer out of bed, get him his breakfast and off to school, then go out to work in the garden. After that there was telephoning to organize some volunteer committee, or canning in the Duncan Kimball cafeteria for the school lunch program, and every other Friday canning for home use, when Claudelle would go with her to the school lunch room. Panimer dreaded those odd Friday afternoons when, riding the school bus past the Clayton crossroads, they might see his mother with the colored woman, waiting together for a ride to Small Hill.

Paula, enervated each evening, but excited with the progress of the war, listened to the same newscaster, usually falling asleep before his broadcast was over. One night a week she tried to stay awake for "Town Meeting of the Air," which she said was a worthwhile program. Too tired, or bored, she hardly ever lasted past announcement of the issue for debate. Usually she would leave supper out for Junior and go to bed. Panimer would

75

be in the house for a moment after school but out again before she could shout a chore to him from kitchen or bedroom. Junior came home at five-thirty, took his shower, and some evenings forgot his supper, trying to get into bed with her before she was too far gone to be roused. She loved to be moved slowly from her drowsiness to excitation so that dream became flesh, then dream again, almost without waking; pleased to serve, in sex as in war, not expecting too much from it, only expecting to be allowed to give.

One afternoon she left the War Worker Sleeping sign hanging from the bedroom door. Junior recognized it for a joke, even understood the invitation. He took the sign off the knob, came roughly into the room, stripped, and, with the day's grime on him, forced a grin from her opossum sleep and a feigned protest that he was too dirty to love as she pulled him down, mumbling all the while that no one seemed to have any respect for war workers. And when they were finished she was mumbling again, something about a new secret at Sons of Clayton; proximity fuses that had to be dried at a different temperature because they went off when they got hot, and she urged secrecy on her husband. Nobody outside the plant was supposed to know.

Junior, suddenly proud of his war working wife, repeated, "Go off when they get next to something hot."

"Like you," she said, and he pulled her close again, quickened, a little surprised. She was making him ready once more. He never ate his supper or got up again that night. As she got up to go to work he laid a heavy arm across her as if to prevent escape.

After that the sign became a sign, for a while meaning yes, then a gentle, no, when Paula came to a period of exhaustion that had begun to erode her zeal. But finally, when hung, it meant yes, come in if you want, I want you to if you want to, and Junior had not thought its use a loss of his rights. If anything its frequency of appearance was more a challenge to potency than its absence a barrier to desire. And Paula saw that this joke between them had become the sweet tool of her disposition. Having accepted initiative, she assumed a delicate responsibility went with it, knowing every evening when he came home he would check to see what the door said, no matter what his inclination.

If they supposed the sign kept their evening intentions from Panimer they were mistaken. The boy had caught on quickly, though surprised at first by the heat of two so old. He knew his father was past fifty and his mother close to forty. When Junior said, "She must want to sleep bad to hang that up. We'd best keep quiet," he knew his son would be going out to roam the corner or sit the store porch as soon as he'd swallowed some food. Panimer did go out, but came back for something he'd forgotten, quietly, and heard their noise in the bedroom, a little embarrassed, a little pleased. After that the sign became a sign for him too; on the evenings it was posted he left the house immediately and stayed out late. When he came back he would sit for a while in the kitchen. Sometimes his father would come tiptoeing out of the bedroom, excusing his dishevelment with, "Don't make no noise, she's sleeping," but it was no use lying since they both could hear her making some last adjustment for a final hour of sleep before she would have to get up and go to work.

For that hour father and son would sit together, the man telling the boy stories of how he had come to Clayton with Paula, how they had run away from Perryville, Maryland, in a Chevrolet coupe and Panimer's grandfather hadn't even bothered to chase or call the police on them. And there were parts of the story Panimer would ask him to repeat again and again, as if his own memory could not do them justice, though detail and nuance never changed; how his mother, beautiful now, was even more beautiful then and had meant to be a writer—was that educated—but had run away with him instead. How they had crossed the Potomac River at Point of Rocks and wandered for several days through northern Virginia until, their money almost gone, the coupe ran out of gas on the Wye Bridge Pike and he and Paula had walked to a gas station where the Pike crossed a railroad track. "It wasn't even Clayton then. Just a gas station. Wasn't any Chain Food or Jew store or nothing.

Hardly even a house if you didn't look close. Just Lamartine's Mobil. He ran it himself back then.''

Lamartine had come out of the garage and before he'd pumped a gallon tin of gas for them he'd hired Junior. ''On sight you could say,'' though Junior had never been sure whether it was the sight of himself or Paula that had attracted Lamartine, who had said, ''You got a bad arm, hunh? Don't matter. We ain't hanging wallpaper.'' So Junior became garage handyman. Lamartine found them rooms in a cousin's house and their wandering elopement was over.

''What about the time you told 'em what was wrong with the car just listening to it and Mr. Lamartine asked did you want to run the station and you told him no.'' It was a set piece that began with his father doing odd jobs and pumping gas until the day they began to discover his talents, the day Junior had called into the service bay, ''It ain't ignition. It's the carburetor,'' which advice Lamartine and his stumped mechanic had ignored, their straightened patience only aggravated by the handyman. After they struggled for an hour without result and supposed the carburetor was the only thing left to check they began to take it off the car. ''You don't have to take it off,'' Junior called from outside where he'd started his lunch, only casually interested in their problem.

The mechanic mumbled to Lamartine, ''What do he know about it?'' but Lamartine, annoyed with the wasted hour and the diffidence of Junior's effrontery, called back, ''You think you can fix it?''

''Expect I could,'' Junior said, coming inside. He studied the engine for a moment, half a sandwich hanging from his mouth, then gently cupped the glass bowl of the carburetor in his hand, and deftly as a chef performing one-handed separation on an egg, reached up around it and unloosened its casing. Gas began to drip into his cupped palm. Grabbing a screwdriver with his free hand he began to make an adjustment underneath. He squeezed, ''Start it up,'' around the sandwich still dangling from his mouth. For a minute neither Lamartine nor the mechanic moved. ''Start it up,'' he repeated. The mechanic got in and started the car as Junior's hands continued moving in delicate unison until the gas stopped dripping and the engine hummed, then slowed to its normal idle. Junior wiped his hands, pushed the sandwich into his mouth and savored it for a moment before swallowing. "Was just off its seat a hair. Got a little sediment into her," he said. They were still standing a little slack-jawed over his performance when he walked outside to finish his lunch.

Lamartine, ready to expand his enterprises, had asked Junior if he wanted to run the garage, not understanding the man was not interested in responsibility, would rather perform, even astonish, at any job he might be given, but was then going to retreat into the menial's role he liked best, the remove from which all efforts were insured against lost face, the stance from which he could best surprise people. And the mechanic, who had been prepared to dislike, even hate, and challenge the newcomer's encroachment, found instead that Junior's self-effacement forced friendship on itself despite the little victories of skill that belittled those around him; more, that Junior could be used over and over again to rescue him from his incompetence, never asking credit or seeking his job. Lamartine saw what was happening but could not coax ambition from his extraordinary handyman, no matter how he tried. Each time he suspected Junior might be restless he would raise his salary a nickel an hour.

Over the next several years Lamartine's business spread into excavation, construction, and road contracting, in competition with Earl Jackson's company in Stilson; the two men's distrust and loathing for each other had grown from feud over a wedding that had never taken place to secret and not-so-secret bidding for contracts. The principals of the aborted wedding were to have been Jackson's niece Phyllis, Jackson's shotgun, and Lamartine's young brother Francis, then thirty-six, who had fled rather than admit to, or claim, a paternal obligation whose exclusivity he had sufficient reason to doubt. It was the same girl, hardly out of high school and seventeen years his junior, whose name had been carved in bark, indelibly inked on the blue cloth covers of dozens of loose-leaf notebooks, scratched on school buses, walls, and furniture from Clayton to Stilson, even splashed in paint on the Washington & Old Dominion Railroad overpass; the girl whose reputation had marched on before her as she advanced through the Clayton County school system in a kind of bemusement, at once smug and mindless; untaught and unteachable, her teachers bracing against the devastation she worked on their classrooms, not only deface-ment of desks and walls, but also the reduction to mooning bewilderment of their young scholars, the boys, their heads turned and groins overheated at mere mention or sight of her name, which was everywhere, and girls, wondering when they might catch up, or if they dared to. She was never flunked: not one of those teachers would risk a second season of the same, so that Phyllis sat through all those school hours in a kind of triumphant satisfaction, unblushing in her sincere confusion over the simplest algebra problem or rule of spelling.

Soon after that non-wedding toward which she had been racing through all her non-academic career and which left her ebbing honor in the hands of her uncle Earl, Junior had chanced upon the Clayton corner with his new bride and was im-mediately hired by Lamartine. On that same day Junior had caught sight of Phyllis Jackson, standing across the road as he waited with Paula for the tin of gas. The girl, her pregnancy still invisible to the town's eye, though familiar enough to its ear, had gotten in, or been pulled into, a green Packard sedan and been driven away toward Stilson. The scene was not lost on Junior, whose own history till then had been a wandering through places and women, and in this, only the second week of his marriage, he was a little surprised, even dismayed, at his turned head.

In the next months Junior became an object of the two con-tractors' competition. The stories of his hidden skills passed back and forth between Clayton and Stilson until he had become a kind of phenomenon, his worth inflated as much by rumor and tug of the two sides coveting him as by the real skills he posses-sed. Earl Jackson had approached him personally and through intermediaries, only to find Junior's allegiance fixed.

Lamartine, discovering Junior's talents one by one, had once prevailed on him to be chief carpenter of a housing job, and the promotion had almost driven him to defect. It was a disaster; Junior would not tell anyone what to do, would not give orders. Carpenters cursed one another. If Lamartine had not seen his mistake and withdrawn Junior's authority, the roof of the new house might have pitched forty degrees on one side, sixty on the other. As it was, the ground floor rolled over uneven joists. Mocking his own leadership, Junior said the place made him seasick; he was secretly grateful when Lamartine relieved him of command. But his salary was raised once more, against bruised feelings.

Panimer would say, "What about that time you worked on that house and the man wasted all that wood until you showed him how to cut the angle on it?" And Junior would explain how the boss had discovered he was a carpenter too.

Through this gradual encroachment Junior had begun to make Lamartine dependent on a truck driver, which is what he eventually allowed Junior to call himself, though at two dollars and seventy-five cents an hour he was the most expensive truck driver in Stilson County. Lamartine put one of his fleet of dump trucks at Junior's disposal, which satisfied the man's view of himself, or the only view he cared to show the community. Lamartine knew he could send Junior into any emergency, that Junior would appear and fix the unfixable, would roll up to a job in the truck, pretend not to know why he'd been sent, wait for some mechanic, stonemason, carpenter, or bricklayer to confess his dilemma, then, without show, solve the problem. After which he would drive back to the Mobil Station, whose upstairs rooms were Lamartine's office, and wait for his next assignment, which might only be hauling fill dirt; as happy with that as anything else.

By 1931, long after most of Lamartine's men had been laid off, the depression had touched, but not hurt, Junior; he was still getting two dollars and seventy-five cents an hour, his boss was still afraid Earl Jackson might try to hire him away, might use the hard times as an opportunity to sneak up on his handyman. It was not as if this were a hardship for Lamartine; even in those years Junior was more than worth his salary. And by that time Lamartine was rich enough to afford the depression too. His most expensive equipment—two dozers and a back hoe—he owned outright; Junior could keep them in working order while they waited out the trouble. When contracts came again, he'd be first in line. And was—slightly ahead of Earl Jackson. Lamartine, hunkered down with his handyman in the Mobil station, was beating the depression. He'd cleared his first hundred thousand dollars putting in the Stilson water and sewage lines, somehow underbidding Jackson in the man's own home town. He'd never had any use for the stock market. Nor had he much faith in banks; he invested only in himself. He used banks, but only if they would invest in him. When his loans were paid he never kept much money in them; just his business account, not his savings. Less afraid of fire destroying his cash or someone stealing it than letting another man hold it for him, he kept most of his profits hidden in his own house.

Panimer liked Junior's stories of the depression years, hearing in them more than the resourcefulness of his father continually unmasked as hero, but a kind of unyielding trust between him and Lamartine, a respect that had nothing to do with liking each other. Panimer did not need this explained, it was patent. His father and Lamartine were not especially comfortable in each other's company, did not consider themselves social equals, nor did they want to. Junior referred to Lamartine as "the old man" and Lamartine to him as "the truck driver," Junior dependent on dependency, Lamartine on being boss, though he possessed none of his employee's skills; the one, talented liege to the other's incompetent sovereignty.

Sometimes Junior mentioned Phyllis Jackson in his stories of the early days in Clayton, but she appeared always as spectator, never as participant, and Panimer would nod when her name was mentioned. Not blush, just nod, and Junior would again suppose his evasion effective. If his son asked "Who was she?" or "What was she doing there?" Junior would say, "She was just a pretty girl around town," or She was just there," supposing that satisfied Panimer, though he had discovered this Phyllis was the same whose name, years later, had still not been washed or worn from all the public surfaces where so many swain had marked it.

Junior knew Phyllis Jackson had left town an unwed mother, and he knew the bastard child was not the only reason for her leaving. Phyllis was driven off by the very attention she had once sought. Her name, even after graduation from Stilson, had begun a life of its own, had reached such saturation that it no longer needed her presence to perpetuate itself. It had become a joke, an obscenity. Boys who had not known her had begun to carve and paint it around the area until notoriety became vulgarity. After Phyllis appeared on the railroad bridge it worked its way toward the center of Clayton, painted on the road itself, then through the village and out the other side, heading down the Wye Bridge Pike toward Washington. Until it showed itself on the Virginia end of Wye Bridge over the Potomac River, and finally in huge letters on the river's palisade, a sheer rock face that seemed impossible to scale, much less write on; the message, a demonstration of the painters' daring rather than devotion to the name they painted.

Phyllis could have lived with, even delighted in, the notion that all those boys—some of them men—had been there, that is, to see her. But that was absurd, impossible. There was not time in the day to charm, much less be escorted by, all who had written **PHYLLIS.** She could not abide the idea that her name had been taken as public property.

As it was, auto passengers from Washington, crossing Wye Bridge, might have joked they were entering Phyllis, not Virginia, and by the time they reached Clayton they might have supposed the town fathers had renamed the place for a woman. Her name was written large on its few commercial establishments. It would be painted, painted over, then painted again.

Each new, more prominent, appearance of **PHYLLIS** added

to the pent anger and anguish Earl Jackson felt for his niece's condition and the good name of the family. He drove up and down the Pike late at night, shotgun beside him, seeking the painters; would gladly have left buckshot in back or belly of any of them.

But it was Phyllis who felt the true loss of her runaway name, a name gone out of control, way ahead of her ability to live up to its notoriety: there were no more men—or boys. Even those who had risked the association during her pregnancy and first year as a mother, those who had dared escort her into the Stilson Cafe before retreating with her from community view to some dead end dirt road for whatever encounter they might coax out of her, no longer looked for her at the Clayton corner, or waited for her uncle to leave their house in Stilson so that they might idle the engines of their Fords at the bottom of her driveway, as they slid down behind thin steering wheels.

No more. She had her standards, understood their hesitancy; she would not go an inch further with them if they would not be seen with her at the Stilson Cafe.

Junior had been reminded of his mother whose bastard child he was. A woman who had cast herself out of a coal town's stunted society, gone to live in a cabin in the woods outside Clinton, Tennessee, where men came to see her. He did not see the difference—that his mother had never lost the company of her men, that her name had usually been whispered, not shouted, had not been written on the community's public buildings.

Junior was proud she had stood her ground in that cabin and been pushed around by no one. She had not fled; he had. So that when he watched the progression of Phyllis to **PHYLLIS** it was not without sympathy for the girl. He had sought her out, all the while insisting to himself it was not her that aroused him, but her plight.

11

Nancy McConkey allowed Hiram Johnson to sit beside her on bus 47 each day but not even his seniority could compensate for the boredom he excited in her. Eventually she made a point of evading his approaches, out-hesitating his hesitancy in finding a place to sit, each of them looking around as if they had forgotton something, or as if they couldn't make up their minds, pretending not to notice each other's indecision. This had gone on for a week or so until Hiram was forced to see it for the rejection it was and Panimer took new hope in the sight of her looking for a place to be alone or at least away from Hiram, wondering if she really wanted to be alone, teasing himself with the forbidden place beside her, at once daring and not daring to test her affection, all inside the safety of his imagination. She was not making it easier; the shyness she felt, which she might have intended as a kind of neutrality if she had considered it at all, was seen instead as hostility, or nothing better than indifference, and Panimer was as intimidated as the rest, balancing the chance of rejection against the possibility another might win a daily place beside her. He followed little scenes out to the limits of his pessimistic fantasy, most of them ending in catastrophes that lost her forever, like sitting down to talk to her and being unable to begin, or beginning with something she would ignore, or sneezing and having his nose run right down to his chin and nothing to wipe it with.

So that when he did catch the courage to sit down beside her and discovered not only that he could talk but that she would answer, smile, even laugh, and once more nudge close to him and ask if his scars still hurt, he was overwhelmed. He began to nurse new ideas about her, wishing she were a little taller and thinner, even as her plumpness excited him. And each day when he transferred to the bus for Small Hill, leaving her behind in Clayton where anything (anyone) might happen to her, he sat down to reveries of her hand on his, in his, more, until sometimes he made his eyes tear.

His days existed for his afternoons, which existed for the ride between Stilson and Clayton, the time before and after which all thought drifted forward and back over Nancy. Until Hiram Johnson Jr. came back through the bus one afternoon with Ronald Pride, the two of them pushing aside the younger and smaller as they came. Passing Panimer and Nancy, Hiram said, "That girl wears falsies."

"That stuck up little freshman bitch?" Pride answered.

"Yeah." They went by, all the way to the back of the bus before making their slow, offensive way to the front again, this time stopping beside Panimer as Ronald asked Hiram, "How do you know?" and Hiram said, "I felt 'em myself."

"Bull," Ronald said, pushing Hiram in the back, trying to make him hurry, but Hiram braced his feet in the aisle, grabbed the seat on either side of him, would not be pushed, still watching Panimer so there could be no mistaking that he, not the girl, was the object of their abuse. Nancy was looking at one of her books as if she hadn't heard but Panimer knew she had, knew he ought to do, at least say, something. But there was nothing for it. He spent the rest of the trip in shame, wondering how he was going to deal with this, knowing it was just the beginning. When he got on the bus the next afternoon he had rehearsed his response for hours. No matter how he imagined the beginning, who spoke first, or whom he attacked, the end was always the same; he was beaten to the floor of the bus by the two older boys and woke up wounded, with a grown-up leaning over him, wanting to know his name.

What actually happened was worse, though it left him unhurt; the whole thing unresolved, in fact more dangerous because there was a spoken promise of vengeance. His plan had been partly fouled by Nancy, as though she had guessed what might happen.

She stood on the bus by a seat until she had forced him to take the window side, so that when Hiram and Ronald came back to taunt them she could be talking to Panimer, pretending not to notice the affront.

"You didn't feel her," Ronald said.

"How could I? Wasn't nothing there," said Hiram. This was followed not by laughter, but a challenging silence, the two of them waiting to see, not if they had hurt the girl, who was closer to tears than anger, but if they had hurt the boy. Panimer stood on the seat, then almost stepped in Nancy's lap as he moved across her, leaping, arm cocked for Hiram's head. There was time to duck his punch but not the flying body, which knocked Hiram backward into another seat. Then they were wrestling, Ronald yelling, "Keep off him. It's a fair fight," at a boy who was trying to get them apart, then "It's none of yer business," as the boy persisted, and, this failing, Ronald went after the peacemaker, and another boy after him, which might have brought the whole bus to riot but for the driver, who had been watching in his mirror and was on his way back as soon as he saw Panimer jump into the aisle. At first sound of the adult voice it was over, before either had satisfaction of the other's pain. The bus driver pulled them apart, and took Panimer's name. Always someone wanting to know, or take, his name, which annoyed and confused him. He had a notion everybody must know him, or about him. Children knew him well enough; it was adults he had hidden from.

After the interrupted fight there was whispering around him:

". . . the one wouldn't pledge to the flag."

". . . he doesn't do a thing for the war."

". . . that I don't see how she can like him at all."

"Lives with the colored at Small Hill."

Nancy and Panimer sat together again, Nancy next to the window this time. As they passed the Clayton crossroads she said softly, "There's your mother." Paula was standing on Station Drive with Claudelle, hitchhiking. Panimer would not look.

"That's his mother," he heard behind him. Then "Which one?" Laughing.

Roland Lewis had three dollars and a half-dozen gas coupons, more than enough to take his parents' car for the evening and leave the tank as full as he found t. He and James picked Panimer up at Small Hill corner and they drove toward Clayton, at once looking for trouble and not looking for it, telling each other they were, and hoping they were not. The Lewis brothers had watched the fight on the bus from a rear seat and, like most of the others, had taken no part in it until it was over. Then, apologetic, even angry, they discussed revenge on Hiram, who had himself promised revenge on Panimer. They were driving to the village to look for him, though none of the three knew what they would do if they found him.

Hiram would probably be standing around the garage with Ronald Pride, discussing the war—how bad they felt about not being in it, how after graduation, not even their parents could stop them.

Panimer knew Roland Lewis wasn't a fighter—more smooth mouth than muscle—and James wasn't big enough and neither was he, so what could they have been thinking other than that there would be some way to avoid the whole thing once they got to Clayton. Panimer, Roland, and James were each dependent on what they took to be the others' determination; they had pried themselves into it, not so much with dares as denials of fear. What none of them would have done alone, together they could not avoid. They went, nervous in their boasting, Panimer unaware Roland had a twelve-gauge shotgun in the trunk. Roland, though he had shells in the glove compartment, had no intention of using them. At least not when they started.

James begged, "Lemme drive. So's you two can jump out easier and get him," not because he was really afraid—like his brother and Panimer, he doubted anything was going to happen—he simply wanted to drive. But Roland had the wheel and wasn't sharing.

It was already dark. In Clayton they turned on Wye Bridge Pike and cruised past the service station. There were two figures standing in the doorway of the closed garage but neither looked like Hiram. Roland said they might as well drive to Wye Bridge and get some gas. The others agreed, James saying, "Yeah, and if we're going all the way there you better let me drive back," to which Roland only grunted. It was seven miles to Wye Bridge and Roland drove slowly; he knew this is what they had really come for—the drive—but he also knew that they had to pass the Clayton corner again on the way back. They could avoid it by taking the river road all the way from Wye Bridge to Indian Falls, then turning back to Small Hill on Station Drive. But none of them would accept the shame of evasion. With a presentiment of unavoidable trouble Roland slipped the shotgun out of the trunk into the car's back seat after the attendant at the Wye Bridge station had pumped their six gallons, all their parents' B sticker allowed. That amount of gas and the loose ration stamps Roland pulled from his pocket in abundance, and the gun aroused the attendant. He called Stilson.

James moved into the driver's seat while Roland was out of the car and would not give it up. The brothers argued for a moment, then Roland relented, climbed into the back seat with the shotgun, but not before he had taken two shells from the glove compartment.

"What's that for?" James asked, a word ahead of Panimer's echo. "We're not gonna use it," Roland told them. "It's just in case."

"In case what?" this time their question exactly synchronized, a pitch higher.

On the way back James drove even more slowly than Roland

89

had, maybe trying to delay their arrival in Clayton, where Hiram Johnson was sitting on the steps of the Jew store with a half-dozen others, his face in full profile as their headlights swept the corner and lit Station Drive.

"Did you see him?" Roland asked.

"No. D'you?" James said.

"No."

"Me neither," Panimer said, each of them hot with his own lie and trusting honest oversight in the others, hoping no one would suggest going back to make sure. No one did. They might have got to Small Hill without trouble if James had been driving faster, but he was making his pleasure last. Before they reached Saw Mill Road they began to hear the horn behind them, a rising wail that gradually overtook them. The persistent noise came alongside. "Don't let him pass," Roland shouted. A flashlight beam waved across the front seat. At first they had supposed it was a drunk. But the car was edging closer, signaling for them to stop. There were no police lights, nor even a siren, only the horn. "Just keep driving," Roland yelled, James accelerating, confused by the light in his face. Panimer could make out only the cropped head of an ununiformed driver who must have had an elbow on the horn to leave a hand free for the wheel, because his right hand was still busy with the flashlight.

The two cars were going at least fifty, weaving together and apart as if connected by elastic. Finally their front fenders collided. The gun went off in Roland's hands. Panimer, who had been leaning forward, encouraging James, retained his head, which might otherwise have been blown off. He thought for a moment he had been shot; or that a single ricocheting pellet was embedded in his neck. In those first seconds after the explosion, he looked around, felt himself all over, disbelieving he was still intact because he could not find what the gun must have done—anywhere—unaware of the jagged wound that had opened the car's roof to the night, just above the window, where smoke poured through the hole. James lost control, or nerve, and they went skidding across the shoulder and came to rest in a shallow ditch.

The chasing car had skidded to its own halt when the shotgun went off, then raced backward, leaving black marks on the pavement in its haste to be away, missed a driveway it was trying to turn in, then sprayed mud and gravel as it wag-tailed onto the road again and sped back toward Clayton. They did not find out until the next day it had only been Osmond Clarke's son Bobby, a boy Roland's age, and already a volunteer fireman in Stilson. They would have known why they were being chased if they had paid closer attention as they drove through the village; their headlights were the only illumination in the whole place. Hiram Johnson and his friends had been sitting in darkness because the village siren had only minutes before sounded blackout. The gathering on the Jew store steps had yelled and waved fists at the passing car, which paid no attention as it turned the corner.

Bobby Clarke, assigned to patrol the blackout in Clayton, had run for his car and chased them up Station Drive.

The first phone call following the incident was from Earl Jackson to Mr. Lewis, the second from Mrs. Lewis to Paula. After that there was no keeping track of the sequence. Bobby Clarke, returning to Stilson through Clayton, had told the gang on the corner he'd been shot at. Callers to the principals' families had begun to get busy signals; only those on party lines could listen to a continuous discussion of the event. Jane Settle had broken into the network somewhere toward the beginning, thus had all the issues ready for Clayton's Notions in the morning. As she listened in on Mrs. Clarke and Mrs. Jackson she hardly kept herself from breaking in with, "But which one was it shot at Bobby?" and later almost pulled her hand from her phone's mouthpiece to console, "you must be just worried sick."

The high sheriff in Stilson had first heard about the boys' pleasure ride from the gas station attendant at Wye Bridge but had considered it just a nuisance call, not worth a trip into Clayton. Afterward, when he heard from Osmond Clarke that Bobby had been shot at, he drove from Stilson to Small Hill, found Mr. and Mrs. Lewis lecturing their boys, examined the hole in the roof of their car, and, satisfied the shot had been accidental, left the matter in the parents' hands. Officially, it was dead.

In Clayton's Notions, opinion was divided; Valerie Jackson believed the shooting was deliberate, Wilma thought it accidental, Jane straddled, coaxed each of them to convince her.

Bobby Clarke told the gang at the corner, "They had a gun. They shot at me."

"That little son of a bitch shot at him," Hiram Johnson said. "Panimer tried to kill Bobby Clarke," but they were still angry at the Lewis brothers for driving through the blackout and endangering the town—"That's all the Germans need is one light and they could bomb the factory and the whole town with it."

They waited a long time to get Panimer, uncertain what they wanted to do to him, whether they wanted credit for it, or whether it was going to be so bad that they did not. Because they supposed he would tell and if they were going to uphold the county's honor against a little traitor they did not want to get in trouble for it. They watched for their chance, waited through the month that remained of school, counting the days until they would be soldiers, while the little turncoat rode bus 47 with the girl who they decided didn't have any sense, or self-respect, to be seen with the boy who had shot at a law officer—"Firemen are police in a air raid warning," Ronald Pride reminded them. They went for their service examinations and Hiram was rejected. They told him he had something wrong with his blood and sent him back to his own doctor with a note, which he tore up, keeping his rejection, and his disease, a secret, still counting with the others the days separating them from uniforms.

Panimer waited with Nancy on her porch while she argued with her mother, then her father, about where they were going.

"Just around," Nancy said.

"Around where?"

"Down to Peterson's maybe."

This was unacceptable to Mrs. McConkey, who was watching Panimer through the screen door, waiting, until he saw he would have to be definite or lose the evening or be confined to the McConkeys' porch.

"We're going to Peterson's for ice cream," he said.

"You come right back."

12

They were walking free, their imaginations way ahead of ice cream as they went by Peterson's Drugs, even ahead of what they had allowed themselves the night before in their sweet, hot love, which they supposed unequaled in the village as they argued, "I like you more," "No, I like you more," and on and on until their declarations began to heat the thoughts of what was coming, what would be granted and what withheld by tender agreement. They were already aware in their first, guarded sharing of flesh that each little abstention was itself a kind of devotion that could further heat their affections and their bodies, though this self-denial revealed itself to them primarily as the boundary of propriety—what was right and what was wrong. And as they walked across the field behind their old grammer school to the edge of the woods where they would make their evening's nest in orchard grass, Panimer was thinking, "I will not even try this time. She'll ask or we won't touch at all," ashamed of the last time when she was aroused from a sweet moaning to utter, "No," and remembering with a holy respect the rules she had made without words, as if to say, you can touch me here, but you can't touch me here, guiding his

hand to license and from the forbidden, none of these places
having names they had ever spoken to each other. Tonight, if
she did not signify, he meant only to talk, though he might be
thinking of her nakedness, and his own. No matter if she teased
along his thigh while *she* talked, her voice without a trace of
understanding of what her fingers had already accomplished
(She must know, he thought, she *must* know what is happening), this time she would have to encourage him because he did
not intend to hear that sudden, firm "No," which would wrench
him from what he had supposed was a shared abandon, back to
the rules he had so reverently agreed to.

They found their place, sat and talked, Nancy holding his
hand, telling him, "You have nice hands," and asking "Why
does your mother like the colored so much?"—more curious
than accusing.

"I don't know," he said. "She doesn't like 'em all that
much."

"She must," Nancy insisted. "She's always with them."

"So?"

"Nothing." Nancy had not meant to provoke him. She held
his hand tighter in apology, but let go when he did not respond,
then remembered, "Daddy says she's the only one up there
seems to know there's a war on."

"Up where?"

It was too late to renege; she had to answer "Small Hill,"
which twisted his face in a way she had not seen before. She
could see the evening's tenderness slipping away. And she grew
petulant as his back straightened against the criticism; she was
thinking, "Well, it's true isn't it? It's nothing up there but a
bunch of colored women and a junk man who won't give his
scrap for the war. And the price man and his wife who let their
boys go pleasure riding against the law and flouting the black-
outs. And that tramp Farmer Kreutz who never was a farmer,
never was anything but lazy, and spends all his time cheating the
rationing. And you." All of this gathered from her parents who
did not want her running with the boy people said acted like a
traitor. Nancy said none of this, but touched a finger to her lips,

then reached with the finger for the scar on his chin, which softened him beyond the reserve he had sworn himself to, all that falling away and more as she said, "Panimer, when I have our baby I don't want you watching."

This overwhelmed him, how far beyond their rules her imagination had run as they slipped further. Their bodies began to heat the tall grass to warm damp in the dew, the steamy itching of their nest a further excuse to escape into writhing as he marveled at what she had said. She had delivered him way beyond his present inclination, beyond this embrace to marriage, even beyond the secret business of making a baby to the mechanics of its delivery. The thought of so distant a future unsettling him and at the same time allowing him a vision of her nakedness, and his own; his moving hands now licensed absolutely he supposed as she whispered encouragement. What boy his age had ever known so much? None in Clayton, he was certain, as he wondered how to ask if she would show herself to him. He would promise not to touch a thing if that's what she wanted, he would help her, then she would help him; thinking of shared nakedness and thinking of nothing as the grass beneath them took the hot print of their prone form, and his hand slipped beneath and beyond their rules and she said, "No."

Panimer was furious with himself. He would not speak to her on the way home.

"What's the matter?" she said. But he would not even mumble, nothing, so she chattered aimlessly, wishing she had not said, No, but not wanting to unsay it. He left her at her door without kissing her, or wanting to. Turning away, he crossed the porch and saw four boys watching him.

They began to chase him as soon as he was out of sight of her porch, following him across Station Drive toward the Duncan Kimball yard. He vaulted the fence. They were still a safe distance behind but he tried to hide behind the school. They were not fooled but saw him as they came round the building. Running again he beat them to the edge of the woods. He was certain if he did not get away they were going to beat him up, or worse. Why else would four boys chase one without even announcing the chase? He would have outrun them in an open field—he was extraordinarily fast, faster than any of them though they were all two or three years older. But at the woods edge he lost that advantage; within moments one of them tripped him.

Surrounded, he began to flail as the four of them lifted him by arms and legs which pumped against their grip. Spread between them, his pumping raised and lowered his body in crazy jerks as if an epileptic seizure suspended him in convulsive flight. "Put him down," one of them said, "he's a tough little bastard."

One grabbed for his belt while the others held him against the ground. Squirmig, he turned himself over but was still pinned beneath them. Through all this he had not said a thing, simply struggled in animal fright, not focusing on faces or voices, only on shapes to be fled and force to be met by counterforce. Identification would have been difficult in the double dark of night and forest. He knew Hiram Johnson and Ronald Pride were not among them, but he knew with the same certainty that these must be their friends, part of the same enemy. And he understood, as an animal might, their attack had design since there was no discussion; the only sounds among them the grunts of their exertion. While three held him fast, one tore the buttons of his fly and pulled his pants down. Exhausted, his legs ceased to pump. There was only an occasional spasmodic movement of an arm or foot. His pants were at his ankles, a further shackle against struggle. His shoes were in the way. They were removed, thrown in the woods, then his pants were all the way off and a hand reached up for his underpants. His body twisted in a final paroxysm before yielding completely; he imagined them staring through the dark at the center of his nakedness. One of them said, "Look at. He had his cut." He did not understand how they could see while he could not. Another said, "We ought to rub his little ass in poison ivy," the first sign they were not in absolute agreement about what they would do to him, and the first assurance it was to be something less than death. His heart slowed in its retreat from terror and now he thought of them as stupid.

"Yeah."

"No. Just what we said," he heard.

"This'll teach his little bollocks what a blackout is. He won't see any light back here."

"You're gonna show a change, boy, start talking right about this war." As his body had gone limp, denying them the treat of struggle, now his mind flexed against argument, against any answer.

"Do you hear?" They were dragging him backwards. "Stand up." He would not. They grabbed his shoulders, pulled him up against a tree. He did not scream as they stretched his arms out behind him. They did not know how badly they were hurting him. They used his belt to tie his wrists behind the tree, then his pants, which they stretched behind the tree, to tie each ankle. Hobbled, foot and hand, naked below the waist, he twitched, waiting to be beaten. He could not see them, even their shapes, nor hear them; he supposed they were behind him, whispering, and as he waited, a new fear climbing to his head through groin and stomach kept him rigid against the tree. He waited, still could not place them, until even that notion of mutilation subsided and he realized they were gone.

They had judged well. His vigil, sleepless against the rough wale of locust bark was not vengeful or whimpering; he was poised, not to alert those searching for him, but to avoid discovery, with never a thought that he might starve there or die of exposure. Even halfway through the next day, when he could have been heard by Lester, who sat each day on the steps of the school, he did not yell. He was still hoping for unassisted escape, though his wriggling had not even begun to loosen the bonds. Even in the afternoon, when he heard his father and mother and Claudelle calling from the schoolyard, he did not respond. By then several groups were searching for him. But all he could think was, "What if they find me?" Worse, "What if *she* finds me?" because by then he knew that Nancy would have been questioned. And in his sleepless exhaustion, arms and legs numb, he still insisted: They will not find me like this. I will not let her see me naked.

Eventually Mr. Johnson walked right into him. When they untied him his knees buckled. He could not walk. They tried to lift him but he pulled away from them. It was a while before they understood his reluctance. Someone walked back for a pair of trousers.

"The snotty devil didn't say so much as thank you," Mr. Johnson told the others. Panimer had been able to walk out of the woods, leaning on one of them. But he answered no questions. They left him for a moment on the Jew store steps while they went to find his parents. When they came back with Junior and Paula he had disappeared again. He was walking up Station Drive alone, not thinking of his two-day-old hunger and thirst, or even of revenge, only escape to Small Hill.

13

They want a blackout so bad, Panimer thought, I could give them one. But for the moment he put the idea out of his head; he was so distracted by the memory of his night in the woods and notions of what they might try next, that he hardly paid attention to what his father was telling him. Paula had missed her shuttle bus, overslept while Junior sat with Panimer in the kitchen talking to the boy about his mother.

"Them Sons of Clayton is making double profit off her and them colored she works with. She hasn't even got sense to ask the extra gas ration coming to her."

"I could get her some extra at school," Panimer said.

"You been messing with counterfeit stamps?"

"These are just like real. I know a boy his father gets all he wants. You can't tell the difference."

"Don't bring none around here."

Panimer had only been trying to help. He would not speak to his mother when she woke and came bleary and scolding into the kitchen, annoyed with them for letting her miss the bus. But his hurt was already diffused by the time Junior drove her to work. He was proud of both of them; of his mother because everyone said she was doing more than anyone else in the county for the war, of his father because he was skeptical about the whole thing.

I could give them an air raid he thought again. It was a lonely mischief he was drifting into, a matter between him and the siren—all that non-noise that could become a high screaming tied up in the little electric box with the lever on it. Panimer walked onto the kitchen porch and put his hand on the lever; he never suspected his alarm would reach the three miles into Clayton.

It was no great coincidence that he gave the signal for imminent attack without really meaning to. What other way would he have approached it but tentatively so that after the siren had whirled to its highest pitch his hand raised the lever again, more to relieve the ringing in his ears than to silence a false alarm, and the noise wound down, close to stillness; so taken with the long slow rhythm of this that his hand was forced to it again. From the porch he saw a light in one of the colored shacks at the corner go out, but did not connect this with what he was doing. Once more he raised the lever to hear the receding wail. Another light went out. His hand continued on its own, pleasing his ear. He looked toward the Lewis house and could not see the second-story lights. He took a mindless pleasure in the gathering darkness and the noise as it washed and ebbed over the land, clearing away the last illumination save a glow in the mist over the hollow, over the huge building.

For several minutes he was charmed by this, the loudest noise he had ever made, connected to the effect only by his fingers. When he finally stopped the telephone was ringing: their ring, two longs, one short. He woke to his connection with Small Hill, with Clayton, and began to run. Down the porch steps, down the hill, across the skin diamond. He slowed, looked back, heard his father's car skidding into their driveway, knew he must put more distance between him and what he had done.

101

He walked into the woods at the edge of the ball field, made his way along the dark path toward the junkyard hill.

The siren reached Clayton only as the faintest wail. It might have been taken for the horn of a distant car if any had noticed it at all. But it carried clearly the mile and a half to Saw Mill Road, to the next warning station where Harold Johnson was preparing a Stanback powder and water against his regular headache. He listened in disbelief to the undulating signal, the blue alert, imminent attack. There had been no announcement of a practice alert. He ran outside, cocked his head to the sky for the bomber engines he'd been trained to recognize. There was only the clear wail of the siren, which seemed to be coming not from Clayton but from further out Station Drive. He hurried inside to call the Small Hill station, Junior's number. The phone rang and rang, much too long, he thought. There was no answer. He tried to call the Stilson fire department, center of the county's warning system, but misdialed and heard a lady's voice, "Is it you again?"

"No," he said, ashamed, replacing the receiver in a gentle haste. He did not want to call Stilson anyway, did not want to play the fool for one of Earl Jackson's men who would be on duty there. Lamartine would be angry if he made a mistake, if he made Clayton a joke for the Stilson people. He would call the Clayton station instead. It would only be Ronald Pride or one of those young corner boys on the night shift there in the office over Lamartine's garage where the town's new siren had been installed. Harold's head throbbed as he looked for the garage number. Then his hands would not hold still, he was too nervous to dial. He could not ask help from the operator; one of the Settle women worked nights in the Stilson exchange, and what if this were all a mistake; thinking how he would be ridiculed at Clayton's Notions if he failed. If Clayton's Notions were not bombed to extinction. In his flutter the alternatives were negative—risk a false alarm or risk the community's annihilation. He chose the warning.

As he raised and lowered the handle on his alarm box his

headache disappeared. All fear subsided as he did his duty. He felt his house vibrate with the rising pitch of the siren; watched with satisfaction as his hand drove the alarm, the rising and falling noise extinguishing house lights in widening circles around him. But still there was the glow of Clayton reflected in the low haze over the village. When his three-minute signal had been given, the last whine driven into the night, he heard his telephone. As he turned to answer it a flash split the Clayton sky. A moment later he heard a violent explosion. My God, I was too late, he thought. They are bombing us. He could not hear their engines. "The Germans are bombing us," he screamed at the empty night, but his voice cracked and broke; he hardly heard it himself.

Another sharp light flew into the air over Clayton. Not lightning, it moved from the ground upward, and the sound that followed was not the crack or reverberation of thunder. More like dynamite. They were bombing for sure, bombing Sons of Clayton, he supposed, grateful he had not given a false alarm, certain he had done his duty well because the village's own siren could now be heard—so loud that more than a mile away Harold felt pain in his ears and supposed his headache was returning.

Clayton had been late getting its siren but when it came it was the best. "It's gonna be something that'll wake Jackson up over in Stilson," Lamartine boasted. He was right. It was a Victory Siren from the Bell Laboratories and was meant to be powered by an ordinary automobile engine. But it was going to be put on the roof of Lamartine's Mobil and Lamartine was going to make the decisions about it; he wasn't going to have anything ordinary. It was a twelve-cylinder Packard engine they hoisted to the garage's second story with a crane; the weight of the thing requiring new shoring under the decrepit floor.

They had been warned about it, that it made the loudest sound in the world, and Lamartine told the boys who sat listening for enemy planes and tending the engine that would force air through the siren's spinning blades: "Don't rev it up all the way just for a practice alert. It'll break your head." What he meant was eardrums. And each day the Packard engine was disengaged from the Victory Siren and started, cleaned, oiled, its gas checked, made ready for Lamartine's inspection.

"I could send a signal 'crost the river with it," Lamartine said, "let those price men know there's people over here," but what he was thinking was he could be the loudest patriot in America if he wanted, louder than Earl Jackson or anybody in the Stilson fire department—their siren couldn't touch his.

Ronald Pride, sitting upstairs in the garage, next to the Packard engine, heard what he supposed was the Saw Mill Road siren and could not understand why. No one had told him of a practice alert. The window was open wide for the sound of bombers but all he heard was the distant siren. There was no sign others in the village had noticed; the ring of lights still burned around the Sons of Clayton fence, and a few scattered house lights were visible though it was past midnight.

The boy had only a moment's anxiety from the noise. As he stood at the window a small building in the middle of the Sons of Clayton lot came apart; he saw pieces of wood and tarpaper and glass riding up into the night on a ball of light, floating up and up, then spreading and settling back in silhouette against the plant's lights. Moments later the brilliant center of the explosion still shone on his inner eye, the noise still sang through his head. His senses had not shaken these memories when it happened again. He had not even thought of the alarm. This time it was not a single explosion but a series, six small buildings in a row going off like a giant string of Chinese firecrackers, blown into the air in sequence, but syncopated, each noise and flash pretending to be the last, but lying, until Ronald understood he wished they would stop, and he cursed the last two explosions for surprising him again.

He could see people running across the low field toward the creek; by then he knew it was an emergency worthy of alarm. But his siren was meant for air raids, and he was not sure what had happened, trying to sort duty from confusion. There were fires in several of the demolished buildings but it did not occur to him to call the Stilson fire department. He was trying to keep track of what had happened, was happening, because he supposed himself the lone observer of this tragedy—someone must be dead, he thought—and he would have to report what he had seen; already composing his answer, "It was just like they jumped up in the air, one at a time, right down the line till there wasn't any line left, and then I . . ." at that moment remembering he had done nothing, thinking he ought to give the alarm perhaps since the result wasn't much different from a bombing. He wondered if it might not have been a bomb in the first place, and he remembered the siren he had heard and wondered if it had not been a siren at all, rather the whistle of a bomb falling right on the place everybody knew was so high on the German list—Sons of Clayton.

He ran across the room and pushed the starter. There was immediate ignition, and in his haste he did what he had been told not to do. After putting it in gear he gave the engine full throttle. As the noise began to swell he walked back to the window. It was still rising as he watched another explosion rip skyward, light appearing to penetrate the roof of the main building in the center of the plant even before the building had come apart, tearing a seam along the roof's crown, escaping before the force of the explosion had raised roof and beams into the night and sent the walls flying sideways. This time the boy's senses were tried beyond endurance. He blinked against the flash, then felt the percussion as walls and floors of the garage absorbed the shock waves. The windows shook in their casements though he could not hear them. Again he was trying to clear his head of this confusion of light and sound. He felt a sudden sharp pain, was surrounded by a rushing wind, confusing because he could not feel it. It was as if he had crawled into a giant seashell, was now receiving a surrounding but unidentified noise that arrived from a great but indefinable distance. Until he realized in panic of lost faculty it was the roar of no noise at all. He knocked the base of his palm sharply against his temple, but only screamed in pain at this further attack on himself. And the scream arrived from that same strange middle distance as the airless wind, was distinguishable from it only as still more pain. The whole garage was vibrating now, and Ronald stood rigid in his fright. It was now long after the last explosion but glass had just begun to fall from the window over his head. Totally disoriented, he trembled with the building, and was only moved to leave the garage when he took the sudden notion it was about to be target of the next German bomb. He ran down the stairs and out into the night of fires and running shadows, forgetting the siren he had left at full throttle, which had broken his eardrums early in its attack on the air around it, had then broken every window in the garage. The noise had still not leveled at peak. The forty-foot pane in Chain Food across the street cracked, was about to fall to the pavement, and all the windows on the near side of Duncan Kimball, two hundred yards away, would be shattered before the siren was finally shut down. Glass fell from windows all over the village.

14

The newspaper paid 32-point capital respects to the dead, nine women and three men; carried sub-headlines for the maimed.

One Woman Blind, One Boy Deaf
In Night of Homemade Terror

A few of the dead had been known by face in the village, none by name. They had been transients, temporarily settled in the trailer park, latecomers who were forced to take the night shift. Relatives came for their bodies, took them home for burial. But no kin could be found for one of them. Her body lay in the Stilson funeral home for two weeks while they waited for some clue to her origin, for someone to come forward and claim her. No one came.

It was Arthur Settle who first suggested a monument to her memory—though none seemed to remember her. Others seized and clung to the idea until it was done. The town needed it, something to relieve its sense of injustice that no sons of Clayton had been lost in the tragedy. But it was Settle and the other partners in the plant who would not let go, even when it was determined there was no public plot to accommodate tomb and memorial. The village had no common then. Regardless, they would adopt this mystery woman for their own, their orphan in death, even before they were sure she would remain unknown, because they needed concrete evidence of their misfortune.

Jewel Lamartine's men finished the concrete, as his back hoe had dug the grave, right in the middle of the crossroads, down through the alternate layers of gray and red stone and the old track bed of the country trolley. They built a little traffic island at the intersection of Wye Bridge Pike and Station Drive; buried their unclaimed war worker beneath, and placed the obelisk donated by Stilson Monuments above. The stone said Here Lies A Patriot. From the steps of the Jew store a boy could sail pop bottle caps and just reach it.

When the rumors started it was too late to dig her up or remove the monument. The rumors would just have to be buried with her, and blame shifted to shoulders of the quick; they couldn't expect blame to lie still with the bones of a hero, not after inscribing a stone to her patriotism and placing it in the center of their best traveled paths. Maybe the doubting began just to fill empty space in Clayton's Notions. Valerie Jackson mused, "Now why would it start in number twenty-seven? That building wasn't supposed to have anything but drying ovens in it."

The deaf boy Ronald Pride had pointed to one of the smoldering foundations the next day and said, "That was the first one." After that the newspaper's sequels began to refer to building twenty-seven. The rest of Valerie's information was from the *Journal* too. She was only begging questions again, the same the whole village had been asking itself. If Arthur Settle had sat in the notions store with sister and friends the plan for the monument might have been delayed long enough to catch the mistake. At least he would have caught the ladies' skepticism: "How could she have been an unknown soldier? She had to have a name, didn't she? She was on the payroll, wasn't she?"

108

The mystery worker had given a name and told the employment clerk she was from Richmond.

The Richmond police and newspapers were informed. They found no past address, no trace of a relative, no recollection of her name. Her trailer was searched. There was nothing with her name on it, not even a letter. There were several books about American history and a biography of Thomas Paine; all these recorded in the *Journal*'s eulogy under the headline, An American Patriot, the title of the biography. Which had first excited Arthur Settle's pride in the woman. And Wilma's doubt. "American revolutionary," she mumured. Still no one said sabotage, though all had pondered the possibility. Not even when they learned the woman had been working in number twenty-seven did they come out and say sabotage. Would she have blown herself up on purpose? But what if she had been inept, or hurried.

Sons of Clayton could not explain the explosions. They defied sense; the drying ovens had been inspected the same night. They had been operating at lower temperatures and for a shorter time than usual. At first there had been talk of human error and room for human error, and other catch cries as weightless of blame. But somewhere in their search for cause they would have to stumble on intent. They did. "If nobody knows where she came from and nobody knows her name for sure, maybe she was keeping it all a secret." Valerie's observation turned them; the mystery woman beneath the crossroads began to move from martyr to suspect.

Then they began to wonder about the two survivors of building twenty-seven—Paula and the colored woman.

From Marcum's junk hill Panimer had heard the alarms he supposed he had set off in sequence. He had watched a truck disappear around the cinderblock wall. Two more tractor trailers were waiting to get inside. There was commotion at both ends of the long wall, arguing about the lights, whether or not to turn them out. There had been three sirens going then, Clayton's and the Saw Mill Road station, and, coming down

Station Drive from the direction of Indian Falls, the air horn of one of the county warden's Paul Revere cars that had been scouting for pleasure drivers when the deputy warden driving it heard Clayton's alarm. He raced toward the village, looking for blackout violators; he, too, thinking this must be the real thing, indignant when he saw the bright haze over Small Hill hollow, angry as he came close enough to see the giant war installation was the only thing illuminated anywhere in the vicinity, the place bright as a carnival with all the truck lights and lights along the fence. From the air it could not have been missed, its perimeter outlined and the huge building itself defined as bull's eye by the floodlights under its eaves.

The deputy warden barely made the turn into the driveway, slid to a stop just short of a trailer's mud flap. He had come through the gate just after the truck, ignoring the man who stood waving against his entry. He understood he was not meant to be there, would not be allowed in the building, did not want them to think he was trying to get inside, so stood beside his car and called to the men he could see trying to close the sliding doors in front of the place, "Get those lights out."

Panimer heard this, then from the far end of the lot, "Get him out of here."

"It's the warden's man."

"Get him out."

"It's an alert."

"Damn you," the deputy warden called, "it's a air raid."

"Get up here." Two men at the rear of the building disappeared through the back door and a minute later emerged at the front. "Put him in his car and get him out of here."

"He says it's not a warning. It's a air raid."

"Wasn't no notice of a air raid."

"Can't you understand?" the deputy warden said. "That was the attack signal." For a moment they all stopped and listened to the Clayton siren. "That's strange," he said. "It's on steady now."

"Get him out of here."

The deputy was sidling away from their grasp, still remonstrating, moving closer to a view through the great sliding doors though this was not his intention. Now they moved between him and the doors, the guard dog growling at their side.

"I don't care what's in there," he said, moving backward, "I'm just telling you for your own good. Get those lights out."

Panimer still heard them arguing as he climbed the fence. There was an opening in the back doors, wide enough to slip through. He moved closer, not walking, trotting, maybe running again from the new trouble he had made for himself by setting off the alarm, maybe looking now for trouble with a larger debt, something that would make punishment for the last redundant. He did not hesitate, slipped inside and stood still. It was too dark to see anything. He could hear the idling diesel of the truck they were loading or unloading, the driver cursing the dark. The inside lights had been turned off against the chance the deputy might see what was in the building.

Panimer moved sideways, his back sliding along the metal door. His eyes were not adjusting, but he sensed huge shapes around and above him. He was thinking, what if the dog smells me. He moved past the door, along cinderblock, one hand feeling behind him in fast contact with his line of escape. His shoulder touched something. He jumped backward. And lost contact with the wall. There was someone behind him; he could not tell how close. He moved again, stumbled into a pile that fell away in front of him. He was lying on paper. It felt like newspaper. He heard, "Hey. Is that you?" and from his other side, "Is that who?" Steps came toward him from both sides. He moved forward again, bumped into another wall that felt like a stack of newspapers. Trying to correct his course, he veered to the other side and knocked into a ragged wall of something harder. If I'm not careful, he thought, I might walk into a cage full of foxes. But if they shine in the dark, I'll see them before they see me. Maybe the paper's just for the floor of the cages. It'd take a lot of paper for that many foxes; these notions interrupted by the voices behind him.

"D'you knock this stack over?"

"You musta done it yourownself."

"I didn't."

"Well it don't matter if you did. It wasn't sorted."

"I said I didn't. And this lot's not got to be sorted. He said he's calling it all number one mixed and let them worry about it at the other end."

"Who *did* then?"

Panimer moved ahead again, away from resolution of the argument, and bumped his shin on something that rang like a steel drum. He lifted his foot to clear the obstacle and bumped his shin in the same place, producing the same noise. The voices behind him were suddenly quiet, then coming toward him again. "Didn't you hear it?"

"Well turn the lights on."

"Not yet. Not until he says."

Panimer turned left, into a soft, ragged wall, then right, into another. He leaned over and felt the steps of an open metal stairway, groped for a handrail, found one, and climbed. After the first dozen steps he went up more cautiously, feeling for a landing. But the voices were coming closer below him; he would have to climb quickly again, risk their hearing him. He tried to lighten his tread, putting more weight on the handrail. The rail fooled him, it was too long. His foot came down on a step that was not there, hard on a metal floor. They must have heard, he thought, but no one was coming up the steps.

He was shuffling forward on a catwalk thirty feet above the ground, about to step onto air when the lights came on. From this height he commanded the building's whole expanse, horizon to horizon. He blinked, not just against the sudden light, but the revelation that seemed no revelation at all; only paper, waste paper of every description, as far as he could see, scrap, great stacks of it rising halfway to the roof and running the length of the place in sinuous lines. Narrow paths crisscrossed between them, a maze of tunnels that seemed to have no pattern. Down the center of the building was a wide lane for the trucks; one of them still waiting to be unloaded.

Panimer was so high above the floor the towering stacks of paper did not shield him from the men who were now huddled at

112

the front of the building. If they looked his way they would see him. The height began to frighten him, this and his lack of cover; he was swaying when they turned and saw him, at least seventy-five yards away, looking down on them. From that distance they could not make out his face or even tell it was only a boy. In fact they turned back to talk to each other for a moment before realizing he was not one of them. When they looked up again he was still swaying. He saw them coming toward him, spreading out in several paths through the maze; then felt himself falling, heard himself yelling. An instant later he was teetering on a great stack of magazines that moved under him; then falling again, riding down on a slick cover, next to a woman in a bathing suit; beside her, *Life* flashing above a prone soldier as he and the magazines bridged the path below, tumbling into the next line; which was a triple stack of newspapers. These too were knocked sideways against the next row so that widening waves of paper began to move across the floor of the great building, blocking pursuit by the men who, temporarily stymied, turned to wider routes through the maze. Now they came more cautiously, supposing the spreading commotion must be the work of more than one intruder. One of them saw Panimer lying in the paper and tried a direct course to him through the fallen scrap. The man pulled himself up by a bundle string and dislodged several tons of *Weekly Readers,* which fell on his back, pinning him in the rubble. The boy was up and solving the maze for the back doors, then racing the dog for the fence.

15

Paula had liked working with Claudelle and the woman from Richmond called Nadine. Their names were frequently on the office wall, on the plaque that said War Workers of the Week, and once they received special mention at a plant ceremony and certificates of their patriotic efficiency. When Sons of Clayton got new contracts that required retraining staff they were among the first night-shift workers taught the new methods. In tacit competition they pushed each other to new quotas, their hands passing swiftly over the drying trays as they moved fuses and small shells to and from the ovens and into packing crates. To Paula it was at once mindless and satisfying. Work for the simple, she said, but she intended to be best at it. When the three of them were transferred to proximity fuses they understood the honor. They had been trusted with a secret project and a new routine.

When there was nothing to do but wait at the ovens they talked, joked, happy in their productivity. Claudelle and Nadine told stories about men that Paula smiled at but could not laugh about. Under cover of night and in the secrecy of the factory building Nadine felt at ease with the colored woman though she would not parade her friendship before the village in daylight as

Paula had insisted on doing. While Clayton slept these three laughed and sang at their work, Claudelle leading them in their favorite "Praise the Lord and Pass the Ammunition," and sometimes singing to herself homemade hymns of confession and salvation.

Nadine gained Claudelle's confidence quickly even though Claudelle saw it was a nighttime friendship. Instead of Paula and Claudelle inviting the new woman from Richmond into their discussions, it was Claudelle and Nadine who tolerated Paula. When Nadine explained how she was running from her husband Claudelle understood immediately that Nadine was covering her trail, was not telling them the truth about her home, much less what her real name was. She accepted the woman's lies. Paula believed them.

On the night of sirens Paula had arrived late, interrupted them in something funny and secret; when she walked in they stopped laughing and looked at her as if she might have heard what they'd been talking about. She relieved their guilt, beginning for them. "I missed something."

"You're late, honey," Claudelle said, "Junior been keeping you late again?" and new laughter broke out between the colored woman and Nadine.

Paula, dropping her eyes, unable to laugh with them, said, "I'm sorry I'm late," flushed with the notion they knew these things about her, upset that her intimacies with her husband provided their amusement. But she wanted their confidence, could not show her annoyance. Without her to coax them with her steady cheerfulness they had fallen behind the night's schedule, and she said, "I'll have to hurry and get us caught up."

"Caught up to what?" Claudelle said.

"She wants to win the war all by herself," Nadine said.

"Then she got to have that man to leave her alone."

"I'm sorry I'm late," Paula said again. "They didn't wake me up."

"Wasn't no war ever won in bed," Claudelle said from the packing case where she had sat down next to Nadine to watch

115

while Paula struggled to keep their three positions running at capacity. They sat and watched with amusement and respect, even pity for the woman's intensity, until the exertion of running from oven to oven finally broke her rhythm. Her fingers no longer obeyed the speed she asked of them; she was near tears and still they sat hiding their shared amusement from her. They did not mean to hurt her, only wanted to play a little, and Paula would not play so their fun went on. As she went down the row of ovens Nadine snuck along behind her advancing the bell timers so that she could not possibly keep pace.

In a respite before this next cycle began to ring Paula sat down with them, out of breath, trying to make them understand how important this was. "The war's as good as touching this continent right now," she said. But how could she explain her enthusiasm for the work. She did not want to antagonize them but maybe they would understand if she told them, "In the Aleutians. They're in the Aleutians."

"The which?" Nadine said.

"Islands, honey," Claudelle explained. "You hadn't heard?"

"Who's in the islands."

"The Japanese," Paula said. "And they've got bombs they send up on balloons that blow this way in the wind. They could be dropping on the U.S.A. right now."

"That wouldn't be in the newspapers?" Nadine asked.

"Wherever they hit they hush it up," Paula said. "If the Japs knew it was working they'd send more."

"Go 'way from here, woman. No bombs coming here," Claudelle said. Then, "Where'd you hear that?"

Paula jumped as the first oven's bell rang behind her. "Already?" she said. "Mr. Lewis told the boys. Won't you help me?" The second bell rang and Paula jumped again. She'd hardly begun to unload the first trays.

"Them Japs," Claudelle said, "they're lightweights," repeating what she had heard Joe Louis say on the radio. Again Nadine tried to advance the timers behind Paula's back. Claudelle, thinking of Japanese balloon bombs, was tired of the game, tired of Nadine's meanness and Paula's eagerness. Nadine was pointing at a timer, inviting the colored woman's complicity, but she ignored it, called out to Paula, "It ain't time yet, honey. Come on and sit down."

Paula looked around the room for Nadine, then asked Claudelle, "She didn't play with the switches again?"

"You come on and sit down."

Paula turned around once more, caught only a glimpse of Nadine, who had been reaching for a timer when the fire ball appeared at the tip of her fingers so that Paula's last vision was of a woman carrying fire, and as she staggered from the building, leaning on Claudelle, her mind's eye was fixed on that blond statue consumed by its own torch. Paula was stumbling forward, screaming backward for the last light she had seen, as if recovery of the vision might lead further backward to its undoing, cancel the awful crunch she had heard as Nadine's head opened against a steel pipe and her clothes caught fire.

Then there was a second explosion and darkness that would not go away, with Claudelle calling "Over here," while she waited for the light. Claudelle grabbed her arm. "This way." The colored woman dragged her from the building, yelled at her to watch where she was going, screamed as the next building blew up behind them. There were others running with them, out the gate, turning back along the fence toward the creek. She was still waiting for the light when a new series of explosions sent them reeling sideways, away from the fence and they began to hear the rising whine of the Victory Siren on Lamartine's Mobil.

"This be the Jap bombs. It's a air raid," Claudelle was shouting as she picked herself up and began to run toward the creek; Paula calling from the ground, "Where are we? Claudelle?"

The colored woman turned back for her. "It's the balloon bombs," she said, "cause it isn't any airplanes up there. What's the matter with you? Here."

She helped Paula up, led her by the hand all the way to the creek, where they hid under the bank while the white woman waited for the light.

117

The searchers were still casting across the marsh at dawn, sending back for fresh thermoses of coffee. They had found eight bodies, knew there must be more but were not sure how many. Some of the night shift had run from the plant and kept on running, all the way to their trailers, and some, with cars, had tried to get their trailers off their blocks and hitched, moved as far from Sons of Clayton as they could, because no one was sure what was causing the explosions or when the next one was coming.

Just before sunrise Paula and Claudelle were still hiding behind the creek bank, within hearing of the searchers. A man had drifted afield from the others, hoping he would not find a body, was startled by "Who's that?" He spun around, but could not see Claudelle who had raised her head over the bank and was calling softly, "Are they done with the attack?"

"Where are you?" he said. He was coming toward them but still saw nothing, was almost stepping on her shoulder, and jumped again when the voice came from beneath him, "Here."

"What are you doing there?" his tone accusing, annoyed at being frightened, suspicious that anyone should be hiding.

"Look out," Claudelle said. "She can't see."

"I can't see you, either...there you are...who can't see?" Then he was trying to pull Paula free of the colored woman's hand, but Paula would not let go.

"Hold on," she begged, her grip fast on the last living thing she had seen, perhaps still hoping this attachment would pull her back to vision. It was so dark. He led them back, holding Paula's hand and Paula pulling the colored woman behind her, begging her not to leave, certain now that it was not night or the cover of trees that was the matter. She was shutting her eyes and opening them again and again, testing; clinging to Claudelle's hand, to Nadine too, or to the sound of the name, repeating in a soft moan, 'Where's Nadine?" until they told her Nadine was dead. There were voices all around her, asking how it had happened, where she had been. She recognized Arthur Settle's voice and Mr. Stockstill's and Jewel Lamartine's, up close to her, then far away and on the other side, then close again; her

118

head swiveled to keep them sorted. They did not seem interested in Claudelle, were not asking her anything. They were trying to pull Paula's hand away from the colored woman, but she struck out at them with her free arm, told them to leave her alone. Neither could have explained anything; both too frightened—Claudelle by what she saw, Paula by what she didn't.

Then Junior was there yelling at all of them to get away from her: "Can't you see she can't see? Come here, honey. We're going to the hospital. Let go."

"No."

"Let go of her now. We're going in the car."

"She can come too."

"Let go."

Paula knew she was in the middle of a circle of eyes. The questions had stopped; now they frightened her with consolation.

"They can fix you right up."

"You'll be just like new."

"They got doctors over there can do about anything."

She heard no confidence, only a kind of callous concern they might have spoken to a broken automobile. There was something less than human about her now, something that could not answer back; already it had begun to change the way they talked to and watched her—this was clear to her, in her sudden knowledge of blindness. She had begun to hear things they did not know they were saying.

Paula's blindness was a fact; it only remained for a doctor to pronounce it, no melodrama of bandage removal after weeks of wondering. It was done, and she was resigned, almost too quickly Junior thought, sensing she was going to be martyr to disease the way she had been martyr to war. That was not quite it, but Paula, grasping the sounds that informed her waking day, was taking a fascination in her own blindness. There was a tension that would keep life tolerable that had to do with the margin between what they supposed she could understand and what she actually perceived, until who she was had disappeared

119

from *their* view. It was a fascination with her *own* invisibility.

Not that people did not talk about her; Wilma Settle the one to observe: "The boy didn't want to be found in the woods and his mother didn't want to be found by the creek," then pausing, as after a profound truth but a truth still in hiding, waiting for Valerie or Jane to seize its implications.

"They're hiding something, Valerie obliged. "I mean all of them up there," and here she meant Small Hill again.

"Ronald Pride," Jane began.

"He's deaf and the Army won't take him," Valerie said.

"And he wanted to go so bad," Wilma said, "but his daddy says it's headaches all the time."

"Ronald Pride," Jane began again, "saw that farm tramp in the middle of it. Going down the Pike with not but a lantern on his wagon so you couldn't hardly see it was him. I've half a notion he must have seen what happened. He knows something."

"And shouldn't have had that light either," Valerie said. "Not in a air raid."

"It wasn't an air raid," Jane said. "What happened was all right here on the ground. And why was he running from it?"

"So he wouldn't get his head blown off?" Wilma said. "All the rest were running. Why shouldn't he? Arthur says half the town was like a bunch of field mice running from a barn owl when that siren started. Not just them in the factory either. Mr. Stevens drove his family all the way to Indian Falls before he turned to think about what he was running from."

"How you go on, Wilma," Jane said. "An owl doesn't shriek to start a mouse. It shrieks to stop it. To make it too scared to move. And Kreutz was moving Roland says faster than he ever moved those mules before."

"Some were too frightened to move," Valerie said, "and some too frightened to stay put. So?"

16

Mr. Lewis had liked to say the Kreutzes were stamp poor. He meant the way some people were land poor. The war had brought the Kreutzes a new kind of wealth. They had more stamps (enough to provide for their five children) than money to use them. The deprivation of war seemed riches to them; they'd never had as much to eat as rationing would have allowed.

"So why wouldn't they try to buy something with their stamps?" Mr. Lewis asked his wife, who allowed further, "So why wouldn't they try to sell them?" Mrs. Lewis sat with a retired judge from Stilson and Mrs. Stockstill on the county ration board, controlling legitimate traffic in food coupons. The board had become a kind of confessional and court, hearing claims and complaints with a flexibility that was bound to be called bias.

The board had received complaints about Farmer Kreutz and considered calling him before it for sanction, not supposing he might put himself in its way with a complaint of his own. The day Kreutz had driven his wagon all the way from Small Hill to Stilson to tell them how he'd been done out of his shoe stamps in a grocery store, arriving in the late afternoon, the dust and sweat of the trip on his face and hands and the smell of mules and unwashed weeks in his clothes, they were not ready for him. Nor for his persistence, which pressed its way into the long line in front of him, the purpose in his eye and odor of his body creating space of their own in the crowded room, advancing out of turn as people fell away before him.

He stood before the petty court, unaware one of its three members was wife of the man he was about to accuse, and said, "The grocery man took my shoe stamps and won't give 'em back," looking right at Judge Preston, supposing the two women who sat beside him must be his assistants. They knew who he was but Judge Preston said, "What is your name?"

"Ain't you known me before? Many times as you blowed your horn at me?"

"You're Mr. Kreutz?"

"Farmer Kreutz. I say the man took my shoe stamps."

"Mr. Kreutz, you know these coupons aren't like money," Mrs. Stockstill said.

"Can't you see I'm talking to this man?" Kreutz said. Then looking at Mrs. Lewis, whom he recognized, "Is it this man supposed to see we get what's coming?"

"This is the food ration board," she said.

"He's got nothing to do with shoes? You mean I come all the way here and can't talk to the shoe people?"

"It's confusing," Mrs. Lewis said.

"Although this is the food board," Mrs. Stockstill said.

"Can't you stop interrupting?" said Kreutz.

"We're all on the ration board," Judge Preston said. "Coupon number seventeen in your food book is for shoes. Now who is it took your stamps?"

"The Chain Food man," Kreutz said. "And won't give 'em back. Said he already turned 'em in to the government people." Kreutz looked behind him, then leaning over to Judge Preston's ear, said, "I don't think he give 'em to no government man. I think he takes the stamps home."

The judge, sliding his chair back, repelled more by odor than ex parte conversation, said, "When the stamps are torn from the ration book they can't be used again."

"Who pays attention to that?" Kreutz said. "Nobody pays attention to that. Now with the gas stamps I can . . ."

"But you don't have a car, do you, Mr. Kreutz?" asked Mrs. Stockstill.

"Got as much right to one as the next. Mr. Clarke, he's the one I got to see about the gas stamps. Soon as I get done with you people. Mr. Osmond Clarke."

"Mr. Kreutz," Mrs. Stockstill said, "there have been complaints about you. You are not to sell your food stamps."

"Who? Who complained?"

"There have been complaints. If you sell your stamps we cannot issue more to you."

"Who complained?"

Mr. Stockstill gave Kreutz food for his coupons just to get him out of the store where he was a menace to trade; slowly walking the aisles, sometimes for an hour at a time, until manager, stock boys, and checkers were all occupied with watching the man's hands and pockets—a waste of their time because he never picked anything off the shelves or vegetable racks, only made feints at a thing he wanted, or pawed something, then moved on to something else he fancied but could not afford. When he came in the store the employees winked at one another, prepared for siege. Kreutz did not talk in the store, only pointed or pawed and Stockstill would eventually follow after him, pushing a cart for him, filling the basket himself with items Kreutz touched, contaminated. If Kreutz hesitated at a bag of coffee or stopped in front of the meat counter Stockstill just pushed the cart past the luxury, and Kreutz would know he had gone too far. It was as if a mute had brought his wife to market to veto his extravagance. When he came to the checkout counter he made great fuss with his wallet, a show of wealth, his family ration books. The checker clipped from them, which is how Kreutz lost his shoe coupons.

"Who complained?" he demanded again. They would not tell him. But he was determined to know, no matter the extra miles he might travel to find out, because that's what he was best at, a clopping pace over the Stilson roads in defiance of the County's traffic that braked and swerved around him, his locomotion announcing his existence: how could they ignore him if he kept getting in their way? A man driving to and from Stilson twice in one morning might pass Kreutz four times, each time cursing the obstacle he presented in the road. When he set out to do something, the distance he traveled was not an inconvenience to himself, but a credit against his purpose to be felt by others. And they felt it, were obliged to his persistence. Mrs. Stockstill's remonstration about his fraudulent selling of ration stamps was just a postponement of the victory that his last eight, mule-drawn miles had guaranteed; they would grant him new shoe stamps, then wonder that he promised: ''I'll find out who complained about me.''

Mr. Lewis's critics in government said he had been there too long, that he held a Resident Chair of Cynicism, was blind to his country's achievement. America was producing more materials faster and at greater sacrifice than any other nation in history. Mr. Lewis said, ''It's a marvelous evil on the other side that's making us look heroic.'' They wondered if they heard him correctly. Then he told them what they wanted to hear: ''In every instance we're behaving patriotically. We do business patriotically, profit patriotically, hold the line on wages patriotically. Why, every waking act is patriotic.'' Then when they were once more secure in his approval he'd say ''and every act profitable.''

Mr. Lewis was carrying the government's battle on price controls to paper companies and the paper companies were counterattacking. One company—Triumph Paper—had fought him from the beginning and he supposed in the end they would win. Their lawyers were exhausting every line of appeal while Triumph practiced every evasion of the price ceiling, so shameless in their aggression and tenacious in their delays that Mr. Lewis thought of them as Germans and Japanese. He said more than once, to no one's attention, ''The war's right here. And we're losing it.'' There were five others in his section working

124

on paper cases. "Imagine it," he said. "Paper. If we can't beat paper, who the hell can we beat?" He enjoyed his part in righteousness, but the tedium of legal particulars advanced his cynicism, made him wry in the way of an overworked man, at once pleased with his effort and suspicious of its usefulness. He told his wife, "They give me an extra ration of gas and a tire certificate so I can drive to Washington every day and get pushed around by paper."

"That's a switch," she said.

On that night of sirens and explosions, close to midnight, coming up Station Drive toward Small Hill, on his way home from a paper emergency, Mr. Lewis was almost forced into the ditch, to make room for Farmer Kreutz driving his mules down the middle of the road; Kreutz's eyes never shifting from the pavement's center, as if his unswerving concentration on the space he occupied and ceded at the clop of several miles an hour protected his wagon against the steel machines. What he ignored could not collide with him. A lantern swung on the back of the wagon. There was no light in front. As Lewis's headlights approached and slowed before him, Kreutz's gaze remained steady on the road. His arm jerked once, petulantly to the side, directing whoever it was out of his way. Mr. Lewis groaned at the inconvenience and whispered "Jesus Christ" as the scent of the procession—mules, driver, wagon—passed between him and the breeze. He heard Kreutz say "goddam fools," and wondered what notion possessed the man that he would have his wagon in the road at that hour.

The next morning on his way back to Washington Mr. Lewis saw the shattered glass of the village on the sidewalks—the window of Clayton's Notions somehow had withstood the attack—and a single fire engine still spraying the smoldering rubble in the Sons of Clayton lot. He wondered what had become of Kreutz, who must have reached the village close to the time of fire and sirens. He was still wondering how it had happened as he crossed Wye Bridge and drove into the first traffic jam he had ever encountered on Canal Road. He could see a line of cars a quarter mile long disappearing around a curve. He was forced to a complete stop. Drivers and car pool passengers were getting out, walking ahead, looking for the accident, then hurrying back to their cars as the line moved again. Once more the whole line stopped. And when it moved again it was at a sweaty crawl; Mr. Lewis was already trapped for the day by the August heat. The oncoming traffic and the stone wall along the canal on the right kept the line honest; there was no passing. But as he turned the next bend Mr. Lewis saw the obstruction, the wagon still heading east. It was Kreutz on his way to Washington, holding the mules steady in their course, and like the mules in blinders, without a glance to either side of him, as one by one the drivers swerved past him at each opportunity, cursing to themselves or yelling back at him; Kreutz muttering "Goddam fools."

By the time it was his turn to pass the wagon Mr. Lewis felt a shame for the traffic's impatience with his Small Hill neighbor, hoped he could sneak by unrecognized, but the car in front of him had barely missed the wagon and frightened Kreutz, who looked around and caught sight of the man he knew. Now it was Lewis who kept his gaze fixed in front of him, avoiding Kreutz, who was calling, "You. Lewis. Where is that opie yea at?" Mr. Lewis, pretending not to hear, pulled around him, once more in siege to that stench which came through the window and hung in the car.

He saw a police car pass, supposed that would be the end of Kreutz's journey.

Farmer Kreutz had left Small Hill late on the night of sirens. He meant to be in Washington first thing in the morning. The first explosion came as he entered the village. The mules lunged sideways in their harness, raising the wagon on two wheels and snapping a line between the traces. Kreutz never budged from his seat. When the wagon righted itself the mules stopped, danced sideways, and went rigid.

"Come up, mules," Kreutz said, and there was no question they would move, experienced in his obstinacy, knowing it was greater than their own. He talked them around the corner, toward Wye Bridge, when the next two explosions made them hop to one side, then the other, before deciding, in unison, their only escape was forward. They bolted down the Pike; Kreutz never looked back to see what had happened, though he suspected the explosives plant was blowing up. This did not interest him. Nor did the traffic he encountered the next morning—so clearly prejudiced against his trip—put him off. He did not know where he would be when he got there, but it was all one—Washington and the price people.

Kreutz was most of the way down Canal Road when a policeman discovered him.

"I'm going to Washington District of Columbia," Kreutz told him. "Can't you keep them cars away from me? It's the price man I got to see at the opie yea."

"You're not taking that wagon to the O.P.A., mister. You're taking that wagon across the river when you get to Georgetown."

"Just the shoe man is the one I got to see." Kreutz said.

The officer, who supposed Kreutz was simply babbling out of fear, left him there, saying, "Hold that wagon until I come back for you." But when he was out of sight Kreutz was moving again. He turned his mules up Reservoir Road, away from the canal, not in fear of the law but in puzzlement. If he was in Washington and had not seen government, he must be going the wrong way. An hour later he was on Wisconsin Avenue, his wheels turning in a trolley track where he intended to keep them, supposing the tracks going down the hill must lead toward government; there were already three trolleys lined up behind him, all their bells working as Kreutz braked the wagon against the steep incline. He paid no more attention to them than to the people staring from the sidewalk. He would have stayed in that track all the way to Constitution Avenue and Capitol Hill had it not been for the foot patrolman at Q Street who risked Kreutz's whip and his abuse:

"Come away from that mule. Look out. You'll pull the wagon out the tracks." Which is what the policeman was doing, having failed to get the man's attention any other way. And Kreutz, seeing his mules being let into a side street, called again: "Well, if I can't use the tracks, how must I get there?"

Kreutz began to explain how it was not that he hadn't been given another stamp seventeen from the sugar book, but that when he took the stamp to Stilson, to the shoe store, they had told him it was out of date, no longer good for shoes; he could still use it for sugar. "I'm going to see Mr. Lewis," he said. "He comes acrost the river every morning. Now would you let go of the mules?"

The officer, satisfied he had removed the man from traffic, and with no interest in the complications of an arrest, turned and walked away; Kreutz calling after him: "If this isn't the sorriest place for information. Come up, mules."

He drove his wagon for several blocks between parked cars on Q Street, then turned right, downhill again, and was soon relieved to see the trolleys in front of him again. He whipped his mules into the busier street, got them turned left and the wheels wedged safely in the tracks once more, relaxing in the notion he must be almost there. The police did not interfere again until there were five trolleys backed up behind him.

"Where am I now?" he said.

"Pennsylvania and Seventeenth," he was told. "You have to get your wagon out of the way."

"Where is it they keep the government?" he said.

"From there on over it's all government," a patrolman said. "You just turn right at the corner up there and keep on straight; But keep your wagon off the trolley tracks." Kreutz drove past a white mansion and around the corner. On his left a marvelous light danced around the edge of a great marquee. As he came closer he could see it was hundreds of lights blinking on and off in sequence, and he stopped the wagon for a moment trying to see how it worked. He was almost at Independence Avenue when he pulled over to the sidewalk and called out to a pedestrian, "Expect I've gone on past the government."

"I'm not from around here," the man said.

"I'm new myself," Kreutz said, but the man was already past

him. He tried to stop several others coming down the sidewalk, but they circled just beyond his reaching arm, walked on without looking back. The next man by he grabbed by the shoulder.

"I'm sorry," he said, "I don't have anything for you." Kreutz let go, but stepped in front of the man, blocking his escape.

"I know I come past the government," Kreutz said. "But how far must I go back to the price people?"

"By golly, I don't know."

"Well it's a sorry town for information."

"All those along there," the man said, "they're government buildings."

"Them tenements?" Kreutz dismissed him, supposing he was misinformed, but others he stopped told him the same thing, that these squat gray rectangles lining the avenue were all temporary government quarters. And all that day he went from building to building asking for Mr. Lewis.

The next day Kreutz told his wife, "Can't just anybody get into the government," a little pleased with himself, because on his third or fourth pass of the temporary buildings he had prevailed on one of the desk guards to check his numbers again and the guard had reached a Mr. Lewis who had never heard of Farmer Kreutz but who came to the front door anyway and listened while Kreutz told his story.

"This isn't in my area," the man apologized, and Kreutz, certain he was about to be turned away again, said, "You any kin to the other Mr. Lewis?"

"I'm afraid not." The man was edging backward. Kreutz raised his voice:

"What is your area?"

"Silk," the wrong Mr. Lewis answered, backing down the hall, while the guard held Kreutz who was trying to follow, calling as the man disappeared into his office:

"Well where's the shoe people?"

It was six o'clock when Kreutz had gone halfway down the row of temporaries again, his enthusiasm renewed by the new shift of guards who had just come on duty; no easier to get past, but new ears for his complaint. He worked his way back to the wrong Mr. Lewis's building and, deciding his best chance was here, demanded of the new guard that he call the man. "Tell him it's Farmer Kreutz," he said. "He knows me." This time the man did not come from his office. It was close to dark when he finally came from the building, not to see Kreutz whom he had forgotten, but to go home. He was not prepared for Kreutz's siege; the springing shadow startling him. He almost began to run.

"I know you just do silk," Kreutz said.

"It's you again. You're still here."

"If you could just give me something says the shoe coupons is coming to me."

"I couldn't do that. I'm in no way connected . . ." He was trying to get past Kreutz, who moved in front of him again, not begging, demanding, "You give me something shows I been here. I didn't come all this way to go back with nothing. You give me a paper says what it is is coming to me—that the shoes by rights is mine. And I can give you a ride wherever it is you're going. That's my wagon."

"No," the man said. "You wait here," and he went back into the building. When he came out again he had the piece of paper Kreutz wanted. At the top he had typed Washington, D.C., then a note of a few lines, which Kreutz did not read, half afraid, the way a schoolboy might hesitate to look at a new report card, nursing his anxiety. He folded the paper five times, until it was not much bigger than a postage stamp, put it in his shirt pocket and buttoned the flap.

At dark Kreutz came back through Georgetown, again using the trolley tracks as a guide. By then he was news on the police radio, but the news was good; he was heading for Virginia. At Canal Road he climbed down to light his lantern. Through the cool dark the mules moved without his attention, and every few minutes Kreutz took his hand from the loose reins to pat his pocket, reassured by the slight bulge. At least a dozen times on the trip home he unfolded the letter, looked at the typing without reading it, folded it again and replaced it in the pocket.

It was before midnight when he reached Clayton and turned up Station Drive. The explosives plant was still smoldering. Mr. Lewis, returning from his day in Washington, caught up with him a mile from Small Hill. The wagon was moving slowly up the middle of the road and Lewis was forced to a complete stop while Kreutz, who had been examining his document again, making sure the typing was still on it, reined the mules over to the side. As he edged past the wagon Lewis said, "Hello, Mr. Kreutz."

"Where was you all day," Kreutz called to the passing car. "I never did find where you work at." By now he was talking to himself but he went on, "The police there never heard of you. But I got the paper for the shoes." He waved the letter over his head.

17

Panimer could not stand being alone in the house with his mother. Sometimes he would stamp his feet when he entered the room where she was sitting to make sure she knew he was there. Other times he would try to tiptoe on the carpet to test her perception but he never could be sure he had fooled her. Once he had come in silently and sat without a sound and just stared, angry at her hands which moved slowly, knitting, feeling for the little knots she made and passed with care from needle to needle, her lips pursed, determined. The boy knew he was angry but did not know why; her crippled industry piqued him. It was his inchoate sense that no handicap short of death could have prevented her contribution to the war, that she had been maimed by that industry and still persisted in it, that she could not even put these woolen squares she knitted together into a sweater, but had to pass them along for someone else's use. He had been sitting there staring for several minutes when she said: "Panimer, will you help me with this wool? Just hold your hands out. Like this." And he had shouted,

"Why are you doing that?" as much ashamed by having hidden from her as astonished she had known it. But there were

132

times when she did not know. He was sure of it. Like the time he had come up behind her as she sat at the kitchen table and watched over her shoulder as she scratched A l o r s M a u p o s in letters like the ones you could see any day on the first grade blackboard at Duncan Kimball. And he knew she thought she was alone because before she had written it she had turned her head to either side, listening, and when she had finished she had torn the paper from the pad, crumpled and carried it to the wastebasket, almost bumping into him on the way. Later he picked the scrap from the basket, carried it to his room and wondered at the crooked letters, remembering the fancy way she used to write.

And the time at the same table he had seen her grope for a spoon she knew was there, her hand reaching gently in the smooth way of the blind, coordination trying to compensate for darkness. She had come close, but missed, then reached off in a cold direction, her palm coming down softly over and over again until she slammed it down; her face raised to the ceiling, jaw flexed. All of this carved in clear relief on the boy's consciousness though he could no more define what it did to him than escape the precision of what it meant. Then she might relieve anguish with her familiar whimsy, tell a visitor: "We started out with three good eyes, Junior and me, now we've only got one between us," this too, was overheard by the boy, who, wondering if something might happen to that last eye, would go to his room to avoid such talk, but would leave his door ajar because he also had to hear it.

And sometimes he would listen behind his door, ear pressed to the crack, while his parents talked about him, or the war, or the accident, which people had begun to think was not an accident but maybe the work of a saboteur. His mother was always trying to understand the war, to fit people into jobs and attitudes that would win it. For a while, when everyone thought it would be over soon, his father would tell her to mind her knitting, not to worry. Then the Germans had done something ugly and people couldn't say how long the thing would go on, and his mother's arguments would send his father jumping and fussing around the living room. Panimer saw it was because he had no answers for them.

For the first several days after his mother's blindness, Panimer was mute in her presence. Junior did not know what to say either. Paula tried being cheery. "How do you like being chef?" she asked her husband. Junior was embarrassed for her awkwardness with her knife and fork and one evening he lunged for her hand when he saw her about to eat a chicken bone. She pulled her hand away from him, anger passing across her face, then disappearing before Panimer quite understood why it frightened him. They sat in pity for each other until Panimer said, "You wouldn't believe what's in that building."

"What do you know about it?" his father said.

"I know what's in it," Panimer said.

"Shut up," his father said. "How do you know?"

"If I shut up, how could I tell you. Because I seen it."

"You just get smart with me now . . ."

"You two stop it now. Stop it before you start," Paula said.

"Don't you tell me you been in that building," said Junior. "Don't you lie to me. Don't you ever go near that place," and Panimer understood he must not talk about this again in front of them. They were afraid he knew a secret that might get them all in trouble.

"You stay away from that building," Paula said. "It's a war building. And if we lose we'll be slaves, won't we? Have to do what the enemy tells us. They can just kill the ones they want and the blind won't be too far behind the colored and the Jews. Your father and his gimp arm might not be worth much to them either. The ones don't agree with them, they'll just disappear in the night."

"They're not going to win, honey," Junior said, but Panimer could tell his father was not sure, and so could his mother, who said, "So why don't they make everybody just cooperate and give everything they got until it's over?"

"You got to have an economy," said Junior. "People got to have money."

"Economy? Is that what it is? With the radio talking about

134

illegal profits and strikes all the time? Who is it is fighting anyway?'' The boy knew his mother was exaggerating. If the radio told you anything, it was who was fighting. There were two sides, though to listen to it you might have thought there were three. There were the Axis and the Allies and the Red Armies. ''I say, until it's all over, everyone ought to give all their time to it and be satisfied with enough to eat. They can get greedy again when it's all over. I mean if it's so serious why shouldn't everyone pay *all* their time to it? And just take what they need to get by on.'' Junior started to say, because it's *not* that serious, but was not sure of that. Instead he told her she didn't understand.

As much as his mother, Panimer was now in the habit of overhearing conversations; she, because she was blind, he, because he was no longer simply alienated from the village, but had begun to spy on it. Mischief and loneliness had graduated to a lonely anger. His mother had been blinded. He had been humiliated in the woods. The same ones who had taken his pants off were the kind who called his father a coward for not being in the Army. The pride and embarrassment he felt for his mother and father confused him. His parents and the women of Clayton's Notions were right; he was looking for trouble. He knew a secret. The building they were all so proud and ignorant of, Stilson County's mysterious war building, held nothing but paper. So why should it be such a mystery? It seemed to him nobody really wanted to know what was in it.

School again. Nancy every day. Nancy in the evening, more than making up for the three blind eyes, and the fourth whose sudden importance frightened Panimer. What if it was gone too? School without Ronald Pride or Hiram Johnson to interfere with the daily rides next to Nancy. Holding hands under their books. And evening promises, half lisped by the girl in the warm of her devotion, the more endearing to the boy for their tremor. His tormentors had graduated. They might have seemed more pathetic now than threatening if the boy had been older. They

hung around the Clayton corner, their war stories forever condi-
tional because they would never go to war—Ronald Pride, deaf,
and Hiram Johnson with the blood disease no one knew about.
Neither acceptable to any service, they could only stand and
wait, loiter on the Jew store steps or around Lamartine's Mobil,
waiting for the war to end, to relieve the shame of not joining it.

Panimer and Nancy had moved their meeting place a little
way into the woods and instead of his coming to call at her
house, they would arrive at their tryst independently, making
sure no one watched them; then smothered, lip and thigh, their
clothes at once aggravating and protecting them, they rushed to
please each other because Nancy would always have to be
home within an hour of leaving her house; she was supposed to
be at the drugstore or doing school work with a friend. They
became dissatisfied, even bored with their unfinished heat,
untangled themselves from each other's hair and clothes. Stopping a moment, a little ashamed of their frustrated writhing,
they would wait while new notions of respect and devotion
washed them clean. Once again they began to whisper their
love. Then restored, body and heart, pure enough to begin
again. Little prisoners, devoted. When Nancy checked her
watch, they hurried out of the woods, back across the field.
They were so in thrall to their devotion that the cyclic
mechanics of their evenings had escaped them; careless of the
path they had worn through the orchard grass and into the
forest, so that anyone, man or dog, might have trotted that way
simply because it led where other feet had gone. And he put her
name in one of the sycamores along the Duncan Kimball fence,
then showed it to her. She scolded him. ''You can kill a tree that
way.'' The name was written so large it almost circled the trunk.
She was pleased; he was hurt.

Their meetings in the woods went on; she offered his hands
new encouragement, license he was unprepared for; uncertain
how to use it. The passiveness he sensed in her left him uneasy.
And one night she had helped him undress her and they had
agreed, again without words, not to misuse that nakedness,
mumbling little sounds of assent or denial, until she was bare

136

and awaiting the attentions of his mouth and hands, which he was too overcome to offer without awkwardness; gaping, looking away, gaping again at the strange body that stretched and curled beside him. It was time to go before he realized his tentative fumbling had disappointed her. Again he knew her notions were beyond his own, but was uncertain whether to question his fears or her modesty.

The doubts did not last, her nakedness in the woods became their regular pleasure, though now with spoken limit: "We can't do that," which he readily agreed to. Which made her wonder. Both of them were too occupied to notice the two older boys who, by the end of that September, had come to watch them in the woods with the same regularity, two spies who had simply

followed the worn path to the tryst, hardly able to see through the dark of night and trees, the soft moaning bringing the scene into relief for their imaginations. They knew she was naked; they came back night after night.

One evening coming from the woods Nancy told Panimer: "I don't want you putting my name around any more."

"I didn't," he said.

"It's on the railroad bridge."

"I didn't put it there." They walked together up the Pike to the bridge so she could show him he must be lying, and there was **NANCY McC** on the trestle in fresh white paint covering the fading **PHYLLIS.**

"You must of," she said. "What was it gonna say?" Underneath her name were the letters **IS**, but the message was unfinished because Panimer had been scared away by a passing car in the middle of his public declaration of love she supposed. She colored slightly, waiting for the confession he did not make, wondering, too, what had been interrupted.

This was only the beginning of the name's circulation; **NANCY** began to appear on sidewalks and walls around the town. Sometimes it was followed by insult or obscenity.

Panimer suspected Ronald Pride and Hiram Johnson. He was right, but only at first, when the name was sparsely placed enough to be passed off as petty vandalism and who the letters stood for was no more significant than their defacement of some corner of the village. One evening on his way to their meeting Panimer looked down at the pavement in front of Lamartine's Mobil and saw **NANCY TAKES HER CLOTHES OFF IN THE WOODS.** It was written in chalk. He stooped to erase it, wondering if Nancy had seen it; worse, wondering who had seen them in the woods. Lamartine's man Billy Paul was leaning against the door of the garage, watching him, grinning. Panimer saw him and stood up as if he'd only been bending for a coin. He walked away, the erasure incomplete.

This was before general appearance of her name had begun to worry her or her family, well before it had overtaken and passed the currency of **KILROY** in the village. But even then Panimer had a notion what might happen if it continued; not only that their meetings might be abruptly altered, his limited license withdrawn, but to be seen with her at all might bring scorn instead of envy. Too proud or shy to be seen with anyone at all, Nancy began to walk the halls of her high school alone, stung by the taunts that grew with the circulation of her name; ignoring Panimer or any other who might accost her when no one else was watching, some hoping to be allowed a favor the graffiti had promised, others just trying to befriend her in her time of need. She ignored them all, and would not leave her house except to go to school.

At first Panimer had tried to undo the notoriety himself, moving around the town under cover of night, erasing chalk, marking over paint, using anything at hand to obliterate the libel. Not that her name had anywhere been placed in arrowed heart or obscene epithet with his own; those who wrote it were too proud to have linked his name with the girl who had spurned them. Whoever wrote it had seen them in the woods, and came back nightly to watch and listen.

It was the message on the bridge that put the thing out of control. It had grown from **NANCY McC IS** to **NANCY McC IS A** to **NANCY McC IS A W**; the writer or writers teasing the community, adding only a letter a week. When it reached **NANCY McC IS A WHO** . . . Panimer had gone out with a bucket of black paint and covered it all. But two days later it had been repainted on the bridge, this time complete. The problem was discussed in the mayor's office, at the weekly bandage-making sessions, which Mrs. McConkey began to skip, and in Clayton's Notions, where all agreed with Wilma, who said, "It's just disgusting, just awful," and what they referred to was the scratched messages but what they were thinking of was the girl's behavior. And finally Jane said it: "She's coming to no good if she don't show a change."

Junior, too, had seen the progression of the obscenity on the bridge, and the frequency of **NANCY**'s, the name perpetuating itself now since most of those who wrote it did not even know the girl, only that it was normal to draw her name in public. But Junior imagined an adult intelligence behind the campaign to ruin a girl. Everyone knew Panimer and Nancy had been a pair. Junior remembered how Phyllis Jackson had been run out of Clayton, by road so to speak; how her name had marched down the pavement until it was written all the way west to Stilson and east to Washington, as if they had given her a choice which way to leave town. And his name had been linked with Phyllis, not on pavement or walls, but village tongues. Paula had never acknowledged it but he knew the reason she'd been so anxious to move from Clayton the three miles out to Small Hill.

18

Panimer had been hanging around the Clayton corner one afternoon, tempting trouble: Ronald Pride and his friends were apt to be there. If they started something he'd stand up to them. At least that's what he told himself. They weren't there, so he sat in Lamartine's drinking sodas until Mr. Stockstill came into the garage and went up the steps to Lamartine's office. The mechanic walked outside and Panimer snuck halfway up the stairs and sat down to hear what was being said above him. There were others in the office. He could hear Hiram Johnson's father and Arthur Settle. There were more. Chairs scraped on the floor. The conversation grew loud and soft by turns: it was something serious. The voices fell almost to a whisper at times, then grew in argument. There were silences. Panimer climbed several more steps to see if he could listen in. Mr. Johnson was saying: "we can't be responsible for another explosives plant. It's too dangerous. Look what happened. It's lucky we haven't been sued. Why, we could still be sued, Arthur."

"Hiram," Mr. Settle said, "someone's got to make those things. This is war."

"Arthur, we built the place too close to town. You know that.

And we took a contract we didn't know how to handle. Two mistakes. We put the plant there because that's where we had the land. Let's at least be honest with ourselves about it." Panimer was not sure who was talking now, but the voice went on. "We've still got contracts. Let's get out. We've got someone to take them over. Let them have control if that's what they want. We can still run the place if we rebuild it." Here the argument grew louder. Mr. Stockstill was almost shouting, "We could have burned the whole town up. We could burn it up again."

"It was a fluke, Charlie," Mr. Settle said. "Just a weird accident. Or for all we know that damn woman blew the place up on purpose."

"Arthur, you're the one who wants a monument to her. Now you're calling her an American kamikazi."

"But look what we're being offered, Charlie. A bunch of paper. What do we know about paper?"

"Don't fool yourself. There's a lot of money in paper."

The discussion had turned against Mr. Settle. The voices were fading and Panimer moved quietly down the steps. As he walked home along Station Drive he said, "My mother should have sued them . . . she ought to just sue them."

Mr. Lewis knew more of human nature than of any particular human; he could predict more about how Clayton would not resolve its shame than what was actually going to happen, or who would be involved. He stood at a remove from the village so it was quite by chance he knew that Paula, his neighbor, now blind, stood accused by rumor of a kind of willful negligence in the Sons of Clayton explosion. He heard the gas attendant at Lamartine's Mobil tell another customer, "Say she might could of done it on purpose. Her and the colored woman." He knew Clayton's war story was not going to end with Paula on trial, with injured innocence in the dock and a narrow but clean victory for justice. The only trial would be a trial by assumptions.

Lewis, pleased with his sophistication in these things, was

141

unaware that he was as much a target of Clayton's assumptions as Paula. Just as he was blind to the home truth that the case he had worked on every day for the last several months, might lead back to the view from his own living room window, the huge building that spoiled his scenery. A view that took in the junkyard man who wouldn't cooperate in the scrap drives, and the two wise-acre brats and their fancy government father (himself) who told them subversive things, like it didn't matter a damn to the war's outcome whether they drove or not. (He knew this to be true, that the government's gas rationing had been conceived as a way of saving tires, saving rubber, and that the scrap rubber drives were largely useless because the old rubber was no good for anything but retreading tires, and there was already an abundance for that.)

His view also took in Farmer Kreutz, whose sabotage was a kind of trial by nuisance; who could handicap the village war effort simply with his intrusive presence, carrying his useless dog-eared letter from one ration board meeting to the next. Now when Kreutz offered it in proof of the legitimacy of his demands he opened it with a kind of crude gentleness and with this warning: "You be careful. You can see you ain't the first one wanted to look at it." The letter promised nothing, neither carrying the imprint of the agency from which he'd cadged it, nor the signature of the man who had prepared it half in jest, half because he could think of no other way to rid himself of Kreutz. As a letter of recommendation it might as well have said, "Give this man a berth, a wide one."

The mayor's man had come to Small Hill to question Paula soon after the explosion but she had only been asked about Nadine, and her answers had only confirmed their pride in the dead woman. She had cried, remembering how hard she could make Nadine work when she coaxed her, also how stubborn she could be.

"I guess she read a lot?" the man said, "Books and that?"

"I don't know," Paula said.

"She must of. We found 'em." The man showed her the

history texts and the biography of Thomas Paine that had been found in the woman's trailer. And Paula remembered how Nadine had got the books, found them in the grass by Stilson High School and had brought them to work one night to ask how much they might be worth. Paula told her she didn't know.

"Well, they're worth something," Nadine had said, and she packed them away in her trailer against the time she'd find a buyer or someone who might trade for them. But Paula told none of this when asked about the dead woman. The mystery of the woman could be solved with heroic notions. Arthur Settle, ending his eulogy over her monument, said, "She was one of Clayton's many soldiers."

They put the books on display under glass in the Stilson public library, and a little flag they'd found on her bureau. And they named a week in her honor. A senior from the high school, an honor student, recognized them when his class marched by the case.

"Those are mine," he said. And he'd tried to lift the glass to show them, but the librarian rushed over and nearly closed the lid on the boy's fingers, appalled that he might have disturbed the memorial. "I can prove it," he said. "That was my summer reading." They did not believe him, or did not want to. He protested as they led him and his class from the building. "I can prove it," he called back at the librarian "I wrote in it."

Alone with her books, the librarian stood over the case, wondering if she should open it and look for herself. She looked, and saw the boy was right. Leafing through the Paine biography she found the page he'd written on, saw several scribbled notes including one the boy had not remembered: Mrs. Fernanda is a old nanny goat.

19

Soon after her blindness they let Paula set up a vending stand in the post office. She sold only stubby, eraserless pencils and little odd-sized scratch pads at first—no candy or gum until the war ended. It was out of character that she should become a blind vendor, stranger still that she should have placed her stand in the center of the village she had once been so anxious to leave. It broke her rules. Charity was to give, not receive, and gossip was neither to be spoken nor listened to. But the stand became her listening station and speakers rostrum. It kept her next to the village at war and this is what she needed most. Then her darkness began to tell her village war secrets.

Once before the war was over she stood up behind her stand and said: "Sons of Clayton could put some money into savings bonds. They're all set up in business again. The accident didn't slow them down much." Mrs. Hewgley who had been talking to Mrs. Stockstill didn't know whether Paula was mumbling to herself or talking to them, but the blind woman bothered her.

"Just a minute, honey," she called. "You be quiet a minute," and aside to Mrs. Stockstill, "She's going on like that all the time now. I can't make her be quiet."

"But they don't put it in bonds," Paula went on to herself.

144

"They want to do good like everyone else. If you do good you can't help getting a little rich from it I expect."

"Oh I wish she'd be quiet," Mrs. Stockstill whispered. "I never know what she means."

"You remember someone was after Panimer. Truth, I never believed those stories about him going in the building. Everybody is afraid of the dogs."

"Hush, honey," Mrs. Hewgley said.

"I started thinking. I thought Panimer's imagination was never that wild, you know, he must be right. But nobody believes it. I suppose that's because they're having too much fun guessing what's inside. I mean wanting it to be something important, wanting it to be secret. But there's people who don't want anyone to know what it is." Across the room Paula heard feet but no voices. "And Sons of Clayton is having all those meetings and Mr. Settle won't let Claudelle clean the mayor's office any more." Paula knew she had an audience; she felt the silence pointing at her. "Everyone knows the plant never should have been built there. Right next to the residences."

"Hush honey. Junior's coming soon."

"But that's where one of them already owned the land."

"The which?"

"And he was a director so that's where they built it. So close it knocked the school windows out. Lucky for them it happened on the night shift. No, it wasn't the siren knocked the school windows out. It was the explosions. Junior wanted to sue. He said he didn't care if Lamartine *was* a director. It was criminal he said. But I told him somebody had to start things. And if they were the only ones with the money and gumption that's the way it had to be. Who else would have done it? Not you, I told him. Not me. It's what they do with the money I can't understand. Don't you know people are getting rich? Junior's making his share too."

Mrs. Hewgley began to make the sounds of her departure. She would come out and push the button to set the lock in the front door. When Paula heard the latch she closed her money box. Then Mrs. Hewgley's hard leather heels crossed the floor to the safe behind the counter. The diminutive clicks as she spun the combination. Lockers clanging shut, and the last sound of the day—the closing window of the post mistress's cage. Then she disappeared silently through the back door. It had been arranged that Junior should have his own key to the back door to fetch Paula each evening. Paula listened carefully for the sounds of these closing rituals. Mrs. Hewgley often left without a word to her; had she understood this dependence on noises she might have disguised her movements or reversed their order in reprisal for the blind woman's obstinate conversation. Even after Mrs. Hewgley had gone Paula continued, "So much happened after I couldn't see any more and that's what makes it so hard to remember." Through the window she heard someone coming across the gravel. Not Junior. "You're too late," she called toward the open window. Whoever it was didn't answer or walk away. They were trying the door. "It's locked," she called, "Mrs. Hewgley's gone home." Still they tried the door. Paula climbed off her stool and felt her way around the stand; she moved across the open floor toward the window, arms in front of her, against collision with what she knew but could not quite trust to be empty space. At the window she called again. "I'm sorry. The post office is closed. If you've got to mail something you can put it in the box out there." No one answered. No one walked back across the gravel. The fumbling at the door latch continued as if no one had heard her. Just another woman who did not want to be recognized by her, Paula supposed. They would go away in a minute and she would never know who it had been. Another piece in the dark world next to her lost forever. That's what she could not tolerate, must guard against. It did not happen often any more; she had ways to provoke them into talking, or walking. Then she would know. She called louder, "It's no use. It's locked." But the noise at the door did not stop. Of a sudden she understood someone was trying to break in. They must know she was there—hadn't she been calling? Backing away from the window, she bumped into the writing stand in the corner and heard the ink well fall and break on the floor. She tried to skirt this accident as she moved away, toward the back of the post office, raising her feet high as she went. But she brought each shoe down in the black puddle, leaving clear tracks with her Oxfords as she felt along the tiers of post boxes and through the swinging doors into the mail room. She knew there was space between the metal package lockers and the wall. She made her way around the sorting tables and squeezed behind the lockers, leaving shoe prints all the way to her hiding place.

The sound at the door was becoming frantic, a rapid jostling of the thumb latch. Then the door was open. She was certain. There were steps across the front room; she did not know them. Then the engine of Junior's truck and a spray of gravel against the back of the building. Thank God he was in a hurry. Quick steps in the front room and the door closing.

Paula was still behind the lockers when Junior entered the back way. She called, "Junior, Junior." At first he could not tell where her voice came from. Then he saw the prints. "Look out, honey. There's someone there. In the front." He went to the swinging doors, looked into the front room, saw the fallen table, the broken ink well and black puddle tracked across the floor, toward him.

"What did you do?" he called back to her, turning, following the prints to where he found her crouching behind the lockers. "What did you do?" he demanded, gathering her up in his arms as if she were a child who'd had an accident doing something naughty and needed scolding and comforting at once.

"Did you look careful?" she said.

"There's no one there," he said. "Look at this mess."

"They got in the front door. What mess?"

"This ink all over the floor. Who?"

"Whoever came in. They must have done it. They got in the front door."

"Did you see . . .? Junior stopped himself too late. "I'm sorry, honey." He walked back to the front room, checked the door. It was locked. "It's locked," he said.

"Well they broke it open," she insisted. He examined the latch; there were no marks on it.

147

"Can't see where anyone forced it."

"Someone came in," she said. "I bumped into the table. But I didn't make any mess." Junior tried to lead her out to the truck. "I can do it," she said. He followed behind without telling she was leaving another set of black tracks to the door. "Don't leave me alone," she said. "Is it dark yet?"

"I got to clean the place up. You'll be all right."

"Is it dark?"

"It's *been* dark."

"You came late for me."

"You wait here. You'll be all right." Junior went back inside. There was a mop sink but no mop. In the latrine he could find no rags or towels, only toilet paper. Someone had left a little puddle on the floor beside the toilet and the seat was wet. Standing over the bowl he held his breath a moment as he pulled the roll of paper off the wall. He was trying not to be mad, trying to understand, but there were dozens of marks on the floor. He got the worst up but there were still stains on the gray linoleum and he knew Mrs. Hewgley would notice them and have to ask what happened, and Paula would tell her story—which even he did not believe. The door had been locked. She'd frightened herself with her own notions. But the stories would start again about her losing her mind. That was convenient for them. It took credit from her speculation about Sons of Clayton and the big war building at Small Hill and Panimer, and who had been after him, or who was still after him. Mr. Lamartine himself had told Junior his wife ought to stop talking about all that, that it wasn't profiting anything and could do innocent folks harm. And it was clear that a lot of them were hanging silently around her blind talk to see how much she knew and how much she might still discover. Junior never mentioned what Lamartine said. He did not want her to shut up. Rather he took a secret pleasure in their discomfit, little enough compensation for the injury done his wife, and him. What aggravated him was her giving them room to discredit her, things like this. He rubbed harder but the stain was deep.

On the way home Paula said, "That door locks itself. They

could have got in and shut the door when they left. And you'd never know." Though she spoke tentatively Junior knew she had no doubt of what she'd heard. She was only coaxing him into support of her story. Which he still did not believe.

"You believe me, don't you? Junior?"

"Look at this. What happened, dear?" Mrs. Hewgley asked Paula. "It goes all the way back behind the lockers. Now how are we going to clean that, honey? Because it's got to be cleaned. We can't leave it like that, can we?" not mentioning what else she'd noticed—hand prints, too, on the floor behind the lockers where Paula had crawled into hiding, Mrs. Hewgley thinking maybe the woman really was insane.

"Someone broke in here last night, Mrs. Hewgley," Paula said.

"That's all right, honey. But we can't leave it like this, can we? You tell Junior it's got to be cleaned up."

"Someone came right through the door. I went to hide and I don't know what they could have done. Junior came and they must have run."

Later that day Mrs. Hewgley told Martha Settle, "She's gone mental. It's pathetic. And she makes such a mess," nodding toward the latrine door. "I think it's her wets the seat."

Ronald Pride's deafness left him to himself. The chance to be a soldier stolen from him, he looked for other ways to be a patriot. What better way than to force patriotism on the mother of a traitor? Even a traitor's mother who did war work. Sometimes he doubted she was really bind and toyed with ways to prove that she was faking. Everyone said Paula thought too much. Ronald remembered his father saying that ninety-five percent of the people were doing their best, so why couldn't she stop looking for trouble?

He thought that he might rob her to see if her blindness was real and use the money to buy a war bond in her name. That would relieve him of his feeling of uselessness. He knew she was collecting insurance—maybe for her own carelessness.

There were even rumors she might have caused the explosion on purpose. But why should she get money? Besides, her son was a little traitor. It wasn't stealing—what he meant to do. He'd put the money where it should be—in a war bond. That would be *his* war work—buying a bond and scaring a traitor.

20

Panimer sat with James Lewis in front of his house.

"Why don't you call her up?" James said.

"I don't want to," Panimer said.

"If her mother answers, you can hang up."

"What do I care?" Panimer said. He could not finish his cream-filled chocolate cup cake. It was making him sick. He held it out to James.

"Sure," James said. "What's the matter?"

"Nothing." Panimer walked into his house. His mother and father were gone. He picked up the phone, covered the mouthpiece with a piece of paper, and gave the operator Nancy's number.

"Is that you, Paula?" the operator said..

"No," Panimer tried to disguise his voice.

"I'm sorry. I thought you sounded like Paula. I worked with her in the plant." The number rang. Mrs. McConkey answered. Panimer hung up. He decided to wait for an hour and try again. But he only waited a minute.

"Yes?" Mrs. McConkey said. "Yes?" Panimer hung up again. He walked out of the house. There was nothing to do.

James never wanted to do anything, never wanted to take his father's car any more. Panimer walked across the field to the Lewises and sat in their car. The keys were over the sun visor. He started the engine and drove to Small Hill corner. James was still sitting on the store porch. "What are you doing?" he called.

"Get in," Panimer said.

"No," James said. "What are you doing?"

"Get in."

"No. You better take it back." James would not get in. Panimer turned the corner and drove toward Clayton, speeding as soon as he was out of James's sight, free again, flying down Station Drive faster than he'd ever driven before, thinking to himself; I didn't steal it, James knows I took it. He felt safe under the canopy of foliage that hung over the road, making a tunnel for the humming car. He was unaware that the telephone wire running along the road, overhead, had already sent the news past him. "Panimer stole the Lewis car." Osmond Clarke was waiting at the corner when Panimer ran the stop sign in Clayton.

When he stopped him, Clarke gave the boy every chance—he was Junior's boy, he deserved a chance. "If you're on your way to collect scrap or anything like that it's all right. I know you just borrowed the vehicle."

"I don't do collecting," Panimer said.

Mr. Clarke put him in the patrol car and took him to the Stilson police station. As they came back through Clayton, Ronald Pride and Hiram Johnson watched from the Jew store steps. "Do you know how much those boys hate you?" Mr. Clarke said.

"So?" Panimer said.

Panimer would not admit to having taken the car for any particular reason. "I don't know I don't know I don't know why I did it," he yelled at his father."

"Don't you know there's a war on?" Mr. Clarke had asked him.

"He ought to be in a reformatory," the police chief answered for him. To Panimer it had just been another afternoon's excitement; it had nothing to do with war. He had lost track of who he was in the community's sight—rolling scourge of the home front, junk car kamikazi, enemy frogman who had sunk the Duncan Kimball navy, breaker and enterer of their secret building how many times over, giver of false air raid warnings. All of these things they believed about him but could not prove. They thought of him as a traitor, a saboteur; they were watching for him to give himself away.

Paula worried less about Panimer's delinquencies. In fact she had come to a sympathy for her son's diffidence, not just because she perceived a community prejudice against him, but because she was now certain someone was after *her*. Someone was. She begged Junior to come earlier for her at the post office. He always promised he would but when five o'clock came he would still be busy with his comings and goings for Lamartine. She knew he doubted her story of the burglar. And she was never sure how late it was. It was harder for her to keep track of time now. She sensed this was more than the loss of clock faces or even the angle of daylight. Without access to the sight of any motion it was difficult to reckon a passage of time at all. All she knew was that time took longer now. She had turned inward to the sound of her heart, but dwelling on life's fragile rhythm made her nervous. Besides, she was scared too much of the time, her heart was useless for a clock's second hand—too often it raced beyond reckoning—even had she cared to try. It raced now as she heard footsteps in the gravel again, and the fiddling with the door.

"No one's here," she called. "They've gone home." She was sure it was the same person. What she could not understand was why they would persist when they knew she was inside. "You can't get in," she yelled. "It's locked," but already she had begun to feel her way into the back room again, wondering why she had been so stupid. Why hadn't she said, "We're waiting for you this time. Come ahead if you dare. Because you're doing burglary and you're going to be arrested." Too late. Whoever it was was inside the door again. She could hear steps on the linoleum.

Whatever was going to happen was taking too long; frightened beyond sense, she began to beat on the backs of the metal lockers she hid behind, as if that booming reverberation through the building might end her insupportable fright, maybe wanting whoever it was to find her. She had carried her fear of the intruder for three weeks. When silence came back it was not silence but the sound of steps in the front room. She knew it was a man. But it was as if he had heard nothing, was maybe ignoring her just to frighten her. Whatever he was doing must have been interrupted by Junior's truck pulling up in the back driveway, and she heard him hurry to the front door and close it firmly as he left. The door would lock itself again. And they would not believe her.

The next evening the post office door was tried again. Paula sat on her stool, a policeman from Stilson on one side of her, Junior on the other. "See?" she whispered, then, to prove the rest of her story, she called through the open window before the officer could stop her: "It's locked. They've gone home. You'll have to come back tomorrow," the last of it muffled as the policeman tried to cover her mouth with his hand, which Junior tried to push away, their cross purposes surprising them almost as much as the voice which came from outside the door:

"Well *you're* in there. *You* open it," as the latch rattled. Paula knew the voice immediately and knew the shuffle that would accompany it. They waited, the latch still sounding impatience until the policeman, hand to open holster, opened the door and Farmer Kreutz tried to walk past, or through, him to the mail slot, brushing aside the officer's question, "What are you doing?" and declaration, "You're under arrest."

"I got to mail this."

"You could have put it in the box outside."

"No sir, it's got to go first thing."

"Well hurry up and mail it 'cause you're coming with me."

On the way home with Junior, Paula said, "He couldn't be the one. The real one didn't talk or pay any mind to a thing I said. Didn't matter whether I rattled the lockers or what, it didn't bother him. Besides, Farmer Kreutz shuffles in boots. The one I'm talking about, his heels click. And when did Kreutz ever ignore anybody? He comes right at you till you have to back up. He never snuck anywhere."

She was right, Junior thought, Kreutz never did anything without putting himself in your way, but he said, "The blindness makes your mind too active, honey." It was all strange, he admitted, but the strangeness was Paula's.

The Stilson police got nowhere with Farmer Kreutz. They wanted him to admit he'd broken into the Clayton post office twice (with intent to mail a letter) but he kept saying, "I would of if I could. You damn right," and they believed him, even while they tried to coax a confession. They were familiar enough with the man, knew he would be proud to tell them he'd broken into the post office if he had, because he'd already told them more than they cared to know about why it was necessary for him to get inside; to mail the letter which kept coming back to him marked "Insufficient Address," which he'd been trying to make Mrs. Hewgley deliver to the government pecker who'd tried to make a fool of him. "Mr. Lewis. Not the one lives in Small Hill. The one works on Independence Street, Washington, District of Columbia." That's all he'd had for an address—that and U.S. Government.

"I found him, didn't I? Why can't she find him?" Kreutz demanded of the police. "That's what we paying her for, isn't it?" The commotion at the desk attracted a crowd of three sergeants and a state trooper as Kreutz began to interrogate the captain. "I say that's her job, isn't it? 'Course it is. If she can't find him, then we got to have someone can." He could take his wagon to Washington again, the captain suggested, and find this Mr. Lewis for himself, but Kreutz's concern was now his abuse by the U.S. Post Office, motive enough for him to break into the building, the police thought. Except for one overriding piece of evidence to the contrary—Kreutz denied he'd done it.

Against the captain's wish, then against his command, Kreutz again began the story of his note from the Mr. Lewis in Washington and how what he had to say to him was all in the letter that the post office would not deliver. He had told it twice in fine detail and was beginning again when they realized what he wanted was a place to spend the night in Stilson. They obliged him.

21

Panimer knew the sound of a bullet passing over his head. He and the Lewis boys had taken the twenty-two down to the baseball diamond and each one had stood on home plate and while the others stood in center field, they had taken turns firing over each other, partly to see if they could ever be soldiers—to shoot as much as to be shot at—partly to find out if a bullet went "ping" as in the war comic strips. In fact, it snapped and whined as it hit the trees. The same sound he heard now as he came around the corner of his house. He did not move. Then the same sound again. Hit the ground, the sergeant called in the comics. He hit the ground. And looked up in the kitchen window, where his father was laughing at him. He walked down to the corner, supposing it had just been someone careless with a gun in the woods. But he heard the snap over his head again that week while he sat on the junkyard hill, and this time he ran and kept running till he was safe in his house. He told his father someone had been shooting at him. Junior thought it was the boy's imagination. But now he was in siege to the fear of his wife and his son. In the village no one spoke much to him any more. But he had never gone out of his way to talk to people. He supposed it was simply silence in payment of silence: That suited him. Until even Billy Paul grew quiet around him at Lamartine's. Something was happening to his family.

Just the night before Panimer been on the junkyard hill staring at the gray building, thinking long thoughts of paper and of blindness. So lost was he in contemplation of a one-eyed set of parents he did not notice the approach of a stranger. When he did look around he was more taken by the man's business suit than his sudden appearance.

"You live around here?" the man said. Panimer nodded in the direction of his house. "Not much to do around here I guess." Panimer shook his head. "There's just not much here." The man was looking at the gray building. "What's that?"

"Not much," Panimer said.

"But it's huge."

"It ain't much."

"It must be."

"No."

"How do you know?"

"It isn't. I know."

"You know what's inside?" Panimer regretted telling the man anything. "If you know what's inside there you must know a secret."

"Who are you?" Panimer said.

"If someone really knew, I wouldn't think they'd want to tell. I mean they could be telling a war secret. Looks to me like no one's supposed to go in there."

When he was sure the man was gone, Panimer got up and walked down to the fence, hoping to avoid the watchdog. A car pulled into the driveway, blinked its lights once, then turned them out, and continued rolling toward the huge building's entrance. As it fell under the front spotlight Panimer recognized it as Arthur Settle's Packard. The great doors rolled open for it and it disappeared inside.

Paula slammed her cash box down on the candy stand several

times. The fiddling at the post office door continued. She was alone this time, but she was not going to hide. "My God, he must be deaf," she exaggerated to herself. "If he can't hear this, he *must* be deaf." And of a sudden she knew it must be Ronald Pride. Ronald had just solved the lock again and was standing inside the door as her head turned toward him and he supposed she was staring at him because she began to nod the short nod of recognition. Not trusting her blindness he moved behind the bank of post boxes at the far end of the room. Paula knew he was waiting there but did not know why. Now she wanted to hide, wanted to get up and walk back to the mailroom. But she did not trust his deafness. In their double doubt they waited an unconscionable time. Until he peeked around the tier of post boxes and saw her still staring right at him. He ran for the door, slammed it behind him.

Paula could not tell them it was Ronald Pride. Even if she'd been sure of it she could not have proved it, certainly not by her own blind witness. If you could not prove, you ought not to mention, much less accuse. She lived alone that week with her suspicion of Ronald Pride. Then, in rage at Junior's disbelief, she felt through her bureau for the War Worker Sleeping sign and hung it on their bed post. This time it meant, Make yourself a pallet on the floor, or anywhere else you like because you're not sleeping with me.

Junior apologized. But not until whoever it was had taken Paula's cash box, had walked right into the post office a few evenings later and fairly pulled it out of his wife's hands; Paula having sworn to herself that this time she would not budge, that without eyes she would stare the man or boy down, as Ronald had vowed to himself that he would not be cheated again by that false stare. This time both achieved the bravery they promised themselves. And Ronald took, grabbed, the cash box out of Paula's hands, while Paula said, "It's Ronald Pride, isn't it? It's you, isn't it?" And the boy left her the sound of his footfall.

Now familiar with the intruder, Paula could challenge him again, wanted to. Junior would not allow it, would not let her stay in the post office alone. Neither would Mrs. Hewgley, who stopped calling her mental and now said, "She needs trouble," somehow blaming the theft on her.

Why was the big building still a war secret, Panimer wondered. In night silence he lay on his bed watching leaves sway behind his dark window, making figures out of shadows; thinking, if someone wanted to shoot me they could just shoot me, that easy. So they're not trying to shoot me, they're trying to scare me. And they are. It's Hiram Johnson and Ronald Pride. Because they think we shot at Ronald. He got up and pushed his bed away from the window.

Jewel Lamartine asked Junior what he knew about the big building, tried to ask casually, but it came awkwardly and with advice: "War secrets got to be kept." Junior heard more patriotism in Jewel's voice than anxiety. Still, it was strange. Why should Lamartine be asking or telling him about it? He knew the stories of his son's prowling around the building. They had come to him through Paula by way of James Lewis. He had not confronted the boy with them; maybe afraid his son would admit to the mischief. Nor did Panimer tell his father that three strange men had come to speak to him on three occasions, all of them hinting at the building's importance, almost begging him to tell what he knew about it, then warning that if he knew anything he ought to keep it to himself, that he might tell a secret that would be used by America's enemies. America still had enemies, they told him. "I still got some too," Panimer told the last one, a man whom he'd seen on one of the Stilson fire engines, which connected him in the boy's mind with Earl Jackson and Redmond Clarke. If you were a volunteer fireman in Stilson it was because one of those two men liked you; it was one of those two who decided what was serious and what was not. He knew how they could all laugh together in the firehouse and then do something cruel. He had seen them do cruel things.

It was their kin and acquaintances and the people like them in Clayton whom Panimer was half afraid of, half despised—them, the painters and carvers of things they knew nothing about, whisperers and shouters of ugly words and names of people they did not even know; them, the depantsers and cause of his affliction, the loss of Nancy, who might be gone for good now; the ones who painted Nancy on roads and buildings; and those who read it, and leered or clucked or grinned or laughed. And somehow connected to them were the ones who sought him, sometimes warning, sometimes threatening or begging for a pledge of silence, which he never took.

When he took his own brush and can of white paint to leave the message that would embarrass or anger them, or both, it was the first time he had said to himself, Now I am going to do sabotage, now they can call me traitor if they like and I don't give a wild rat's ass, because that's what I'm going to be. If it's a war secret, or whatever, I'm telling it. To anyone who can read. And he waited one evening on Marcum's hill until the German shepherd was inside being fed. Then he walked down the hill with the can of paint and brush, made his toe-and-finger way up the chainlink fence, which had three new strands of barbed wire angled outward at the top since he'd last climbed it, these only slowing him temporarily and only because he had the can of paint hooked over one arm. He was up the steel ladder at the corner of the building, climbing to the ridge and halfway down the other side of the roof by the time the dog was outside again. It was barking, jumping up at the ladder when one of the watchmen came out for a look; Panimer was already and beginning to paint in great letters that would be visible to all traffic on Station Drive. The watchman climbed the ladder, began to scale the roof, stopped, climbed back down.

Overhead Panimer was finishing the first of his huge letters, taking his time because they must be legible; everyone was going to know this secret. It was even going to be visible from airplanes—so large and carefully drawn no one could mistake it. The simplicity of it encouraged him, made it the more fun to be taking their wild notions of luminous foxes, deadly weapons, poisons so strong they would kill you if you came near them, these and all the other ideas that made their building special, taking them and writing them into nothing in one word. The way they had taken one name and written it everywhere, read and

161

scorned it, until the person it stood for—Nancy—was forced into seclusion, so that now there was not even hope, not even the silent shape of her body to scorn him as he passed her in the school hallways, her chin angled against conversation. Even just her there to ignore him was better than this nothing.

He was painting a sign, knowing it was going to upset them, not fully understanding why. And this was not going to be enough; he was going to paint it everywhere. He was going to hurt them with signs. Damn them. Damn her. His eyes filled with water as he painted.

The word was finished. He stood up and realized how steep the roof was. On his hands and knees again he made his way up to the flat ridge, then down the other side. He could not see the dog, or hear it. He backed all the way down the ladder, and was most of the way across the clearing when the dog heard him. He made it over the fence, but not with his can of paint or brush. Men were coming out of the building now, but Panimer was already running up Station Drive. He ran beyond the corner and was still running when a car stopped beside him. He supposed he'd been caught but the driver leaned out and asked, ''What's the matter? Need a lift?''

''That's all right,'' Panimer said. ''I mean yes. I need a lift.'' And he got in and had calmed enough by the time he got to Clayton, where the man let him out, to know just what he was going to do. If he'd done sabotage, what matter that he should be a thief as well? There was no one at the Clayton corner. A bare light shone on the front of Lamartine's Mobil. He walked to the back of the garage, knocked a pane of glass out of the back door, reached in and opened it. He knew where the paint was, a whole shelf of it in the back room. Without light, he felt along the shelf, took the fullest can he could find. Several brushes hung in front of him. He took the largest. Outside again, he walked down the Pike toward the railroad trestle. He climbed the bank beside it, walked onto the bridge and climbed over the side to a girder. Sliding his feet and the paint can along this metal beam he made his slow way, painting the word again. A car approached and passed under him. He did not care, kept painting. He saw his work was good. The steel sections of the trestle's side made a frame for each letter. Finished, he walked back to the corner. Now there were buildings to paint. He'd have to be more careful—people might be watching through their dark windows. He did the sides and back of Chain Food, then wondered why he'd hesitated to paint across the whole front window. He did that too, then walked across to the Jew store and did four sides of that, then the window of the notions store and up the street to Peterson's Drugs, catching the radio repair shop on the way. He still had more than half a gallon of paint when he came back to the corner. He'd forgotten the post office. When he'd finished that he came back to sit on the Jew store steps and look at what he'd done. There was only one public thing in the village he had not touched—the monument to Clayton's first war hero. That was a gravestone; he would not paint it.

Panimer was still sitting there an hour later with the paint can when the wagon approached from Wye Bridge. It came first in silhouette of mule and driver, the lantern swinging behind. If he was going to run or hide he had plenty of time. He knew it was Kreutz, and Kreutz's mules moved slowly. The boy did not run. He might have sat there all night if Kreutz had not pulled the mules up in front of the store steps and challenged his silence.

"What you doing there?"

"Sitting here."

"What you doing sitting there?"

"Nothing."

"Get in." Kreutz was offering him a lift to Small Hill.

"I ain't in a hurry."

"We won't be nowhere in a hurry."

"Yeah, you can give me a ride." Each having made clear he was doing the other a favor, Panimer climbed onto the back of the wagon with his can of paint. In the lantern light the can said Porch and Shutter, **DARK GREEN**.

"What you got there?" Kreutz said, thinking maybe the boy would give him something for the ride.

"Nothing."

"Well how far do you want to go? I wouldn't ask nothing just for a mile. I wouldn't ask a man his money just to take him that short a way."

"I don't want to go nowhere." Panimer said. The man and boy were attracted to one another's rudeness.

"That's all right too. I'm coming from Washington District of Columbia myself." Kreutz said. "It's how come I'm so late."

"Ain't you going to tell the mules to move?" Panimer said, intrigued by the man and the wagon.

"Come up, mules," Kreutz said. "I had to take my letter myself. The post office woman couldn't get it there." Panimer was not really listening. He was leaning over the back of the wagon, painting a dotted line toward Small Hill. He began to hear the steady click and creak of the wheel, began to count the revolutions. Every fifty turns he painted an arrow on one of his lines, all pointing toward home. Kreutz had not turned around on his board seat, had no idea what the boy was doing, but raised his voice in petulance; he was getting no answers. "I say she couldn't deliver it. So I took it myself. You hear?"

"I hear," Panimer said.

"He wasn't there. A whole new bunch was moved into his office. One of those temporaries and you couldn't tell it from none of the rest. No wonder the woman couldn't find him." Panimer raised himself; the blood had been too long in his head. The lantern did not give enough light for him to see the trail he was leaving, but Kreutz had been making it easy, guiding his mules as he always did, down the center of the road. "So I found another government man and he was about worse than the other. Said all these stamps I got is worthless. 'That part of the program's over,' he said. I struck him. He stopped talking so much."

"Could you stop the wagon a minute?" Panimer said.

"What you got there? What are you doing?"

Panimer was off the wagon, painting words on the road. They had come halfway to Small Hill and there was not much paint left. He would have to space the arrows wider.

164

"You ought not to be doing that. What are you doing?"

"Just showing how to get there."

The wagon was moving again, the boy listening to Kreutz now, but still counting the wheel's click behind the man's voice, making his arrows on the road at regular intervals. "I told the man I been buying food with them this far, I expect I'll keep on. They're worthless, he said. But I'll tell you, that Chain Food man, he makes good on them." Panimer knew what he meant, how Kreutz would hang out in the Chain Food, fingering everything and blocking the aisles; none of the village women caring to push their carts past his ragged beggary, and if they ordered him out of the store he would loiter right by the door, making all traffic flinch. And if the police came to take him away he could outlast that banishment too, even enjoying the public accommodation as he served his twenty-four hours, knowing he would be back when it was over. It was easier for Stockstill to pay him off as soon as he arrived. The boy had seen him do it, fascinated by the transaction at the checkout counter where no money changed hands, only coupons, even though he understood what Stockstill and all his checkers and even Kreutz knew—that Kreutz was such a well-calculated aggravation, such a perfect nuisance, he could have had the food for nothing. The ration stamps merely gave his pride a currency. He did not mean to give them up even when the war was over. Kreutz was going on in the dark now; the lantern had burned out. No matter, he thought. There was no traffic at this hour. It was after three a.m. though neither man nor boy knew it; neither cared. They were almost at Small Hill corner. Panimer was almost finished. Kreutz was saying, "You started them sirens, didn't you. The night your mother went blind." The boy pulled himself upright on the wagon, startled, not just by the intrusion of a truth so private, but that Kreutz should know anything about it.

"What are you talking about?"

"I know the first sound come from this way. And I know your mother and daddy wasn't home. I passed your daddy driving your mother to work. I was on my way to Washington District of Columbia when the whole thing went up and . . . ."

"So?"

"And what I don't see is how you knowed there was going to be them explosions." Kreutz knew too little and too much; there was no way for the boy to deal with him. He said nothing, went back to painting the line. They were almost at the drive of the huge building where the last arrow would point when the first dim wail of the sheriff's siren reached them. Panimer splashed the arrow onto the pavement. "Get the wagon out of the road," he yelled as the headlights shone over the rise behind them. The car was coming at great speed. There was hardly time to yell at Kreutz again. He would not have changed his course anyway. He meant to deal with the approaching automobile the way he dealt with all—simply by staying in its way until the driver knew that he, Kreutz, could not be pushed aside just with noise or impatience. The sheriff was coming seventy miles an hour or more over the crest at Small Hill; there was no way he could avoid the wagon. There was time for Panimer to jump clear; the brakes singing out above the receding siren, then metal and wood in collision. Kreutz catapulted from his seat of defiance into airborn somersaults onto the the road's shoulder in a tangle of arms and legs, only one of which was broken. The mules were destroyed, and the wagon, and most of the car.

Hospital and then jail for all three of them—Panimer, who had only been scared, the bleeding sheriff, and Kreutz, smelling of soap and disinfectant, his leg in a cast, and nervous at being so clean. Before they got out of the police car and into the jail Kreutz began to tell his side of it. "I don't know where he got the paint or nothing else. I just carried him from Clayton to Small Hill. I was on my way back from Washington District of Columbia." They put man and boy in the same cell, Kreutz still explaining, "I can prove it. Here's the letter I was taking and I couldn't even find the man. They already took and cleared him out of his building. You don't believe it, look for yourself. And it's all right with me if the post office woman keeps her job. She couldn't a done no better." But they were not listening to Kreutz; they were going after Panimer, asking him, "Have you gone crazy, boy?'' Not because it was the worst vandalism they'd ever seen, or even that they thought Panimer should spend the night in jail. It was because the Clayton mayor had got so upset; he and Lamartine and Earl Jackson. All of them up in the early hours of that morning on the telephone. Stockstill too, and Hiram Johnson, Senior. Until the sheriff's office had realized it was something more than a naughty boy with a paint brush they were after, though none of the complainants had said just what it was. Their urgency was evident enough in the pre-dawn hustle to remove or obliterate what he had done; soon after sunlight every word he'd painted in the village had been washed or smeared with turpentine, or painted over. But there was no chance to undo his work on the road before morning. The arrowed lines led straight to **PAPER**, and the word on the warehouse roof was undetected, or unreported, until the middle of the day, when it too was erased. Mr. Lewis had seen it first, passing Small Hill corner on his way to Washington. It had surprised him, but in a half mindless way. Paper was his thought and quest. Here was the word to greet his morning drive. But it struck him whimsically, as coincidence; he made no connection between the building and paper. It was odd, but it was not significant; as if he understood the flat surfaces of Stilson were blackboard to the county's passions and silliness. Later he said, ''That boy's trouble was he didn't know how to get into trouble. Not like my two. That one always left his spoor, whether he was taking his girl into the woods or vandalizing the town, he had to leave a trail.'' The last one he had made led right to his own hand and paint brush. And that morning Lewis had driven against the boy's spoor, against his arrowed directions to the warehouse, not even connecting the green paint on the road with the green word **PAPER** on the roof, preoccupied with the rationale he had conceived for his government's last brief in the case of U.S. vs. Triumph Paper.

22

Everyone was waiting for the end of the war. The radios were on all day and much of the night that August. Two bombs had been dropped on Japan. Farmer Kreutz said they were called Adam bombs because they were going to knock the Japs back to the beginning. Panimer sat on the steps of his house those long August evenings watching his mother grope her way around her victory garden. She was after the county prize again. Junior had helped her plant her rows straight but she had trouble telling weed from vegetable seedlings. The rows began to veer off here and there in cultivated curves. When the weeds had grown large enough for Paula to feel the difference she took them into her tender care along with carrot top and beet green, no matter that they might be producing thorns or bitter leaves. Junior hated that she would not let him help, and grew angry as he tried to show her weeds from vegetables, but then he came to think of it as a good place for her to be crazy in. A place where no one else would notice her. It kept her from talking to herself around the house. "I'm going to win the prize this year," she would announce at supper and Junior would get annoyed or tears would come into his eyes and Panimer would stare at the ceiling.

It was that kind of evening when the news came. They had eaten an early supper. Panimer was sitting on the steps when he heard the Saw Mill Road siren. His father came running out of the house. "It's over," he said. "Come on, it's over." He was shouting to Paula.

"What is it?" she called. "What's over."

"The war! The radio says the Japs give up! Come on."

Paula raised herself slowly from her stooped position. Panimer watched her hands go to her face. She was crying, almost losing her balance, then stumbling out of the garden and up the hill. Junior already had the truck started. She ran to the noise and climbed in.

"Come on," Junior called to his son. "We're going to the village." But Panimer waved his disinterest and the truck spun away down the drive. He did want to go to Clayton but not with them. He wanted to see what happened when a war was over. Horns were sounding from all directions across the countryside. He began walking down Station Drive. Cars came spinning past him, paying no attention to the thumb he begged with, in a hurry themselves to see what happened when a war was over, happy in the machines they would again be allowed to operate anytime, honking without stint.

Before Panimer arrived the horns had begun to gather around the Clayton corner, in front of Lamartine's, in the little space in front of the Jew store, in the Chain Food parking lot. From a mile away he heard them. He was coming at a dogtrot now, not wanting to miss anything.

He saw Farmer Kreutz ahead with his new mules and wagon, a present from his brother in the next county. Kreutz was going to Clayton, too, but not to celebrate. He knew his wealth of coupons was now in danger. Panimer overtook and passed Kreutz without looking back, yelling , "Get that damn mule flesh out the middle of the road." As the Clayton corner came into view down the last straightaway he could see there was no activity, only the cars raising their shrill din at one another, and more of them coming, homing in on the metallic racket they meant to join. Even before he reached the corner the sound annoyed him. What could anyone do in that racket? How could they think of their victory—if that's what they'd come for—in the midst of that? For the boy it was like horns after a football game. It was not the players themselves you had to worry about but the ones who rooted for them. These people with their horns parked and pointing at the corner as if they were trying to raise the dead. That's what it seemed to Panimer now; horns in a circle around the crossroads, all pointing at the monument to the woman who had worked with his mother. She was under there, dead. They were disturbing her deadness; he wished they would stop. He saw Mrs. Green putting her American flag out the second floor window of the Jew store, and heard Jane Settle say, "It's all right with me. It's her flag too. I don't care if she broke the rules and put too much butter fat in her ice cream. It was the only place for homemade ice cream for four years. And we all bought it from her. I don't care if she did stay open later than Charlie." Panimer had heard all that before; how the agriculture man and the price man had come from Washington and told Mrs. Green her ice cream was breaking the law, and they'd have to shut her down if she couldn't cooperate with the war rules. But she'd kept right on making ice cream the way she always had; let them call it Jew store ice cream or whatever they would, everyone kept on buying it because it was the best, just as the Jew store would always sell wax candy shaped like little bottles, or gums studded with huge teeth, all full of that sweet syrup (the war had given them the bitter aftertaste of imitation sugar). Panimer wanted a set of wax gums now, that and to go and stand in the crowd gathering behind the cars in Lamartine's lot. The garage was closed for the day. He could get lost and watch. Maybe the McConkeys would be there and he could stand back further and watch Nancy, who would not be speaking to anyone but standing in the silence of her pride and disgrace, unmoved by this or any other commotion. Thinking of it later, he was not sure whether she had seen him first, whether it was her signal or his that had brought them face to face there at the door of the garage. She had not tried to avoid him; he was certain of that because she'd spoken first:

170

"You're chewing awful loud, Panimer," and he had almost tried to swallow the wax jaws, choking for a moment on their juice. "What are you chewing?"

"Nothing. Wax candy."

"Gimme some."

"Ain't got any more."

"Gimme somma yours." He was not sure whether to credit what he heard, whether it was only a joke which she herself would be revolted by if she considered it, or the most intimate thing he could imagine. It took him only an instant to decide. He bit the large wad of wax in half and was about to hand her the larger half when she held her open mouth forward and he put it inside for her, carefully, so the juice might not drip on her chin or dress. It was a relief not to have to talk for a moment, not to have to think of something to say, both of them chewing loudly as if, while they were so occupied, conversation was not required; he was thinking that something which had been in his mouth was now in her mouth. What did it matter that they were not holding hands? Or that she was again staring straight ahead, not even glancing sideways at him. He knew she was showing the rest of the crowd it was purest coincidence she was standing next to Panimer, or next to anyone.

"The fire trucks are coming from Stilson," he heard someone say. That's what they muust be waiting for, Panimer thought. Nobody seemed to know what to do. They were slapping one another's backs and looking down the road toward Stilson. One man was yelling, "We won, by gum. We won," as if up to that very moment the outcome had been in question. You could tell the ones who had lost sons and nephews; they were not slapping or being slapped. There were five Clayton families missing sons. They planned to put the boys' names on a bronze plaque to be attached to Nadine's monument. But they had waited for victory to be sure no name was missed; too long because now the surviving families were not sure they wanted their sons' names linked with Nadine or the two women she'd worked with.

171

Panimer saw his mother in the crowd, walking with Claudelle, her hand on the colored woman's arm. It hurt him that she could not walk naturally, especially now, but took those sliding, tentative steps that gave her away; that and hanging on the colored woman. It made him uncomfortable. The people around him didn't like it. He wondered what Nancy thought, wanted her away somewhere with him, alone, could not bring himself to ask, but said, "I'm going around back," began to walk around the garage. When he came to the corner of the building he looked back, saw she had not moved, supposed he had lost her, but could not turn back, could not be that indecisive. He continued around to the back door and sat on the threshhold, putting his head between his knees, the better to feel sorry for himself and to block the noise of horns, sirens, voices. He did not hear when she called to him, even when she bent over him and said, "Panimer, didn't you want to see me?" She had to touch him. Before he even looked up to see what it was, he slapped away her hand and lunged sideways, coming from daydream to alert in the notion he was being attacked, chased, had to get away. When he looked to see what he'd done, her surprise had already turned to hurt. Then disdain, her chin angled once more against conversation; nothing he said would stop her. She was walking away. He had to get in front of her.

Had she tried to get around him, honestly tried to leave? He was not sure. Or had she allowed him to hold her while she argued against it, told him she didn't care what he thought of her anyway because they were leaving again, she and her family leaving Clayton.

"Why are you leaving?" he said.

"We don't like it here any more. The people are no account. Trash the war brought in. My daddy said he wouldn't stay here if they cut him a gold key and made him mayor. Not anybody's money could make him stay."

He heard the lie in what she said, knew that if they were leaving it was because of what had been written about her, her name and what she would do with anyone—not just Panimer—all over the walls and roads of Clayton. He held her there against

172

her will, or her feigned will, and wondered if any of it were true. She'd said she didn't care what he thought of her, suggested that even he might no longer trust her. As if all the times he'd erased her name and the foul language on either side of it he only might have been trying to convince himself it was not so.

"I don't believe any of those lies," he said. "It was just white trash painting them things. They don't know any better." She did not pretend he'd misunderstood, but said.

"Why didn't you stop them?" not tugging now, but clinging to his arm as he walked backwards toward the door, maybe afraid that if she'd kept pulling away from him he'd have let her go. They entered the back door of the garage, accomplices. He locked the door behind them. The celebration was suddenly muted by the double cinderblock walls of the garage and plate glass window, which they would have to walk in front of if they were going to get to the stairway. She knew where they were going because she said, "Wait. You go first." Without hesitation he moved across the room, but glanced toward the window as he went; no eyes facing him, only backs pressing against the glass as the crowd grew in the parking lot.

"Are you coming?" he said, not impatiently, but with tolerance, even affection for her doubt. It helped clear all the painted libel. She stepped quickly and easily, then watched his back as he began to climb. Halfway up he turned to ask again, "Are you coming?" And she began to climb. He was waiting for her in the middle of the stairway. He wanted more than she, or anyone, could have given; he wanted her innocence and he wanted her complicity.

They were safe from interruption now; the noise of the crowd outside did not bother them. Rather it seemed to insure their isolation. They had already undressed themselves when they discovered there was nothing to lie down on, but were staring at each other's nakedness, each wondering if the other meant to ignore the rules this time, wondering if they were only teasing each other again, when he pushed himself against her. She moved backward until she hit the desk but Panimer was still advancing. Lamartine's desk rather than the floor became their first bed. She was encouraging him, he was sure of it, she was guiding him past his plain ignorance into her confidence, into her; all fears of the mechanics of it fell away into himself, into her. Tender, she could not have known more than he, must have been guessing as he was; at once trusting and denying each other's experience as they groped to make it right, and somehow did, attended by the little cries of surprise that were themselves surprises, each to tell a discrete sensation, then reaching for sensation that was not there. It was love beyond flesh until his spasm, and they were once again conscious of their nakedness and of the noise outside, which had never stopped. They stood up, shy and proud, and looked down through the window at all the poor people below them. What did they know of celebration? Panimer held his nakedness against her as they heard and watched the ladder truck and the other engines from the Stilson Fire Department coming down Wye Bridge Pike and around the monument.

A fireman was staggering to keep his balance on top of the prone ladders as he trained the truck's hose into the air and then into the crowd. People scattered and screamed as joy lit the faces of the truck's company. Two of them tried to take the hose. The man holding it made as if to turn it on them and they backed away along the hand rails. He sent a spray directly over his head that climbed fifty feet in the air, catching the evening sun as it fanned outward; he opened his mouth to swallow his homemade rainbow, but fell backward on the ladders, still clinging to the hose, now far behind the nozzle, which leaped from side to side, out of control. He was not hurt, only his feelings perhaps as the people laughed at him. He got up and brought the stream under control again, then turned it from side to side on the people who dodged and ran. Two targets did not move; a boy with his back to the road who could not hear the fire engines coming and a woman staring at it who could not see it. The fireman seemed to accept their challenge with a special glee. He turned the hose on the boy. The spray lifted him from his feet and sent him tumbling along the sidewalk. If his body had fit, it might have been washed into the storm sewer in front of Chain Food. Then the spray was on the woman. The man must have thought she was daring him, because he kept the spray on her even after she had been knocked down, pressing her body against the pavement while his comrades on the truck cheered. She screamed, more in fright than in pain or injury. Then the truck was out of water; the hose gave a final spurt, dribbled, and went limp in the man's hands, and his jaw went slack as he considered the end of his pleasure. The driver had not had enough. He led the procession of fire engines down the drive to the Duncan Kimball playground and there the trucks chased each other in a tight circle of horns and sirens until Redmond Clarke raised his hand to let them know that was all.

Farmer Kreutz, his mules and wagon parked in front of the Jew store, had been a still target for the firemen's fun too. He refused to move and was caught under a steady sky spray until he was drenched. He cursed and shook his fist and turned the mules back toward Small Hill. Junior said it was "Kreutz's victory bath, and he's been waiting one whole war to take it." Then he saw his wife knocked to the ground and went chasing after the fire engine. Restrained from climbing on, he kicked its fender before running back to pull his wife away from Claudelle, who was explaining to Paula what had happened.

"They didn't know," Paula said. "It's all right. They didn't know."

"They knowed better," Junior said.

"Yes they did," Claudelle said. They were still there fixing and unfixing blame when Panimer came running around the back of the garage, barefoot. Seeing his mother already attended, and remembering where he'd just been, what he'd been doing, he stopped, shied away before they saw him. He had a sense the marks of what he'd just done must be visible on him. He wanted to be alone again with Nancy until the evidence had died away. At least until he'd had a chance to look in a mirror and see what had happened. He walked around to the back of the garage again, went inside and up the stairs. She was gone. He sat to put his shoes on.

Lamartine was watching him from the office doorway before

he'd got his second shoelace tied; the man's grin spreading back toward his ears so that Panimer's fright had suddenly turned to embarrassment; certain now that the deed must be visible on his hands and face, never thinking it might have to do with his untied shoelace or that Lamartine might have seen Nancy on her way out of the garage. His face turned crimson in his recollection of the detail.

Lamartine was so pleased in his amusement, "Got tired of the woods, did you? Listen, I know you and your old man pull more outa your pants than the other boys around here. I couldn't afford you people if I paid you for that. When you come to work down here, when you're finished school and all, you'll have to start just like the others."

Panimer got to his feet, stood by the desk wishing the man would get out of the doorway. But Lamartine still laughing, wouldn't move. "You stay out of trouble. Don't be chasing that thing around my garage. I bet she's all right, Hunh?" Panimer was trying to edge past him while Lamartine said, "I know you hit a good ball and run like a rabbit. It's time you left them colored up there and come down here to play with people." The boy was pushing by him but Lamartine went on. "We'll have a team again next year and Stilson won't touch us. You get an average going and there's money in it." Regardless of all the times he'd wished someday he might play for Clayton, might one day win one of the twenty dollar bills Lamartine used to slip to a favorite player for a special hit, Panimer hated him. His father had explained that Lamartine and Jackson always brought fat wallets to the games and half of the money in them they bet against each other and the other half went to buy the victory. There had seemed nothing finer than to play for Clayton and have Lamartine pay you for it.

23

After the war Paula heard so much sitting at her vending stand in the post office she hardly knew what to credit. At first she would say, "Who was that, Mrs. Hewgley?" or "What did she say, Mrs. Hewgley?" or maybe "That wasn't the way it was at all."

Until she knew voice and footfall so well that questions became unnecessary, only a matter of politeness, a way of covering the acuity of her perception and putting passing villagers at ease as she identified and placed them in the four years that had been the war. If she had stuck to questions she might have stayed out of danger, but she had fixed on that time, blacking out all that went before, as all that came after had been blacked out for her, making a war map of deed and motive in Clayton as brightly lit with good works as transgressions, lights blinking and shifting against her darkness as new information came to her.

Her questions became assertions, her blindness its own excuse for candor, as if, being denied light, she was owed these coordinates of the past to cling to. And these became the coordinates of her war map. The day Mrs. Pride came in speaking of the Kreutzes and how they had misused their food stamps,

Paula said: "It was your boy always had the gas coupons?"

"He was a spotter," Mrs. Pride said.

"He was a fine spotter is what I heard."

"Ronald got his extras for being a spotter," said Mrs Pride, turning to Mrs. Hewgley to make sure she heard, and ready to ignore the blind woman, who was saying "I'm thinking about after the county safe was rifled," almost to herself, which brought Mrs. Pride spinning back.

"Do you mean . . ."

"It was food stamps was taken from the safe. Oh no, I didn't mean . . . but someone at the school was getting gas coupons for the children. I still don't know who. Must have come cheap. None of the boys had much money, did they?"

Mrs. Pride turned back to the post mistress, began again: "Kreutz. Charlie Stockstill had a time with him because do you remember when the price people said stamp seventeen in the sugar book was for shoes? Well Kreutz thought the coupons were just like money and he near drove them crazy with hanging around the store like a beggar until Charlie would just let him have a little food for his stamps. And he couldn't keep his books straight unless he paid the difference himself. But do you know . . ." Mrs. Pride, supposing this was between her and Mrs. Hewgley, stiffened as Paula called behind her, "They were in such a bad way, weren't they? The Kreutzes."

"But do you know," Mrs. Pride whispered now, and Paula began to whistle, little parts of scales, shifting keys aimlessly, "But do you know he came back and said Charlie took his shoe stamp and how was he going to buy shoes without it. You know he didn't have any money to buy shoes."

The village began to move more cautiously around Paula's blindness but her probing continued: "Marcum said he never called the police on the boys that night they drove the car into that building but if he didn't, who did? Is that you, Valerie? There was so much strange going on for so long, and all of them blaming Panimer," her hand moving slowly over the stand, feeling . . . three, four, five across the gum to the Beamans.

"Valerie?" But Valerie Jackson, who would want Beamans if she wanted anything, was sliding away from her, across the post office floor, disguising her step, as if Paula could not recognize shuffle or normal footfall of her or anyone else who came in the post office every day. Unless too many came in at once; then she would be helpless, cornered until voices rescued her.

But Valerie Jackson was alone, and refusing to speak. Paula brightened, said, "Please excuse me. I thought you were someone else." Silence confirmed it was Valerie. She was winking at Mrs. Hewgley, signaling for her mail; the two of them looking back at Paula, shaking their heads at the woman whose blindness and presumed derangement had become more annoying than pitiable, centered as it was in the daily path of a village ready to forget the things still troubling her. Paula was saying cheerfully to no one, "Now the Jacksons—I thought I heard Valerie come in. Now she knew something about that big building at Small Hill." Valerie was listening as best she could, her interest in what Paula was saying hidden by a conspiracy of glances with Mrs. Hewgley, their anxious confirmation of the woman's insanity. Paula, obliging that conspiracy, slipping off her point into the familiar, "Junior and I, we started off with three good eyes, and now we've only got one between us. And that's his." And they saw her smile sweetly, watched her hand move across the counter, reach a chocolate bar, close slowly around it and keep closing, until smile became grimace, and candy a mush in its wrapper.

Paula was searching the town's silence for some missing story. All they were giving her was a confusing shuffle of feet. They did not want to talk about it. Not even Mrs. Hewgley, who had been so kind at the start, who had helped her orient her hands among the stock of candy, and talked to her by the hour from behind the bars of her clerk's window. She too was exhausted by the questions, sick of it. She wished Paula gone. Still the blind woman persisted:

"Someone tried to kill Panimer," she said. "Someone called the police on *him*. Now who was it is what I ask myself," but loud enough that Mrs. Hewgley knew she was being asked.

179

"Leave it alone, honey," she called. "Don't get yourself upset again. Junior'll be here soon."

"We've only got one eye between us."

"Leave it alone, honey."

"That's his."

"Honey, don't talk that way," Mrs Hewgley looked up from her newspaper at the ceiling.

"If it was just boys tried to hurt him, that's one thing."

"I can't talk now, honey."

"Sorting again? . . . It's late for sorting . . . I said it's late for sorting . . . I used to think it was just boys tried to hurt Panimer. I knew that bunch of boys were after him," this too low for Mrs. Hewgley to make out—the more annoying because she still felt obliged to answer. She said, "You tease a place, Paula it'll start hurting."

"Junior says forget about it but I can't forget. Something's wrong I can't figure out."

"Hmmmm."

"You'd think we'd been a bunch of traitors." Silence. "Do you think they might still be after him?"

"I say leave it alone, honey. Tease a place long enough, it'll start hurting."

"But it was all part of the same thing. Whatever it was Panimer was getting into. And that huge place out at Small Hill, that nobody knew what was going on in there. I think some people knew."

Panimer found Farmer Kreutz on the Jew store steps. "You know them things I was painting on the road?" he said.

"They got us both throwed in jail whatever it was," Kreutz said. "And my mules kilt."

"Wasn't nothing but the truth," Panimer said.

"The truth don't have to be writ all over. What truth?"

"I'm gonna write it some more," Panimer said. "You want to help?"

"Couldn't. Even if you wasn't crazy."

"They killed your mules. They're bound to pay you for them. The law don't let 'em just kill your mules. And smash your wagon too."

Kreutz considered that for a moment. "Obliged to you," he said, wondering if the boy might be right, if the police might have to pay him even though his brother had replaced them. By the time he got to the Stilson police station it was a demand he presented to the officer at the desk, along with five complete food ration books for the man's trouble. "They're still good all right," Kreutz said. "Don't tell me they ain't good. I use them myself. Anytime. Mr. Stockstill don't even argue about it. He does, you let me know. Believe me. It don't matter the war's over."

The officer put the ration books in his desk and locked Kreutz up once more, but in a few days he was out again, pestering the police again for his money.

After the night in jail with Kreutz, Panimer had been released with more warning than punishment. He did not even have to clean up his painting; the village had been in too big a hurry to get itself cleaned up. As he drove back through Clayton with his father he could see his work had already been erased; the lines and arrows remained on Station Drive, but none of the words, and the huge **PAPER** on the roof had been painted over by the evening. They thought that might be the end of it. It was not. He painted, they erased. It had been a mistake to put him in jail for a night, making an issue where they wanted none. If they were going to stay his hand and paint brush they'd have to find a quiet way. Still he painted, and they erased. He did his work under cover of shadows and of night. It came to be a game for him, watching to see how soon they would find and wipe clean his latest painted word—**PAPER**—pleased with their hasty response to each new appearance of the word. He never bought the paint, only stole it—under porches, out of cellars, garages. They never caught him stealing—must have known who it was—but could not or would not stop him, waiting for his obsession to run its course, supposing that ignoring might finish it. They had not considered that it might be catching, that others finding nothing in the word but its ubiquity about the village might take it for their own pleasure, just as a pastime, not knowing what it meant or caring, just repeating what everyone else was repeating. Doc Peterson couldn't keep crayons or chalk stocked on the variety shelf in his drug store. He thought he knew what they were going for but wouldn't deny himself a sale on the mere presumption. The word even appeared on the Potomac palisade. Panimer might have stepped aside now and let disciples of the fad continue what he'd taught them. But he was not finished. The others could take care of buildings, store fronts, sidewalks; his own pleasure was the road, and the warehouse itself. He could see it was a terrible problem for them—how to keep the painted arrows and the word erased from Station Drive. At first they'd left the arrows alone, only covered the word, sending the gravel and tar crew from Lamartine's up and down the three-mile stretch between Clayton and Small Hill as if it were the season for pothole patching—an expensive way to erase paint, but a price they could apparently afford because they patched all over, potholes or no. Panimer painted again. Other boys unwittingly helped too this time, following the fad. And every week or so the patching truck would be sent out again, embarrassing Junior, who would sometimes be in charge of the crew. The sheriff had begun to patrol the Drive at night but there were not enough police cars or deputies in all of Stilson County to stop the dozen or more village boys who now participated in the wanton sport, striking anywhere along the road, anytime, jumping from the woods with cans and brushes to leave the word of the moment, until they saw headlights or heard the hum of tire and engine along the macadam and fell back into the woods. The road would not stay clean but became playground to the young people's end-of-war celebrating. Their only game was **PAPER**. That and the arrows leading toward Small Hill. Most had painted for the sport, though Ronald Pride and Hiram Johnson supposed the arrows they drew toward Small Hill pointed shame at the hamlet where Panimer lived. Station Drive had become such a mess of patch and paint that Lamartine and others had already decided on a complete resurfacing.

Then the painting stopped. And whoever had been so anxious to keep the road erased must have supposed they'd won with patience. The resurfacing began. Lamartine and Jackson shared the contract—or everyone just supposed there must be a contract, that the state must be helping the county pay to rid itself of the village's mindless self-desecration. All except those doing the work. Junior knew it wasn't an ordinary job. Lamartine had as much as ordered him to supervise the three-mile repaving without pay, and Junior had agreed without argument, or any conversation, silently acknowledging his son's responsibility. Who else was working the road for nothing, Junior wondered. Was the stone and tar coming free from somewhere too? He did not ask.

The road was more of a mystery to Paula. Panimer, driving her to the village for her monthly permanent, had not told her why he was taking the back road, but she could tell the difference and immediately wanted to know why.

"Because they're repaving the Drive," he said.

"They just finished patching it two weeks ago," she argued.

"Don't ask me," Panimer said.

"It's not right," Paula said. Then "Somebody's getting rich," and he knew she meant Lamartine or Jackson or both of them, "But it's hard work. I mean it's no more than right they ought to be paid well for it. And your father can thank his lights they are."

"Oh Jesus, Ma, can't something be right or wrong for once, not both all the time?"

"Panimer. You don't talk to me like that." She was right, he thought, he had never spoken to her that way. "You must be tired, dear. What have you been doing?" She knew by his silence she was aggravating him. "Well if I could only see to do it myself I'd get a home permanent kit. Then you wouldn't have to bother driving me."

"Oh, Ma." He did not want her talking that way, but also, just now, he didn't want her talking at all, not while he was thinking of how he'd attack the new surface of Station Drive, and how he was going to get Kreutz to help him do it.

Now his silence was aggravating *her*, and she said, "And I don't want you down there in the junkyard any more." He knew what she meant was she didn't want him messing around inside the fence around the great secret building, much less inside the building itself, as if it really was a secret any more. What surprised Panimer was how much was known and how little was talked about. He was sure they all knew about the warehouse now, even his mother, because he'd heard her wondering aloud about it: "It's more than one of 'em trying to keep that place hushed. How many is it?"

But Panimer supposed no one knew more about it than he, simply because he was sure he was the only one who'd broken through its several lines of defense to see what was inside. He was not aware how far his propaganda had taken them, even against the village will to disbelieve it. He had caused their secret to be repeated so many times they hardly realized themselves that they'd made the connection and had come to accept it: the great building contained paper and nothing more.

He had no inkling that minds beyond his own had taken that simple truth and begun to weave their notions around it; his own mother beyond all the rest, sitting at her candy stand, making them all uneasy with her musing and speculation.

Mrs Hewgley, trying to quiet her, said: "Oh, you know men. They just wanted people thinking it was something important in there. They didn't want people saying Clayton's war secret was only paper."

"If that's all there is to it," Paula said, "why is everybody trying so hard to pretend they don't care who knows it? You can tell it gives them all the silent creeps." Paula was certain now there must be a second man in Clayton with an interest in the building. "Someone's got to own the place," she announced one day to a full post office. "Who owns the place?" But since there had been no antecedent to her question, her audience could take ease in another example of her advancing derangement. "Maybe outsiders came in," Paula continued.

Paula would never have spoken out this way before. But now

her blindness protected her; she was free to do as she pleased behind that screen of her imagined invisibility. All of them might be looking at her, or maybe none of them; what did it matter? She was sure though that a daily audience came to listen for her mumbling; all turning the combination locks of their mail boxes, fumbling longer than necessary, busying themselves with mail chores, talking aimlessly with Mrs. Hewgley, until Paula said, "It's not just Panimer wrote those things on the road. There was others doing it too." The fumbling stopped. "Whoever leased the land for that big place, they had to have help from somebody around here. Who was it helped them?" There was a sudden business of voices. Her questions came without warning, dropped on their daily congress, as little bulletins toward her solution of the last mystery of the war.

So many sons dead, so many people here who did so much; the sacrifices past and forever, the handsome photos of uniformed sons, dead and medaled, on desks and dressers, sons of Clayton; and mothers, knitting, writing letters, some for sons they did not even know, doing so many other things with such good cheer, happy sacrifices in the war against abominable things; and fathers, their sweat in the earth of victory farms and gardens. Harold Johnson was dead of blood pressure—his heart strained with his ears to hear the noise of enemy bombers that had never come; even sons at home, Ronald Pride deaf from devotion to duty. And Paula, blind from war work. Why this gnawing at what was not quite right?

It remained to see whether she, making patterns of the silences around her probes and questions, would come to the simple truth of the thing before Mr. Lewis, who had all the facts of the case before him in his office and still could not see it. What his own picture window daily tried to show him, the affront to his scenery that he had sworn to undo when the war was over. He knew there was a case against Triumph Paper. The company's books were inconsistent. There were vouchers and bills of lading for tons of scrap paper no one could find. He had the crime; he needed the body.

Lewis had spent months fighting Triumph over their grading

system, supposing this had been the company's easy path above the ceiling price. Then his own government had undercut him, writing law forbidding the price office from establishing product grades that had not existed before the war, even though this ruined his control of paper. Furious, he had come to believe, and accept, that Congress would defend business even at the expense of victory. He had tried a new tactic, investigating the company's operating procedure, hardly realizing he was stepping way beyond his charter and duty, seeking crime where he had no reason to believe any existed, never supposing he might be probing the secrets of his own village. And he had caught them, found them charging an extra dollar a ton for their scrap under a rule allowing the surcharge if their point of shipment was not on a railroad. They were growing so fast, buying into other companies so quietly that he was not aware of all their holdings but he knew they had two warehouses in Trenton, right around the corner from each other with a connecting private alley, one of them with railroad frontage. Triumph was using the non-frontage building as its shipping address, charging the extra dollar. A District Court found them lacking candor, upheld Mr. Lewis. Triumph appealed and the issue became fuzzed in niceties of definition, meanings of simple words and phrases that had once seemed so clear to Mr. Lewis—point of shipment, weighing and storage phase, point of accumulation. The petty chiseling had heated Mr. Lewis's cerebral patriotism, kept him warm in pursuit of righteousness, distracted him while Triumph's more important secret lay before him, unexplored.

Now, with the war over, Lewis wanted to bring the company to book, let them make restitution, if not in cash, at least in shame. What work had they done toward victory? If they behaved like that in war, what must they do in peace, he wondered.

186

24

What would Panimer do in peacetime? There came a week he was beset with adult advice, all of it confusing, as if people sensed he was on the edge, about to do something from which there would be no recovery. "Stay out of trouble," Paula begged, "Stay away from that building." She knew there were men who would like to see his mouth stopped and his hand stayed from further painting. He listened to his mother without arguing. "Listen son," his father said, "you got to stop this nonsense with the paint. And don't tell me you ain't doing it. I know you started it." Seeing Panimer was about to argue, he raised his hand, said, "No. Don't say nothing. Don't." He sat down with his son in the kitchen and from nowhere began to talk about Phyllis Jackson, to console him for the loss of Nancy. "They said I liked her," he said. "What if I did?" already half admitting what he was about to explain in detail, whether his son was ready for it or not. "I wouldn't cheat your mother," he promised the boy's darkening face, lying a little to keep the truth from coming too fast. "I mean your mother and I, we love each other. You know that. Now she's blind, I love her much as I ever did." He supposed the boy needed reassuring. "This Phyllis, she got in the same kind of trouble your Nancy did. She got herself a reputation and couldn't get rid of it. She knew I liked her. But it was only just glances made her know it." Panimer was moving around on his chair, wanting and not wanting to know what his father was wanting and not wanting to tell him. "She'd just sit around the garage waiting for a chance to talk. Earl Jackson couldn't stand it. Didn't want any of his kin hanging around Jewel's place, much less getting familiar with his men. Least of all her. Playing peekaboo behind all that hair of hers, all the time signifying. But I could see none of that satisfied her, that she was tearing herself apart with all that lip twitching and eye batting, not meaning any of it. Except for me. Wait. I'm not bragging, or proud of it. Just telling you so you'll understand. What she thought she wanted was me. And no more experience than a puppy not licked dry. Oh she was pregnant all right. But I don't believe she hardly knew how she got that way. You know what I'm talking about?" he stopped suddenly, inquiring of the boy's reddening face; a blush was all the answer Panimer could manage. "Yeah. You know. Well, it wasn't me got her that way. And it wasn't her being that way caused her to leave the county. It was what Earl Jackson saw happening to her name and his. He'd pull up in front of Lamartine's in his Packard, wouldn't even turn off the highway. Just wait for her in the car. When she saw him, she'd get herself one more orange pop and sit up on the soda cooler, drinking it slow as she could. And if there wasn't anyone listening she might ask could she talk to me alone sometime."

Panimer relaxing in the rhythm of his father's memory, now giggled with the vision of a woman, her pouty lips around a soda bottle, her eyes playing over the room for contact as she drank and her uncle's jaws jacked higher and higher as she let him cool his heels.

Junior told him of the evening she had come to him unasked, after everyone had left the garage, told him she was "in a bad way," and asked what should she do. They had gone upstairs together. "Lamartine doesn't keep nothing up there you'd hardly want to sit on," Junior said. "Much less lie down on."

Marcum let the war take his rubber, but he'd never let it have the chassis—all the rusting shapes he loved, the metal covering his junk hill, all the way down to the fence around the huge building; their sheer bulk and occupation of the landscape giving security, never mind that it was as hollow as the cars themselves. He would not cede them to patriotism, outside scrap dealers, or any force in nature outside of weather and rust. During the first two years of the war, while the cars were still precious stores of parts, he had sat up late into the nights, in the upstairs window of his auto shop, watching for prowlers, parts thieves and vandals. Even when the bodies contained nothing more of use he had sat up to watch over them, keeper of his auto graveyard—they would have to last till the fighting was over. When more would come to take their place. His early vigilance had saved Panimer from the Phaeton he had guided into the cinderblock wall. Now he watched the boy again as Panimer came in the evenings to sit on the hill, sometimes to walk down and climb the fence around the forbidden building. Once he had seen him climb onto the roof, other times watched him disappear into the building's back door. He sensed in Panimer a reverence for his graveyard as he watched him make his careful way around the sleek shapes, sometimes stopping to rub his hand over the gentle curve of a fender. And he admired the boy's real prowling, the stealth he assumed as he climbed over the fence to do whatever it was he did in that strange outsized building. Marcum resented that it had ever been put there, a wall against the growth of his auto field.

Panimer had traveled alone around Small Hill corner for several weeks. James Lewis did not want to run with him any more and Roland had not yet flunked out or been dismissed from his military prep. Panimer began to miss his school bus on purpose and Small Hill had been watching his truancy, especially Marcum. Day and night he watched the boy's aimless wandering from the room above the auto shop. One night he saw another man spying on Panimer under a light behind a far corner of the great building. Instead of putting the dog on him or coming after him, the watchman had let him climb the fence and enter the back door. Several minutes later Panimer came out again, still with no one bothering to follow or arrest him. He came back over the fence and climbed halfway up the hill, where he sat down.

If he had not been walking in to do business with them, he must have been walking into a trap, and Marcum was certain Panimer had no business there. So why hadn't they sprung their trap? He came down, hoping to warn the boy of the danger he might be in and ended up talking about himself, wanting to say, "Don't run, it's only me," but instead, coming silently to within several yards of him, startled him with, "Good evening boy. What you doing?" Panimer swung around, but did not try to run; the man was too close.

"Nothing."

"I seen you go in that place down there."

"So?"

"They seen you too. Did you know they seen you too?"

"I didn't do nothing to your cars."

"They could arrest you."

"It's nothing but junk cars here anyway," Panimer said, which would have angered Marcum except that he knew the boy did not mean it.

"That dog could chew you up," he said. "Ain't you afraid of that dog?"

"That dog can't catch me."

Marcum could not scare the boy so he began to indulge himself. "I had a dog once," he said. "They kilt it. I never got another. One of 'em run it over. Never even scraped it off the road. Didn't even tell me." Panimer said nothing but, of a sudden, felt sorry for the man who seemed to share the same unnamed and widespread enemy. "Then they come and asked would I sell them some land, and could they have my cars at a special price, and why wasn't I helping with the war, and didn't I like my country. I told them all to get the hell away. They called me names like you never heard. Said it'd serve me right if the Japs took my cars in the end, and the Germans got my land."

He saw he had turned Panimer's head. "They're out for you," he said. "You better duck. They'll get you."

Paula thought there might be someone else after her now, not just the Pride boy; someone trying to scare her, maybe even to do away with her. One afternoon she recognized Mrs. Stockstill's step, then heard her whispering with Mrs. Hewgley. "Is that you, Mrs. Stockstill?" she called. Their voices shifted audibly to the subject of farmer Kreutz.

"And do you know he's still coming around with those stamps and making Charlie give him food. And another silly letter. Everyone knows all those stamps are counterfeit. Where did he get them anyway? But the war is over and him still getting away with that foolishness. I can't understand it. Can you?" she cued Mrs. Hewgley.

"Uhm uhm uhm," Mrs. Hewgley said, the note rising and falling, indicating Mrs. Stockstill should continue. But Paula called, "They're so badly off, aren't they? His wife and children. Don't have a thing, do they?" Mrs. Stockstill had her stamps and had mailed her letters; she would have left the post office immediately rather than talk to the blind woman, but Paula called, "Mrs. Stockstill. Could I ask you a question?" and rather than have anyone else hear what Paula would say, Mrs. Stockstill had walked over to the candy stand.

"Keep your voice down, honey. What is it?"

And Paula said, "Isn't your husband one of the investors in the paper business?"

"Are you all right, dear?" Mrs. Stockstill said.

"I know he was trying to do right by the war. Of course he was. Everybody was. My boy too. Mrs. Stockstill? Panimer was too, you know. Somehow he just got off on the wrong foot and couldn't get back in step. That was all. You worked so hard too. I know you did. All the problems you must have had on the ration board."

Mrs. Stockstill had begun to back away but Paula raised her voice as her audience receded, until her audience was the whole post office, all of its morning traffic, all of them puzzling with what she was saying. It was so easy to Paula—a notion, but so concrete, so obvious. If there was nothing in that secret place but paper, and certain people were so ashamed of it, then the paper must be tainted. Black market paper. At once a notion and a certainty flashed in her darkness. And if certain people were so troubled by it, maybe they had bought in, maybe they had been tainted themselves, maybe they had known all along it wasn't luminous foxes, or rare metals, or secret weapons, or anything fancy. Just paper. They would have been the ones who went silent when all those rumors were current, the ones who'd made you think they were privy to the great secret just by their smug silence, content to let others spin the fancies. And they had known. They must have found out early that what they had invested in was not quite right. Or maybe the same ones who had coaxed them into it had also convinced them it ought to be kept a secret; maybe convinced them the enemy would like to know where acres of paper were stored. Paula had been certain Lamartine was one of them. Her memory of his silences assured her. Now she felt certain of Charlie Stockstill to. But she had no idea how close she was to the notion that would connect them all.

Ronald Pride walked into the post office, went straight to the candy stand, and told Paula: "Don't try to talk to me. I couldn't hear nothing you'd say. Here's your money. I didn't want it anyway." He tried to keep his voice down, not sure how loud he was talking. "I was going to buy a war bond with it." Before Paula could speak to him he'd already walked away from her and out of the building. Mrs. Hewgley had guessed what he'd done and put an end to it, told him he'd need another signature to buy his bond. Ronald had mumbled something and fled. Kept from his scheme to correct Paula's patriotism, the boy had hidden the money in his house, wondering if Mrs. Hewgley would tell his mother, wondering if she'd tell Paula, wondering if she'd tell anyone. He'd only been trying to help win the war, he told himself. Why shouldn't he admit what he'd done.

"Did you hear that," Paula called.

"What, dear?" Mrs. Hewgley said.

"Ronald Pride gave me the money back. I knew it was him. Did you see him?"

"I'm busy, honey. What's the matter?"

"Didn't you see him?"

"No. Who was it?"

Paula knew Mrs. Hewgley was lying. Why was she lying?

25

Paula wanted to leave the post office early that evening; she had enough news to readjust her war map, to set the lights blinking again, to make her darkness worthwhile. She supposed she could connect the lights best in the privacy of her own bedroom with the door closed. When the truth was born she did not want anyone watching or listening. Mrs. Hewgley called the Clayton Taxi Company for her. Their car was busy. It took an hour for it to come, and by then Paula was shaking in the fear and excitement of her discovery. She was safe; no one wanted to kill her. She was sure of that again. But how many times had she come to that and then been dislodged from security? No, she was certain now. There had been a stupid, impetuous boy who wanted to scold her, that was all. Why would they want her? She only talked. Talk erased itself in the air. Paint did not erase itself.

The ideas were coming to her so quickly now, and there was no one to share them with. The whole village had invested in paper. That was their secret, now hers. She had to get home, had to get Junior home too, and Panimer. She was sure her son was someone's mark, that they would kill him. All they needed was for him to present himself as a convenient target, one whose position might establish their innocence of ever having aimed at it.

It was a new taxi driver; she did not know him. But Paula said, "If you see my son on the road would you tell me. Hurry please."

The driver caught her urgency, was going sixty, even sixty-five on the straightaways, and begged her not to lean out the window. Closing quickly on Small Hill, he was thinking if he averaged sixty, it would only be a three-minute ride. He began to time himself. It was a pleasure to use Station Drive now that the high-crowned tar and gravel surface had been replaced with smooth macadam. They'd even painted a center stripe on it. Paula was leaning so far out the window, wind tears streaming from her eyes, that the driver guided his right wheel by the road's shoulder, thinking this would keep the woman safe from passing traffic. Whatever speed he could manage was unnecessary. Panimer was for the moment safe at the other end of Station Drive, coming toward the same corner at a tranquil mule-clop, sitting beside Farmer Kreutz with whom he'd spent the afternoon riding down the Pike, making plans for his last painting attack and flight. Panimer indulged Kreutz's notions of revenge only to secure his place beside him on the wagon seat, not just for that night but into the distance beyond Stilson County, into the future, as long as it might take. If he could encourage Kreutz to share revenge, he might force him to share his flight; mules, wagon, and driver to be at his disposal until the search was over. Then he could dismiss them. They argued what their route would be, Kreutz returning again and again to the two people who would have to pay. There was Mr. Stockstill in Clayton, whom Kreutz had learned was the one to report him months earlier to the rationing board—never mind that Stockstill was the one who had fed him all those same months, and never mind that (and this Kreutz could not have known) the method of reporting had been for Stockstill to roll over in bed, on the edge of sleep, and tell his wife that something had to be done about the pest in his store, and she ought to be the one to do it since she was on the rationing board.

"After that grocery man," Kreutz told the boy, "then we got to get over to Stilson and see about the one sprayed me with the hose." For neither of these missions did Kreutz hold the least notion of violence, only anticipating his usual tactic, simply to confront them with his presence and their sin, until they might pay in apology or currency. Panimer argued only over the order of their route. Clayton first, he said, and Stilson last, with Small Hill in between, to make one last trip up Station Drive with his paint cans, and one last ascent of the war building's roof, before going to West Virginia. That's where his longest thoughts were; with Nancy, who had run that way with her family. He knew Stilson was west of Small Hill. So when they had finished their evening's work they would go to Stilson. Then find the highway that went to West Virginia. Whether they could escape detection before clearing the county line would depend on Kreutz's skill with his new team and plain chance, because their mule-pace was not going to outrun the sheriff's van or half a dozen cars of his deputies that might chase them. Meanwhile the mules were not doing well. "It's this new damn road makes them nervous," Kreutz said, "Makes them want to skit sideways."

Paula's taxi driver never saw them. He was already back in Clayton before the wagon reached Small Hill corner. Paula called Lamartine's and made Junior promise to come right away and look for Panimer on the way. But Junior never saw the boy; by the time he came up Station Drive in Lamartine's truck, tapping the floorboard with the accelerator in his aggravation, Kreutz had pulled the wagon into Saw Mill Road to argue again with Panimer about which way they'd go when they got to Clayton. He was not getting anywhere with the boy, who had turned stubborn to the point of jumping off the wagon and finding some other transportation west, when Kreutz relented, realized he was enjoying the boy's company, even offered to let him drive. As if Panimer, who had once driven a Phaeton, could be excited by the reins of two mules. Behind the road bank they heard the truck and watched Junior disappear down the Drive.

196

"Yeah, let me have those reins," Panimer changed his mind, nudging the man aside. But he could not even make the mules go forward, much less turn around, as he slapped the leather along the animals' backs, causing only their ears to move—swiveling several times, then lying straight back. Kreutz, his chin moving up and down without sound, as close as he ever came to amusement, pushed the boy aside, and they were back on the Drive, moving again toward Clayton. Panimer pretended not to be interested in how to drive mules, as he watched the way the man worked hands and voice together, then gave the mules silence for their cooperation.

They pulled up in front of the Jew store. Kreutz went inside and begged a packaged cupcake before he went to Chain Food to confront Mr. Stockstill. Panimer wandered off. Kreutz was a long time finished with Stockstill, having settled for apology this time rather than food, when Panimer came back, ducking around the corner of the store with three cans of paint. The weight made him limp along in his hurry.

"Ain't that heavy, is it?" The man said. "I thought you wasn't coming."

"They're full," Panimer said, climbing on.

Kreutz was already past the corner, heading toward Stilson, when Panimer jumped down from the wagon, pulling the paint cans with him. "All right, all right," Kreutz said, "We'll go your way." He turned the mules once more, even then knowing the boy was going to have the law after them again, maybe even before they got to Small Hill, and he was not entirely displeased with the prospect.

The Drive was deserted but for the wagon under the rising moon. Panimer asked Kreutz for more speed. He was letting the paint dribble slowly from the can over the back of the wagon. It spilled back and forth across the center stripe in lazy curves. Every few hundred yards he would jump down with his brush and leave an arrow on the line pointing toward Small Hill. A single car passed them in the whole hour it took them to go the three miles, swerving around them, not interested in their work. Kreutz turned the wagon left on Small Hill Road, then drove right into the skin ball diamond and stopped in center field at the edge of the woods. "How long you going to be?" he said.

"I won't be long," Panimer said, disappearing under the trees with his last can of paint. Trotting along the path, which he knew even in darkness, he emerged at the top of Marcum's junk hill, making a perfect silhouette of himself in the moonlight. Two sets of eyes watched him as he waited, gathering his nerve. The watchman was crouched and ready at the great building's corner, and Marcum looked on from the window of his room above the auto shop. Panimer waited only a minute before making his way among the used cars, down the hill and over the fence. The two observers wondered at the ease with which he scaled the angled strands of barbed wire at the top, as if he'd had basic training in that very maneuver. Down the other side, he was already at the back door and inside before Marcum could get down his steps and outside to warn him. Marcum followed the boy's path down among the cars, watched and waited, then climbed the fence himself.

26

"Where's the fire?" Paula said. When Junior would not answer, she screamed, "Where is the fire?" Sirens were wailing up Station Drive. "I can smell smoke right here in front of the house. It's down there, isn't it?"

"Listen at all them engines," Junior said. "Stilson don't even have that many engines."

"It's in that war building, isn't it," Paula shouted again. "Isn't it? The fire's in that war building. Junior?" Junior was looking down toward the hollow where billows of smoke rose in the moonlight. But he could see no fire. No light in the sky at all, only smoke, great clouds of it, drifting over them now, so that the landscape darkened suddenly. "Junior, Panimer's in there. I know he goes in there. He's in there."

"He ain't in any fire," Junior said. "You wait here." He ran down the hill.

An hour later smoke still poured from the war building's eaves, but none of the gathering crowd at the fence had seen a flame. "What is it in there could just make smoke like that?" Claudelle begged of a resting fireman.

"Can't see to tell," he said. "Can't get in there for nothing."

Several times they had entered the back door in their masks, but none had got more than a dozen yards into the building. They could only train their hoses blindly and hope it was not an electrical fire.

The watchman whoever he was, could not be found. Redmond Clarke asked all around who was in charge and got only a grunt from Earl Jackson. "I can't send them any further till I know what's in there," Clarke complained.

"No, don't send them in," Jackson said. Lamartine was asking the firemen what they had seen, all of them playing with their secret, which had once more been translated into letters if they had only backed far enough from the building and trained their searchlight on the roof to see **P A P E R** in huge, fresh, white letters on the hot metal.

No one was trying to be a hero, not even Junior, secretly certain as his wife that his son was inside. He wept, walking slowly back and forth along the fence, staring in at the walls and roof, trying to create a place from which the boy might have escaped. If he were not inside, Panimer would be watching with the others. Junior saw Lamartine; he moved faster along the fence, weeping aloud now.

Clarke was on his radio trying to find out who called in the alarm, but the dispatcher had no name. "You supposed to get a name," Clarke yelled, then relented. "Was it a man or woman?"

"I couldn't tell you," the dispatcher said. "Sounded to me like a colored." Clarke walked along the fence asking the colored of Small Hill who had seen it first, and had they seen anybody go in or come out of the building. But no colored was going to get involved with Redmond Clarke and the Stilson Fire Department. Someone back in the crowd said, "The old man went in there." But when Clarke called, "What old man? Who said that?" the voice disappeared.

Later Junior heard Clarke tell Lamartine, "If anyone's in there, they're dead." The building smoked that way all night. Nobody got inside. Junior finally told the police Panimer was missing. And the word passed through the crowd and was soon altered. The boy's in there, they said. Junior's boy. When they could get inside they would be looking for a boy burned in his own fire, they said, a dead arsonist.

All night long they came trickling through the house, some to console, others to question, to carry out official, or presumed, duties—the sheriff with two of his deputies, Redmond Clarke, their voices distant, reaching for authority while they tried for dignity and sympathy. Paula sat in the kitchen, wept out of tears since just after midnight, now listening closely for detail and tone. When terror for her son became insupportable, she drifted into calculation, reckoning with her war map. There were hushed conversations all around her, men talking to Junior, women talking to her; she was connecting the voices—of Claudelle, who stroked her hair and held her hand, of the Lewises, the sheriff and fire chief, of Lamartine and Mrs. Jackson. Even the Stockstills—all roused in the middle of the night to see a two alarm blaze that was not a blaze, but smoke. Who had roused them all, what chain of phone calls? Was Clarke disappointed, Paula wondered. But why shouldn't he be? He'd come to fight a fire, hadn't he? What was Panimer to him? Just a nuisance. More than a nuisance?

"When did you see him last?" Clarke said. The same silly question all of them were asking her. And, "Did he ever say anything about that place down there?" As if they didn't know Panimer had painted the road and building. Only Mr. Lewis, honestly ignorant, asked the sensible thing, but quietly, close to her ear so that she was sure it was meant only for her: "What is it they're hiding from you?"

"They're not hiding a thing from me," Paula said. "They're hiding it from themselves. But I never knew so many was in it." Paula was talking to herself now as much as to Mr. Lewis. "There wasn't a one of them would have done a single unpatriotic thing. Someone got hold of them, you see? Wasn't a one of them would have tried to kill Panimer. It was someone else," sobbing dry sobs now. "They wouldn't mind if he was gone, but I can't believe . . . There's no secret to it."

"You mean they all know what's in there?"

"They tell me it's written all over. Haven't you been looking?" Mr. Lewis tried to guess for a moment what it was he must have been looking at but not seeing, maybe knew even as he asked, "What is it in there?"

"Not a thing," Paula said. "Not a thing but paper."

"What kind of paper?"

"Scrap paper. And Panimer," she wailed.

"But the place is too big," he said. "There's never been that much paper in one place." Mr. Lewis had his missing body; Paula and Junior would have to wait for theirs.

The building was too wide open when Panimer went in. He saw that, but assumed carelessness rather than purpose in the non-resistance that was drawing him further inside, then up the iron stairs with his paint can and brush. He could explore further this time. A door led off the catwalk into a loft. He went through it, then out the other side of an empty room into a long passageway that seemed to lead across the width of the building. It was like a covered bridge with windows in it. He wanted to be in the center of it looking through the windows, down on the people who thought they had a secret.

The door closed behind him. He spun around, then scolded himself, ashamed for his little moment of panic. It must be on a spring, he thought. But what if it locked itself from this side. He thought of trying the knob, but did not want to. He whistled to his soft step down the passage—low whistling—and supposed it was very casual. He stopped and through the windows saw the long stacks of paper towering over the aisles that ran between them. He imagined himself looking down on a paper city lit from the sky by rows of electric stars. Then the gates to the city were closing, the huge front and back doors rolling shut automatically. And the stars were going out, row by row, over the deserted streets. Only his bridge was lit. Two shadows appeared at an intersection. They hovered in the center of it and became two men in front of a flickering light; their busy hands moving above a growing flame. Then the lights on his bridge went out and there

202

was only the little fire in the intersection, and the two men moving away from it, disappearing behind the tall buildings, then showing themselves again in the middle of another intersection. They hunched over another flicker of light, a growing flame; warming themselves. But on so warm a night? Panimer saw smoke cover the last of the light, then no more light. He ran, clutching his can of paint only because he had forgotten it could be dropped. With only his memory of the tunnel to guide him he rushed toward the far end, knocking into one wall, then the other, as he went. The door was open. But he emerged into more darkness. Feeling his way along another catwalk, he almost fell off. He came to another set of steps where he could smell the smoke. It was billowing up into the ceiling now. He could not see it, could only tell it was harder to breath. Over his own coughing he could hear a man's voice somewhere below him, calling, "Boy." Steps came with the voice, making the steel staircase ring. Panimer was climbing again, then moving along a flat place, led only by a hand rail. He bumped into a wall, moved backward and knocked into another wall. He could not think how he had come onto the level, moved back and forth, caged. Smoke was making his eyes sting.

"Panimer," the voice called below him again, barely audible, as if muffled by a wall. He sat down for a moment to listen. "How do you get out of here?" it said, "Where are you?" The smoke hurt his lungs too much to speak; he could not sit still. He moved along his steel platform again, his left hand reaching out, balancing against the weight of the paint can. And the hand knocked into an upright metal strip. He clutched it, felt up it to a rod that grew out of it, and along that to another upright, and back again. A ladder. He felt himself stepping out over air, wondered if there were anything beneath him. Climbing, still clutching the can, which was just another awkward part of his body to be moved to safety with the rest of him. He'd only gone several rungs when his head bumped a ceiling, almost knocking him from the ladder. He recognized the paint can now for baggage. But instead of throwing it clear, held it between his body and a ladder rung, then felt above him with his free hand.

He pushed up. Nothing moved. His hand felt its way around a small square frame. He had tried to hold his breath for a moment, then gasped, making it worse. He'd almost decided to let go the ladder, or his fingers had almost decided for him, when his groping hand felt the hasp. It was shut but not locked, would have been easily solved if his mind had been working. But it was chance and his thrashing hand that jarred it loose. He was going to jump when he punched again at the ceiling and the hatch swung open above him. He crawled up into the night, onto the flat peak of the roof, lay down and breathed. The paint can was beside him.

27

What Mr. Lewis learned on the night of smoke would all come to him within the week. He went down to encourage the firemen, afraid, though, that the evidence he had long searched for was going to disappear in one night right under his nose. Whoever had lit it and then poured a tin of kerosene all along the base of one row, must have thought that because it was paper it would burn. But the flame lasted only as long as the kerosene. In the long rows of tightly packed paper the fire took air only along the stacks' surfaces, flames licking along their sides, making great clouds of smoke; after half an hour enough smoke in the building to kill anyone.

It was near dawn before Clarke got his men inside, and with random spraying the Stilson volunteers had put out the last creeping flame. The fire had jumped dozens of rows and not a single stack had been totally consumed; all those acres of paper were only smudged. They had also extinguished the notion that that amount of paper could be eliminated in one night by an amateur arsonist—but not the notion of arsonist. Much earlier the sheriff had assumed there was an arsonist, supposed he knew who it was, and did not believe for a moment that the suspected boy would have been caught in his own fire. The sheriff's van and deputies' cars, all with sirens, had begun to thread their wailing pattern through the back roads, spinning off macadam onto dirt and back again, with Small Hill corner for their intermittent rendezvous. Two of them came near collision there and another two actually kissed fenders at the corner of Saw Mill Road and Station Drive, all flirting with ditches as they went. Their instructions were to find the boy, or maybe the boy and an old man who might be in a wagon together. The deputies had been ranging out and back to Small Hill for several hours when dawn came and Clarke's men had finally entered the building. They found Marcum dead, asphyxiated in the aerial passageway. They would not just be looking for an arsonist now, but a murderer too.

Panimer, his breath restored, balanced himself on the warehouse roof. He could see smoke pouring from under the eaves, supposed there would not be time to paint his message. He would pour it on. On hands and knees, he crawled the word, spilling paint in his path. It was a messy job this time—long stalactites ran from each letter—but still legible. Covered with white paint, he let himself down the outside ladder. If fingerprints were needed, they were there preserved in multiple on roof and rung, embedded in the paint.

He could hear the sirens coming up Station Drive as he let himself onto the ground. He knew Kreutz would leave without him if he did not hurry, and he cleared the fence and ran up the hill, dodging the junks as he went. The wagon was across the skin diamond and turning up Small Hill Road when he caught up to it.

"Why'd you go and do that?" Kreutz said. "Why'd you start a fire?"

"I didn't," Panimer said. "Can't that mule go any faster?" Kreutz was swinging his jaw back and forth, agitated with the chase he now anticipated, already settled in his route, his thoughts leaping zigzag across the county's back roads, all the way to Stilson, even imagining his way through fences, across pastures, along abandoned roads through the woods where he was not even sure the wagon could pass, but knew a police car could not.

They were almost two miles from the corner, still on Small Hill Road and still hearing the fire sirens when Kreutz turned the wagon into the woods. Ahead a cross road cut back toward Clayton at an acute angle around a little power station where Small Hill Road turned to dirt and continued south toward Stilson.

"You can't stop here," Panimer said. "We hardly got started yet," thinking maybe the man had forgotten his promise to take them west. But a moment later a police car came careening around the power station, spinning out in the gravel, its rear end swaying back and forth in a wide arc, then steadying into a seventy-mile-an hour line toward Small Hill.

"Ain't this a damn shame?" Kreutz said.

"What's he want?" Panimer said, disbelieving, or maybe wanting not to believe all that speed could have been wanting him.

"What do you think, boy? They're looking for us. What'd you do back there?"

"Almost got smoked to death is what. And painted their damn roof is all."

"Come up, mule." The wagon was turning back onto the road. In the next mile they had hidden from two more deputies' cars and were traveling again with the lantern out as they crossed the wide lanes of state route 7. The signs said 7 East and 7 West, with arrows. And Panimer, reminded that he was not just running away from police, but toward a girl, begged Kreutz to forget Stilson and follow the arrow west. Kreutz only worked his jaw harder, guiding the mule straight across the highway, then left and right onto another dirt road.

"You won't find the one who sprayed you in Stilson," Panimer said.

Kreutz did not mean to argue. "Who said I won't? Why won't I," he said.

"Because everyone of them firemen is at Small Hill."

"You started a fire," Kreutz said. "Ain't this a damn shame?" But he did not even consider changing the switch-back course he had set that would bring them to the Stilson Volunteer Fire Department, whose parking lot was an extension of that used by the courthouse, the jail, and the city police, and where Kreutz meant to leave his wagon until he had satisfaction from the man who had turned the hose on him. And for the next two hours, while the deputies' sirens circled and recircled the county, closing on the elusive wagon again and again but never seeing it, Kreutz led his mules behind barns and billboards, on trails through the woods the boy had never known existed. Panimer was amazed at Kreutz's skill. He seemed able to separate the noise of each car, always to know his position inside the circle of vehicles that pursued him. Once he said, "That's Jackson's nephew. That's his Chevrolet," and a minute later they watched from behind a honeysuckled fence as the car and driver he'd predicted came by.

Somehow he got them into the center of Stilson where sheriff and deputies never dreamed they would have gone—the chase had been so thorough.

"You can't stop here," Panimer said. "That's the police station right there." But Kreutz was walking across the lot toward the fire station, where the dispatcher sat alone, playing checkers against himself. He was startled to see Kreutz, recovered, and then said: "You take that side over there, I think it's winning."

Kreutz sat down to the empty chair, half warm from its intermittent occupation by the man who had been moving back and forth, the better to beat himself. Before he described the fireman he was looking for, Kreutz had all kings and the dispatcher begged to concede. Kreutz would not let him.

"All right, but let's play another," the man said. Kreutz agreed.

The second game was finished quicker than the last half of the first. Kreutz was much better at beating him than the man had been at beating himself. He told the dispatcher who it was he wanted. A little way into the third game, bored with the prospect of another easy victory, satisfied the man he sought was fighting the Small Hill fire, Kreutz got up from the table.

"Ain't you gonna finish?"

"You tell him I'm looking for him," Kreutz said. "I got to go somewheres. You tell him I'm coming back."

They made it through the night undetected. At dawn Kreutz drove the wagon into the woods and told the boy it was time to sleep. But an hour later they were moving again, this time with some impatience. Panimer was bored with back roads, the lack of traffic, the lack of chase. There were no more sirens. Kreutz led them back onto route 7. They had not gone a half mile when the state police stopped them. Sirens again. Kreutz smiled.

Minutes later the Stilson sheriff was there. He pulled the boy off the wagon and put handcuffs on him. "You ain't got to be so rough," Panimer said.

"You know where they're gonna send you this time?" the sheriff said. Stumped for an answer to his own question, which had fallen on silence, he said, "You'll find out. That's where."

28

The Stilson jail sits behind the courthouse, its back wall of plain brick set with a row of six barred windows, high on the second story. A prisoner looking through the narrow openings sees only the red brick of the wall across an alley. Even standing on tiptoe Panimer could not see down to the heads of the tallest men and boys who came to stare up at his cell. A sign in the alley says: It Is Forbidden To Talk To Prisoners Through The Windows. Mothers and wives regularly disobeyed the order, yelling up to the bars, asking their men what they needed—socks or something to eat—or discussing a paper to be signed, or arguing with them about the fights or drunkenness that had put them there, or promising not to forget them, or promising they would if the men did not change their ways, or promising to relay messages of revenge.

Then the voices in the alley began to talk about him. He heard Johnny Roe Pride say, "He's in that one there. The second one. I could hit him with ricochet. It'd bounce off that wall and go right in his cell. You shoot enough times, you couldn't miss him."

The first day his mother and father had come to visit. "They say you did arson," his mother said, sobbing. "They say you killed Mr. Marcum in the fire."

"I didn't set no fire."

Junior did not want to hear his son lie. "They trampled your mother's garden," he said. "There's nothing left of it." All three of them cried.

"There's got to be an arraignment," Junior said. "The lawyer told me. They can't keep you here without an arraignment. They should of had it already, but the state ain't got the indictment ready."

The community was in no rush to have the boy out of jail. Neither was it in a hurry to try him. But Junior and Paula were in a hurry. They had gone to the lawyer, first for free advice, then to hire him when they realized they might not get their son back—that the sheriff and commonwealth's attorney were going to try to have him sent away. Why was it taking them so long to prepare the indictment?

Panimer's lawyer begged the court for the boy's release to the custody of his parents. The judge said, "No. They had custody long enough. No. It's the court's turn for custody." Neither would the judge yield after the first week when the indictment still had not been drawn. "No. he said. "A man has been killed."

Boys began to gather in the evenings in the jail alley, yelling taunts and abuse at the second window, trying to make Panimer talk. Police chased them away. They scattered, and returned, and were chased again, knew they were not really being chased.

"You killed the junk man," he heard from below. "You killed him." He leaped up at the window, grabbed the sill overhead with fingertips but could not hold on. "Nancy's a whore. Everyone's had your girl, traitor. They throwed the key away—you ain't never getting out."

It could not continue that way, the boy in jail and no charge brought against him. His lawyer, William Settle, a cousin of Arthur's would not accommodate the delay. He would not play his client for more time. He assumed Panimer guilty but after a

211

week of small-town legal charade, he felt himself being used along with Panimer. He threatened petition to the higher court, letters to the governor and newspaper. The pressure was on the commonwealth's attorney to bring the state's case for arson and murder against the boy or to let him go.

The commonwealth's attorney, Lawrence Monroe, who kept his job through kindness of the Stilson County Democratic machine, supposed he had no special interest in the case except to see it speedily prosecuted. But all the parties were confounding him. The boy admitted being in the building, but even after a week in jail would not own to setting the fire. More confusing to Monroe was the company's lack of interest in prosecuting the case—that and their lack of cooperation in finding the two watchmen who had disappeared the night of the fire. He suspected that if there were not the body of the dead junk man on his hands, there would have been no prosecution, that accusations would have blown away with the smoke and the boy would have been set free a day later.

Against instinct, Monroe was about to charge Panimer with murder when his office received a copy of a letter from the federal Office of Price Administration asking the District Court for authority to enter and inspect Triumph Paper's Small Hill warehouse and a subpoena of all their records. Monroe tore up his indictment of Panimer and began again.

The commonwealth's attorney's office in Stilson is not large. It sits in the middle of the town's lawyers' row, a mews of a half dozen attached frame buildings, all in that attractive decay produced by repeated application of fresh over peeling paint. It has a small mahogany desk, property of the incumbent (who maintains a discreet private practice while he serves the state) and swivel chair of modest padding under leather. There are two other chairs in the room for conference but the office is seldom that crowded. There is an anteroom, actually the front hall where his secretary sits protecting his door, and a single long bench where visitors wait admission.

212

Panimer had been led out of his cell and down the street to the commonwealth's attorney's office a half dozen times that week, dragged by the wrist and left to stand in front of the desk while Monroe tried to frighten him with silence until his lawyer, would arrive and tell him to sit down. Once Monroe began his questions before the lawyer arrived. Panimer had been told not to talk, and he did not, which infuriated Monroe and delighted Settle. In the few celebrated cases he had been forced to prosecute, Monroe always prayed for early confession—anything to avoid the niceties of courtroom procedure, which were apt to trip him. He was not articulate, not fond of confrontation. Hardly suited to his job by temperament, he was more honest then anyone imagined. This unfortunate combination of traits left him frustrated. He could not railroad the boy; neither could he just let him go.

"If you didn't do it, who did?" he finally yelled at Panimer. Settle objected. Monroe apologized. Panimer calmly began again:

"Them two men I told you about. They set the fire in two places and then I couldn't see them for the smoke." Monroe did not want to believe the boy. It complicated things. But the watchmen were missing and the Triumph Paper Company said it was not even sure of their names. Then the search warrant was issued for the big warehouse and everything changed. Arthur Settle, the mayor, had come to Monroe and casually suggested Panimer wasn't really a bad boy after all, that maybe things shouldn't go too hard for him, that he had a hard-working daddy and blind mother. Maybe he should just be released while the thing got straightened out. Monroe was a little incredulous. Then Charlie Stockstill had stopped him on the street, as if it were natural that the Clayton Chain Food manager should have been in Stilson on a weekday afternoon, and said, "Shame about that boy, Lawrence. I have a hard time believing he could have done a thing like that." And when Monroe had driven through Clayton and stopped for gas at Lamartine's, Jewel himself had come out to fill him up, and said, "I hope they don't send Junior's boy away for no good reason," but before he could propose that Panimer be turned over to his parents, Monroe blurted, "We haven't even got an indictment drawn and everybody's got the boy hung. What the hell is going on over here?"

The gangs in the jail alley became rowdier. The boys from Clayton would drive to Stilson in the evening and stand under the cell yelling fresh abuse up at the traitor Panimer. He had news for them, but he was not going to waste it on the night air. He could not even see their faces.

His only visitors were his mother and father, and Panimer could see his father did not believe him and his mother did not know how to tell him that she did. Paula was afraid that if she showed him her belief in his innocence it might encourage him to some new act of defiance or abuse that would only lead to a worse punishment. And she already supposed they would try him for murder and further, that their prejudice would find him guilty. She said, "I don't really think you did it, honey." Junior said, "It'll go easier for you if you cooperate."

As they left the building he could hear one of the boys in the alley saying softly, "That's them. That's his mother and daddy. She's blind." And another one, "A son like that, she didn't deserve no victory garden. Or victory neither." Panimer jumped up and grabbed overhead at the window sill, pulling himself up again to the small opening. No use. He could not see which one had trampled his mother's garden. He sat on the floor, his back against the wall, and cried.

The secret traffic to and from Monroe's office could not remain a secret from itself; there were too many people going in and out, their paths bound to cross. Mr Lewis nodded politely to Charlie Stockstill as he walked up lawyers' row, and Stockstill, pretending not to be heading for the commonwealth attorney's office, walked by it on the first pass, then doubled back when he supposed Lewis was out of sight. But Lewis turned around and watched Stockstill go in and Stockstill saw him watching and shook his head as if he were only retracing absent-minded steps.

214

The same afternoon Junior walked out of the office as Jewel Lamartine entered, hardly acknowledging each other's presence, much less where they happened to be passing. And there were Hiram Johnson, Arthur Settle, and Junior again, this time with Paula, and Earl Jackson. And three times in the same day Panimer was paraded up the mews in custody of the sheriff to sit and wait his turn in Monroe's office.

From a trickle of furtive visitors there had come to be a waiting line, not because they were volunteering suggestions but because they had been asked or ordered to give depositions. Slowly Mr. Monroe was beginning to understand what had happened, but still he probed for some weakness in the boy's defense because the truth he'd been driven toward, in spite of himself, was not acceptable.

When Monroe closed his office door to take a new witness inside it was more a formality than an act of privacy; the wall between anteroom and office was more partition than wall so that even a low voice could be heard through it, and Panimer, sitting on the bench, his ear to the wall, had been listening to Mayor Settle avoid the truth.

"He's lying," Panimer yelled. "He knowed what was in there." The sheriff was told to keep the boy quiet or take him back to jail, so Panimer had kept quiet while Monroe finished the questioning, but he could not sit still much longer. Trapped, the whole thing going against him, old men lying, he imagined himself on the way to jail for good. He stood up to get a drink from the water fountain and bolted through the door into the street.

The sheriff was forty yards behind at the end of the second block and losing ground. It never occured to him to pull his revolver, even to fire a warning shot, maybe because he already knew the boy was innocent, that Panimer, not the town, or county, or state, was the aggrieved party. And Panimer never thought he was going to outrun the law without a headstart, was only running because he could not sit still. In fact he had turned almost a complete circle, and was moving across the wide green

lawn of the town common, exhilarated, maintaining speed. He
went leaping up the steps of the courthouse, thinking: This is
where the whole thing was going to end anyway. He couldn't
wait for the ending. Inside, he ran past a clerk and up the side
stair to the gallery, slamming the door behind him. There was no
lock on it; he thought of holding the knob against their turning.
That would never work. He moved a bench against the door,
then another and another, until they were wedged against each
other all the way down to the balcony railing. They could not get
to him now without breaking a piece of their eighteenth-century
courthouse. Pleased with his barricade, Panimer climbed over
it, stood on the railing, one arm around a column, and watched
the courtroom fill up below him.

"Come down from there, boy," the sheriff called to him.
"When I'm ready," Panimer said.
"Look out, he's going to fall. Leave him alone."
"Get a ladder," the sheriff said.
Someone in front of the courthouse was shouting,"He's in
here. Come on. They got him." More were entering the building
now, people out for lunch who were drawn to the commotion.
People from Clayton who'd been waiting to see Monroe were
already there, having followed the chase from lawyers' row.
There was not enough room in the aisles. People were beginning to fill in the benches. The crowd was pushing toward the
front of the courtroom. Wilma Settle, who had come to Stilson
to warn her nephew William of the embarrassment he was
causing the family by representing the traitor boy, had climbed
up into the jury box with Jane to see what was happening and
who was there.
Panimer, looking below him for Mayor Settle and Charlie
Stockstill and the other Sons of Clayton people, saw all eyes
were fixed on him. "Go ahead. Look at me," he shouted, "I
didn't do nothing." He began to walk along the balcony railing,
almost falling before he steadied himself at the next pillar, and
looked down again. There was Mayor Settle right below him on
the witness stand. Settle was bending over to hear advice from

216

Hiram Johnson and Earl Jackson. Jewel Lamartine was with him too, and Charlie Stockstill was pushing his way down the aisle to join them.

"You'd be better off if you just came down now," Mayor Settle spoke up to him. "Nobody's going to hurt you."

"You'd be better off if you wasn't lying," Panimer answered. "You been lying all week. You knew what was in that building a long time ago. I saw you drive your car into it."

Mayor Settle looked around him to see if anyone were listening to the boy. Panimer's lawyer, standing on the witness table, called to him, "Be quiet. You don't have to say anything."

"What the hell is it to you?" Panimer called back, then beneath him Mayor Settle still calm, as if his were the one voice worth listening to, said, "Don't do anything more to shame your family, son."

"Shame them? You blinded my mother."

"You know that's not fair." Stockstill was talking now. "Come down now and save your daddy this embarrassment. We know the things you've done."

"What things?"

"Never mind. Now's not the time for that."

"What things?"

Further back in the courtroom someone yelled, "He set off false air raid warnings is one."

"And what happened when I did?" Panimer shouted back. "Everybody's lights went off but the ones in that big secret building, which wasn't even a secret, because they knew what was in it all the time. And how come their lights didn't have to go out in an air raid?"

"It's not the time for this," Mayor Settle said. "Come on down from there." Someone had finally brought a ladder. They set it up against the balcony. A deputy was most of the way up it when Panimer grabbed the top rung and pushed, sending the officer tumbling back into the crowd. There was screaming and a wave of new threats against the boy. They set the ladder up again and the deputy, unhurt, was about to try again when the rung he held was yanked out of his hand. Panimer was lifting the ladder up to the balcony. "Get two more," the sheriff yelled.

Panimer did not want to lose them now. They were where he wanted them. He fixed the ladder between the balcony and a beam that spanned the room, and climbed further into the air over them. Reaching the beam, he was barely able to pull the ladder up behind him without falling, but once up and braced between this beam and the next it gave him a platform. He began to walk back and forth on the rungs, his aerial act holding them rapt below as he yelled their war secret at them: "Paper. Paper. Paper. And you knew it. Look at them all there together." He was pointing down at the witness stand where Mayor Settle, Lamartine, and Stockstill were clustered with Mr. Johnson and Earl Jackson.

"Get him down from there before he falls," Lamartine ordered no one in particular.

"Paper!" Panimer shouted once more.

He looked down at them. "You want me to come down?" he said. "Well, why don't you just tell the truth then? I ain't coming down from here until you tell that man the truth," and now he pointed at Mr. Monroe. The gesture momentarily cost him his balance. He was beginning to realize how high he was, how unsteady. "If you knew all them tons of paper was up there at Small Hill and nothing happening to it how come you wanted us collecting more? You got secrets all right, but they ain't war secrets."

The heads of the people below seemed to be swaying with him, then they were all turning as their humming voices became a whisper.

"Who's here?" Paula said. "Who are all these people?"

"Everybody," Junior said, "the whole place," advancing into the courtroom, his wife clutching his arm.

"Take me to where I can talk to them."

"No, honey."

"Take me," she insisted, pulling ahead of him, bumping into the crowd. "Where is he?"

"Up in the rafters."

Paula raised her head toward the ceiling as if some providence might allow her a moment's vision, then turned back on her husband.

"Are you coming or aren't you?" she said. And the two of them slowly pushed their way toward the front of the room, past the townspeople of Stilson, past the Sons of Clayton directors at the witness stand, around the jury box where Wilma and Jane stood attending the blind woman's progress. "Where's the big desk?" Paula whispered, sensing her entrance had brought the room to silence.

"You can't go up there," Junior said.

"Where is it?"

"No."

"Take me."

"You can't."

"I'll do it by myself." So Junior was forced to lead her all the way up to the judge's bench where she did not even hesitate or falter but began to speak in a clear voice, without emotion. "Don't try to get my son down from there. You'll make him fall."

Two more ladders had been fetched from the fire department and carried up to the balcony where several men were arguing about how to set them up and who would go up for the boy. But when they saw the blind woman, heard her begin to speak, they fell silent with the rest.

"I know what happened" she began again. "I'm sorry. I got blinded in the explosion. I can't see who I'm talking to. It doesn't matter. Could you wait just a few minutes and hear me?"

"Come away from there, honey," Wilma Settle was calling softly to her from the jury box. "We'll take you home."

"There's some people here who won't like this," Paula said. "I can't hold a grudge in it. But there's been so much pretending like we all didn't know. And my boy wasn't perfect. No one's saying he was perfect. He knew too soon, that was all."

High above them Panimer was trying to win their attention again, walking the ladder, his arms spread. Now he called

219

down, "Go home, Mother. Take her home. She don't know what she's saying. You blinded her. You could be sued." They were distracted for a moment, but the audience wanted more from the woman and even those watching overhead were listening as she began again: "Don't chase him down from there. Don't make him fall. He wasn't any worse than the rest. Because here's what happened."

Stockstill had moved close to the sheriff, was pleading with him to stop the woman, to take her home. "For her own sake," he said, but the sheriff was not going to be seen manhandling a blind woman, and they all listened as she said:

"It was after the explosion. They didn't know what to do. You see it was called Sons of Clayton but the business really come on contracts from this other company, not from the government direct. And that's what got them in trouble. It was this other company that was the rotten ones and when Mr. Settle and them found out it was too late because they'd already let themselves become part of this other bunch." She was going too fast. Most of the people had no idea what she meant. But Lamartine said, "Make her come down from there."

"Is that you, Mr. Lamartine?" Paula said. "I know it was only because you all felt bad about the explosion. That's when you sold out from the explosives company in exchange for the paper business. You didn't want any more to do with explosions. I don't blame you. You didn't know what that paper company was up to when you got into it. You didn't know they were cheating on the prices and hiding their biggest stock right here. You thought it was all part of a war secret. When you found out they were dishonest you were already part of it. You couldn't get loose. My boy went in there and saw what it was. Someone was trying to shoot him."

Paula heard the sound of ladders again. They were setting them up between the balcony and beam the way Panimer had, but there were two of them. "Don't chase him," she pleaded.

"Come on," Panimer called to them. "Come on up." Their pursuit restored his confidence, and with it, his balance.

"Only one of you," the sheriff called. "You others come

down. Don't scare him. A Stilson fireman started up the ladder while the rest left the balcony, shutting the door behind them, as if that might help relax the boy into surrender. Panimer recognized the fireman, the one who had turned the hose on his mother. He taunted him, beckoned for him to come and get him if he dared. The man made it to the boy's ladder and advanced slowly along it. But as he approached, Panimer turned and walked further away, along his beam, then turned again, deft as a goat, to see if he would follow. He would not. The people below, who had been yelling advice, now laughed a little nervously at the standoff. The man backed up along the ladder and Panimer came toward him. The man moved forward. The boy backed away again. The nervous titter below turned to full-throated laughter. Panimer was keeping a constant distance between them. But the next time the fireman advanced, the boy stood still, let him come closer and closer until the man almost touched him. Panimer dropped suddenly and swung from the rungs, under and past him. Before the man recovered he was on top of the ladder again, stepping quickly along it, then down one of the firemen's ladders, the man in pursuit, following down, supposing the chase over. But once on the balcony, the boy raced toward the other ladder and up it to begin again. The crowd below was laughing uncontrollably now, tears streaming from their eyes, as Panimer stood, proud, way out on the far beam.

"What is it?" Paula insisted in her confusion. "What's happening?" But there was too much noise for her to follow Junior's explanation. And then something was changing, the boy was dizzy, losing balance, and she understood as the laughter in the room became a scream as he fell. Close to him they could hear the snap of his leg and the sound as his shoulder and then his head hit the floor.

29

While Panimer lay in the hospital with a concussion and a broken arm and leg, Mr. Lewis found proof of what Paula had said. The Sons of Clayton directors were part owners of the Triumph Paper Company. They had sold controlling interest in Sons of Clayton for stock in the paper operation. And the blind woman had understood their motive. After the explosion they had become frightened, not only for their investment, but also for their responsibility, their liability. They looked for someone to share it with, and found the same company that had given them their contracts—Triumph Explosives. Triumph Explosives was willing to sell part of its subsidiary, Triumph Paper, for fifty-one percent of Sons of Clayton. Then Clayton discovered what it had bought into was in its own back yard—the mystery building at Small Hill.

"Everyone had what he wanted," Lewis told the commonwealth's attorney. "Triumph had voting control of a company that appeared to be a local operation, and local approval and ownership of its secret paper warehouse. And the good burghers of Clayton had what they thought was a safer investment—paper. The Triumph people had Clayton convinced a paper warehouse was a legitimate war secret. It had always been a secret. Why shouldn't it continue that way?"

"Wait," Monroe said. "Why would they put that much paper in one place and then keep it a secret?"

"There were square acres of scrap in there they never reported. They sold shares of it over and over again for stock in other companies. And always to people who thought they were putting their money in a safe, patriotic place." Lewis could see Monroe was a little incredulous. "Look, all they had to do," he said, "was take them inside the huge building and let them see for themselves. There were mountains of it. If you saw that much of anything in one place you'd think it was worth a fortune."

"And the ones who bought kept the secret of their own defrauding?"

"That's it," Lewis said.

"You're telling me Arthur Settle and the rest of them would get into hoarding and blackmarketing and stock fraud and then go gunning for a boy who had their secret? And then burn down their own warehouse?"

"No," Lewis said, "I'm telling you they didn't know. Not until it was too late. They didn't do any of that. They just wanted the boy to shut up and leave them the privacy of their embarrassment. When they bought into Triumph everything was all right. When they found out what was going on they were too much a part of it to back out. They'd signed their names to deals that defrauded others. The same way they'd been fooled. Actually, their stock in Triumph was about worthless. The warehouse and everything in it had been sold ten times over before VJ Day."

"What about the fire? And the boy?"

"The Triumph people wanted the place gone. If fire wiped it out, each investor could think it was his own private loss."

"Uninsured?"

"That's right. A secret. And if the boy disappeared in the fire so much the better. But the goons they hired to burn it were too

223

stupid for the job. It's still there for the investors to fight over. Or run away from."

"I don't believe any of it," Monroe said.

Monroe did believe it. There was no need for further subpoenas of the local people. Regret, apology, extenuation explained away the need, or opportunity, for prosecution. There would be no trial of Sons of Clayton. Or the boy. How to find ill motive in the collective will of names that circled and ran the village? They'd fought the war as long and hard as any. And with as much sacrifice. Not such a wild coincidence that all of them should have been in paper together, their several interests bound to converge in the newest local secret, which turned out to be a warehouse. And an investment opportunity. People had become so wealthy. House mortgages had been paid off, dental work done, all the invisible uses of wealth caught up with. And still there was money. They had found an invisible investment for their not quite seemly capital.

Lewis came to the house several times looking for Paula. She was not at home. He finally found her in the Stilson Hospital waiting outside Panimer's room

"You were right," he told her. "Everything you said in the courtroom was right. But how did you know?" She wanted to say: Just listening. Just listening to all of them, one at a time. But she did not. Lewis would not have believed it anyway. It had taken him all of the war and all the legal resources of his office to bring Triumph Paper to book—to trace their strange non-treasure all the way back to his own hamlet.

"They didn't really mean my boy any harm," she said, hoping Mr. Lewis was not looking for culprits in Clayton.

Panimer, in his hospital room, moved back and forth across the edge of sleep. Awake, he might make things go his way, but asleep, his dreams slipped out of control: the trip was not going well. Kreutz was not cooperating in the search for Nancy. Panimer heard him saying: "You didn't think of that, did you?

224

What we was going to use for money? What we was going to eat?''

"We could stop and get work,'' Panimer said as he saw Kreutz work his gums and spit.

"You said you had money.'' They had spent Panimer's two dollars on soda and cupcakes. It was raining. All they had left was Kreutz's store of rationing books under the wagon seat.

They were in a store. Kreutz tried to use one of his ration books. The store keeper told them to get out.

On the wagon again Panimer tried to save the mission. "We must have come two counties already,'' he said, "and we only been gone a week. Ain't many more miles to West Virginia.''

"How do you know?'' Kreutz said. "And when we get there, you won't know where to find her.''

They were in another store but no one there had heard of Nancy McConkey. They laughed when he said her name. Was it her name they laughed at? He was holding her hand. Or was it her they scorned? She was holding his hand; he could wake up now. But when he woke, drugged, she was not there. To feel her beside him once more he would have to sleep again.

Drifting back, he was puzzled about police cars. The trip West was beginning again, but how had Kreutz got them past all the police cars? There were no sirens. "We ain't taking the big highway,'' Kreutz said. They were following dirt roads, not straying too far from the railroad tracks. Panimer was leaning over the back of the wagon trying to paint a white line down the dirt road. The brush clogged and left meaningless congealed lumps of dust that looked like so many more round pebbles in the road as they moved away behind him. It was not a sign for others he was trying to paint, but directions to himself, his line home. He imagined he could reel it in on the way back if they did not want a line on their road. He did not want to make anyone angry. But there was no line. He looked far behind. There was only the rutted, dusty road. How many times had they turned, and in what directions? "Where are we?'' he called up to Kreutz. There was no answer. He might be a stray forever. Or wake.

Awake, he saw white walls; too bright. He drifted back once more. He was following Kreutz into another store. Kreutz was arguing too much. He was calling the storekeeper long, ugly names. "It's a common critter won't take a man's good war coupons," he said to Panimer. "Could be his mother was a German. His eyes don't slant none." Panimer was trying to pull Kreutz toward the door, but the man was already going for his telephone.

The wagon was on the road again. Nancy was sitting beside him admiring his command of the mules. Kreutz had disappeared. He was not necessary, Panimer was thinking, a nuisance. Then there were sirens and he wished Kreutz back again to help them evade the police. Kreutz refused to reappear. The flashing light was beside them now, forcing them off the road. He would have to go to jail, or wake up.